EROS ELEMENT

A STEAMPUNK THRILLER WITH A HINT OF ROMANCE

CECILIA DOMINIC

Dear Aerin,
you are a treasure!
Cecilia

PRAISE FOR THE AETHER PSYCHICS SERIES:

"This fun, charming series is a must for Steampunk and Paranormal enthusiasts alike! - Leanna Renee Hieber, award winning author of Strangely Beautiful and The Eterna Files

LOOK FOR THESE TITLES BY CECILIA DOMINIC

The Aether Psychics
Noble Secrets
Eros Element
Clockwork Phantom
Aether Spirit
Aether Rising

The Inspector Davidson Mysteries
The Art of Piracy
Mission: Nutcracker

The Lycanthropy Files
The Mountain's Shadow
Long Shadows
Blood's Shadow

Dream Weavers & Truth Seekers
Perchance to Dream
Truth Seeker

Tangled Dreams
Web of Truth

ACKNOWLEDGMENTS

As always, my gratitude goes to those who support me in my writing, specifically my editor and critique group who help to make my books better, and especially to the mentors I've had along the way. Thank you especially to Anna DeStefano, whose enthusiasm for writing is only surpassed by her own talent at it, and James Bassett, without whom I would never have tried to write steampunk.

I also cannot thank my fans enough, especially those who participated in the writing process for this book. Special mention goes to Gary P, who suggested the perfect name for the series villain. I won't spoil who it is here, but those who live in Atlanta and who are familiar with the controversy surrounding the baseball team's 2017 move will know who it is. Also huge thanks to Dawn P for her archaeology advice and direction.

Finally, there are unexpected perks to being an author. Just before I started writing this book, I lost my beloved fifteen-year-old tuxedo cat Bailey to lymphoma. I am happy for the opportunity to memorialize him in the character of Edward

Bailey, who is actually more finicky than his namesake but who would look dashing in a tuxedo if given the opportunity.

ISBN: 978-1-945074-55-4

Edited by Holly Atkinson

Cover by Karri

First ebook edition: August 2015

Second ebook edition: May 2017

This is a third edition of the novel titled Eros Element that was released by Samhain Publishing in August 2015.

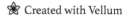 Created with Vellum

1

—————

Department of Archaeology, Huntington University, 08 June 1870

"Perhaps it's time for you to settle down, Miss."

Iris McTavish wrenched her mind into the present and away from the fascinating story the file in her hand told her, of frustration with academic strictures and lack of collaboration. "Not you too, Sophie." She shook her right hand, which one of her dear departed father's files had graced with a paper cut, and stuck her newly lacerated thumb in her mouth.

"I know it's not my place, Miss, but without your father bringing home his salary, how are you going to keep up the household? Cook and I are worried."

Iris rubbed her eyebrows before remembering the dust on her hands. Now she was sure she sported smudges to make her look like a stage actor or some sort of urchin. "I'm working on that."

A knock on the door forestalled the rest of the conversation, thank goodness. Sophie opened the door to reveal a messenger boy.

"Cor," he said and took off his hat with an admiring look at Sophie. "They din't tell me Professor McTavish were a ghel."

Iris stood and drew the urchin's gaze to herself. "Professor McTavish isn't—" The words stung her throat with waspish ferocity, and all she could choke out was, "available." She swallowed the sensation that tried to erupt through her chest and make her burst into tears like a schoolgirl with a broken heart. Yes, her heart was broken, but she couldn't afford silly displays of emotion.

"Oh, well, are you his secretary? Ent no one at the front desk."

"That's because it's summer," Iris's grief burst through as irritable words. "Most of the faculty are off on trips, and the department secretary's mother is ill, so she's gone to care for her." Which worked out well for Iris. Otherwise, the secretary would have breathed down her neck while she cleaned out her father's office. *She never had much use for me.*

"So who're you, Miss? Meaning no disrespect, but I got this urgent message to deliver to Professor McTavish, and if I don't, I won't get paid and we won't eat."

His voice cracked on the last word, and a tendril of tenderness curled in Iris's heart. The poor boy sounded as desperate and panicked as she felt.

"I'll take it," she said.

"How do I know you'll get it to him? My instructions were to give it to him or his assistant."

"Well, then you're in luck. I'm his assistant." Iris ignored the look Sophie shot at her and put on her gloves before she took the message from the boy. "Here's a halfpence for your trouble."

He didn't hide the disappointed look on his face, but he bobbed his head and disappeared.

"Miss..." Sophie said.

"Sometimes the universe drops things in your lap that you

don't recognize as gifts at first," Iris told her. "That's what Father always said." She unfolded the slip of paper and read it, then looked at it again slowly, word by word. It was in English, and the words familiar, but the meaning didn't hit her brain until she read it out loud:

DEAR PROFESSOR MCTAVISH,

Word of your illness has reached us, and we are saddened to hear of your sudden incapacitation. However, we have a project which you will likely find interesting. If you are well enough, we have funding for you and an assistant to undertake a multidisciplinary summer expedition in search of a treasure, the likes of which has never been found. Please join us for a meeting in the Aetherics Department this Monday June 6 in the conference room on the fourth floor at ten o'clock a.m. You will be well-compensated for your time and trouble with bonus once the treasure is located and delivered.

Sincerely, Dean Hartford
College of Sciences

"IT'S FOR YOUR FATHER, MISS," Sophie said. "Not for you. Too bad, it would have been a good opportunity."

"It still might be. What if we tell them that my father is too ill to travel, but I'm his assistant and would be willing to undertake his duties instead?"

Sophie's mouth disappeared into a disapproving line. It reminded Iris of her mother, who would make the same expression whenever Iris would accost her father when he came home to ask about what he'd found on his expeditions, and had he brought anything for her. She later discovered the true reason for her mother's frown, but she pushed those thoughts to the back of her mind as irrelevant.

"But you're not a trained archaeologist, Miss."

"I would be if the University recognized the apprentice system, which was good enough until administrators got hold of academia. Besides, if I acquit myself well on this journey, the University may accept me as an archeology student in the fall. Then I could get a scholarship, which would help support the household beyond the money we'd get for our duties. It sounds like we'll get paid even if we don't find this treasure."

"And what if they find out your father has died?"

Iris patted her hidden skirt pocket, where she held the telegram from France. He'd gone there to see if the warmer climate would help his lungs and passed away at a sanitarium on the coast. She shared it with his chairman before he left for Bulgaria to research the symbolism of the bull in ancient European pottery, and from the department secretary's reaction when she'd shown up the previous week, she was sure the chair hadn't shared the sad news with anyone before he left, likely to keep the fallout from delaying his trip. Everyone knew he had a Bulgarian mistress. The note from the dean confirmed her secret was safe.

Had the death of Professor Irvin McTavish happened a week earlier, Iris wouldn't have been able to work the deception. But now...

"I doubt they will. Circumstances have aligned in our favor." Her shoulders hunched around the guilt sprouting in her chest at having to lie, but what else could she do? If she continued with things as they were, she and her servants would be turned out of their house in the dead of winter, or at the latest in the heat of the following summer if she could manage to sell her father's most precious artifacts. Now determination replaced guilt.

"Get ready, Sophie. You're about to become the assistant to Miss McTavish, assistant archaeologist."

Now Sophie's plump lips hopped to one side. "All right,

Miss, but only because I know we need to do this. But if we're discovered, you're on your own with the punishment."

"I will do my best to protect you should that unlikely event happen." Iris moved to wipe her hands on her skirt, then stopped and looked at her gloved fingers. "Would you mind bringing me some water to wash with? We have a meeting to attend."

∿

AETHERICS DEPARTMENT, *Huntington University, England, 08 June 1870*

Of all the things about the college Edward Bailey liked, the ivy was his favorite. It clung to the buildings, climbing up their stone faces, sending leafy tendrils along window edges as if peering in on lectures. On foggy days, it served as a green veil over the facades and provided a sense of decorum and discretion. He much preferred its jaunty green leaves and steadfastness through all seasons to the flashy color and riot of spring flowers with their pretty lies and false promises.

On this Monday morning, Edward tipped his hat to one particularly long tendril that hung over the door of his department building. He then ascended the cozy stairwell with its wooden rail smoothed to softness by generations of eager, curious students and gave a nod to the three discolored splotches that stood guard around the window in his office. He'd nicknamed them Hickory, Dickory and Doc due to their shapes. A fanciful notion, to be sure, but he considered them to be his guardians as he worked through the puzzles inherent in his profession.

They had not, however, prevented the department secretary, an eager young woman named Miss Ellis who eschewed sensible spectacles for a frivolously fashionable pince-nez, from putting a note on his desk about a meeting he'd neither scheduled nor desired. It was to happen in the department conference room at ten o'clock that morning, which would disrupt his routine abominably and abdominally because he timed his taking of tea such that it would provide a needed urge for a mid-morning break right around ten. Now he would have to make his tea a half hour earlier so he wouldn't end up squirming during the meeting with his chairman and his dean. They'd given him enough to squirm about in the eight years he'd been at the University.

"Well, this is most unacceptable," he muttered before his door opened to reveal the tall blond figure of Johann Bledsoe.

"Usually people talk about my unacceptability after I leave, not before I arrive," Johann said. He sat without being invited and crossed one ankle over his knee.

Politeness kept Edward from saying what he really thought about yet another interruption to his routine—goodness, what was next, a surprise visit from the queen?—but he did give his friend an exasperated look. It was quite rude of him to come in and sit without being invited.

"And to what do I owe the pleasure of this visit?" he asked, although his tone conveyed it was, indeed, not a pleasure.

"I got a note saying there would be a meeting here at ten that required my attendance. Knowing your habits, I took the liberty of coming early and having Miss Ellis make your morning tea so you wouldn't experience any awkward moments while speaking with your supervisors."

Edward's gut simultaneously twisted at the thought of having to leave the meeting to attend to bodily needs and the horror that his friend knew his habits so intimately he could plot to interrupt and adjust them to the whims of others. Underneath, he had a premonition the meeting would be the start of a life-wide disruption, perhaps an upheaval. It was time to put a stop to this nonsense.

"While I appreciate your consideration, Johann, I will not

allow a meeting I neither called nor desired to interrupt this morning's important work or make a shambles of my carefully orchestrated routine, which has been developed through years of study and experimentation for maximum productivity."

"Too late, old boy. Here's Miss Ellis with your tea, twenty-three minutes early. That should give your stomach time to process it before the chair and dean arrive."

Indeed, Miss Ellis walked in carrying a tray with Edward's favorite teapot, cup and saucer set along with a half cube of sugar—she had instructions as to how he liked them split—and two teaspoons of cream in a little pitcher that had been warmed to exactly one hundred and forty degrees. Alongside were two small lemon strawberry scones, their tart fragrance mingling with that of the strong black tea to make for a siren song of scent. Brilliant, now his mind was so confused it mixed up its analogies. He'd never get anything done now.

"Your tea, Professor Bailey."

Edward put his head in his hands. Was everyone conspiring against him? His stomach growled at the aroma, and he glared toward his abdomen. He'd eaten breakfast at the normal time— why did these savage impulses betray him?

"Look at the poor gentleman," Johann said. "He's overcome with sentiment at how well we care for him."

"He's overcome with something all right, sir," Miss Ellis said, a flirtatious edge to her tone. Johann tended to do that to the fairer sex. As for his insouciant secretary, Edward didn't have the heart to reprimand her. Indeed, its caged animal beating— tea twenty-one minutes early—warred with his growling stomach.

"It's okay to emerge from your shell. She's gone. I'll pour the tea."

Edward peeked through his fingers. Johann poured two cups.

"You put the cream in first, right?"

"I've known you for how long? Yes, I fixed it the way you like it." He passed Edward the fixed tea, and Edward almost dropped the saucer on his desk, his fingers trembling.

"Thank you." He would not allow this disruption to turn him into an impolite savage, after all. "What are you doing here? If the meeting is with my chair and dean, what use could a musician be to them?"

"Perhaps they want to talk of a collaboration between our departments?"

Edward stared open-mouthed at his friend. "A collaboration? With musicians? What is this University coming to? I'm a serious scientist."

"Studying something no one seems to understand but you, and that barely."

"I am an accomplished aetherist in my field." Edward drew himself up and gestured to the stack of journals on his desk. "I have articles in all of these volumes."

"As you remind me every time I visit," Johann remarked. He set his teacup on top of the stack.

Edward drew in a gasp. "Move that at once! What if you spill?"

"Then you'll make another pile from among the dozens of spare journals you keep in your closet over there. Now tell me, how are the Duke, Duchess and ducklings? How many do they have now?"

Edward sighed. He knew Johann tried to educate him in social niceties like inquiring about family—his friend had two siblings and two parents, but Edward didn't see the point in asking about them since he never spoke with them outside of mandatory holiday gatherings—and bit his tongue so he wouldn't snap that they were irrelevant to the destruction of his morning.

He filled Johann in on what he knew of the family, but he couldn't focus. When his chair had a chance to inflict an interdisciplinary project on him, trying to stop him would be like keeping an airship from lifting once the gases were heated —it would take more than his measly efforts. Edward hoped that, like an airship, this disruption would float away and disappear, preferably before lunch.

etherics Department, Huntington University, England, 08 June 1870

"I'm not going." Edward didn't mean to sound petulant, but he didn't care. His morning routine had already been disrupted, his tea either too strong or his stomach unhappy with the rearrangement of its habits, and his friend insultingly cheerful about the whole thing. He put his hand on the latest issue of the Journal of Aether and Light. "I have important reading to do."

"You tore into that the day it got here and already have figured out where to incorporate the articles as references in your own research." Johann flexed his fingers. "And if you keep dallying, I'm going to miss my morning practice time, which will make me grumpy."

"Sure, I have to be considerate of *your* desired schedule, but no one cares about mine."

"Come on, Edward." Johann's tone said he grew tired of Edward's whining, as he'd told Edward many times. Johann hauled Edward to standing by one arm. "You can't upset your chair and your dean. They might sack you, and then where would you be?"

Edward always forgot how strong his friend was. "I hate it when you do that."

"Sometimes you need a reminder that you're not in charge," Johann said. "We all do. Now remind me where the conference room is?"

When they arrived in the large rectangular room, Edward first checked the windows, where the week before ivy had covered the panes on the outside and provided a sense of coziness. Now the sun shone in and threw harsh yellow squares on the floor.

"The ivy! Someone's cut the ivy." He dashed to the window and ran a finger over the smooth, warm glass.

"Open the window, will you?" Johann asked. "It's beastly hot in here."

"That's because they've cut the shade away." Edward pressed his hands to the panes, which almost seared his palms. "I suppose it doesn't matter. Nothing important to me does."

"On the contrary, I believe you'll be excited to hear my proposition for you, Professor Bailey." A voice boomed through the room and bounced off the hard surfaces.

Edward tried not to flinch—Dean Hartford had once called him a "sissy boy" when he'd observed Edward's typical reaction to his sudden, loud entrances—and turned from the window. It always shocked him how such a big voice could come from such a small person as his dean, who stood at one and a half meters, and Edward suspected a good bit of that height was due to the lift in the dean's shoes.

"Good morning, Dean Hartford," Johann said and shook the dean's hand. He looked like a blond giant next to the shorter man.

"Ah, Mister Bledsoe, I'm happy you could join us. The rest

of our guests will be here momentarily, as should Miss Ellis with some tea."

"Did you have the ivy cut back?" Edward asked. "It's made the room too warm not to have it."

"I didn't, but I suspect Harry did. It's tearing down your building, Professor. We're taking advantage of the good summer weather to do repairs."

Edward couldn't help but shudder at the name of his chairman, Professor Harold Kluge. The man delighted in torturing him, or so it felt. It didn't surprise Edward that his chair had been the author of tearing the ivy away from the windows and exposing everything in the room to the harsh light. Indeed, he wished he had some of the tinted lenses the Americans liked to wear.

Harold himself came through the door and was followed by a man Edward had never seen. Miss Ellis brought up the rear with a laden tea tray.

"Would you believe she was delayed because she was splitting sugar cubes?" Chairman Kluge asked the assembled with a scoff that poked Edward in the solar plexus. "Have you heard anything more ridiculous? I have instructed her that her job is too vital to waste time on such unimportant tasks."

"I don't mind," Miss Ellis murmured and put the tray on the table. She shot Edward a frightened look that caused him to feel sorry for getting her in trouble. But she should have known better—he'd had already had his morning allotment of tea. Why would she split more sugar cubes?

"I think it's a wonderful idea to make the sugar cubes smaller," the strange man who had come in with Harry said in flat American tones. "Those last few sips of tea end up being ghastly because the regular-sized lumps don't dissolve in time to evenly disperse their sweetening properties to the entire cup."

"My thoughts exactly," Edward said with a told you so look at Harry, who shrugged with his usual good humor.

"Ah, and here's a smart young man," the American said. "You must be Professor Edward Bailey, renowned aetherist."

He held out his hand for Edward to shake. Edward took it reluctantly and studied his unwitting ally. He'd encountered few Americans due to their finances being tight from the economic results of their ongoing "Civil" War, and thus their travel limited. He didn't understand what was so civil about it— beastly business, really. The man looked like a normal gentleman aside from that horrid accent. His dark suit was free of dust, and his graying hair neatly combed and beard trimmed.

Instead of releasing Edward's hand, the American clasped his other one around it. "I am relieved to see you, Professor. I was led to think you may not come."

Edward took his hand back from the man's unrelenting grasp. "I am fortunate to have friends who look out for my best interest." He looked at Johann sideways. "I think."

"You are indeed a fortunate man."

"Professor Bailey, this is Mister Parnaby Cobb," Dean Hartford said. "He has an interesting proposition for us as soon as our final guest arrives. Perhaps we should take our seats?"

Edward would have preferred to be where he could see the ivy, but since it wasn't there anymore, none of the seats seemed right. Finally, he took one beside Johann because it was farthest away from Chairman Kluge, who seemed to bask in the sunshine.

There goes my theory of him being a vampire. Edward took his watch from his pocket and glanced at the time: five past ten. *Five more minutes, and I'm declaring this a waste of my time and getting back to work. I need to set up the aether chamber and tweak the calibrations so the pressure is higher to begin the process of refining it to—*

The sound of scraping chairs brought Edward to the present, and he got his feet under him in time to rise along with the others in response to the appearance of two women.

"And who have we here?" Dean Hartford asked. "We didn't order any files or food."

The young woman in front held out a folded piece of paper. "I am Iris McTavish, Dean Hartford, and this is my assistant Sophie Smythe. You summoned me?"

"I requested the presence of Professor *Irvin* McTavish," the dean told her. "I'm sorry, Miss McTavish, but there must have been some mistake. We're in need of an archaeologist, not a secretary."

"Professor McTavish is indisposed currently, as you know," Miss McTavish, whom Edward found to have a frightening degree of poise, said. "He trained me, and so I am here in his stead."

Edward wondered how she managed to keep her composure under the irritable scrutiny of the men in the room. Well, not of Johann, who looked at her like she was a piece of candy, or of Edward, who truth be told, enjoyed the dean's surprise and consternation. Edward's sense of vindication evaporated when Johann pulled out the chair beside Edward and indicated she should sit there. Miss Smythe took a seat at the edge of the room and pulled a small pad of paper and pencil out of her reticule.

Miss McTavish sat and folded her hands in front of her on the table. Edward noticed the dust smudges at the tips of her gloves.

"I understand this is a matter of some urgency?" she asked.

"Well, young lady, I can't say this has anything to do with you," Parnaby Cobb said. "The journey we're talking about is going to be too rough for a woman. That's why we wanted your pa."

"Journey!" Edward stood. "I'm not here to discuss a journey. I have work to do this summer."

"Hold on," Johann said and put a hand on Edward's shoulder, drawing him back to his seat. "Let's hear what this is all about, and Professor Bailey and Miss McTavish can make their own decisions about their participation."

"And you are...?" Cobb asked.

"Johann Bledsoe, a talented musician," Harry told him. "He is to give this project's cover story its air of legitimacy."

"And the project is...?" Edward thrummed his fingers on the table. He knew it was rude to do so, but he couldn't help it. Sitting beside Miss McTavish made him remember things he had tried hard to forget and would have been able to keep shelved in the back closet of his mind if not for her calm, cool presence. The effort to prevent the memories from spilling out made him feel as if each of his cells was made of aether and insisted on vibrating with the kind of energy he was trying to harness through his experiments.

"The northern American states are running out of resources with this war," Cobb told them. "And frankly, gentlemen, and ladies, we're getting desperate."

"What kind of resources?" Miss McTavish asked.

"Power-generating ones. Coal is getting more and more expensive as manufacturing takes off here and at home. Professor Bailey, you know as well as I that in spite of the excitement around its discovery, aether has yet to prove, well, useful."

"It has a lot of potential, and we're getting closer every day," Edward said. "And I would make more progress if I didn't have to sit in meetings about projects I have no desire to participate in."

"And what about your funding, Professor?" Chairman Kluge asked. "Do you think the money for your little experiments grows on trees? Or in that ivy you're so fond of?"

"Little experiments?" The rest of Kluge's sentence processed through his brain. "And the University funds my research."

"Well, that's the problem, Professor," Dean Hartford said. "The University is growing impatient. The administration had hoped to see a return on its investment in aetheric research by now."

"Science takes time."

"And money," the dean told him. "And if there isn't a breakthrough by the end of the summer, the Department of Aetherics is in danger of being dissolved. We may be able to find a position for you in the general sciences, but it's not a guarantee, and the sole area with openings is the new Department of Geology."

"Geology?" Edward cataloged his experiments in his mind with some desperation. Although he felt close to a breakthrough, it would take him at least until the end of the year, and he doubted his colleagues were any closer.

"There's a chance to expedite your research," Cobb said. "Legend has it that there's an element to be found somewhere around the Mediterranean that can serve as a catalyst to turn aether into heat energy in a safe manner, which is what we need."

"What kind of legend?" Miss McTavish asked. "And what are your sources?"

She startled Edward every time she spoke. His mind tried to ignore her in spite of her sitting beside him, but he couldn't help but appreciate her questions.

"Ancient scripts and tablets, of course," Cobb told her. "A lot of them have been lost to time, but enough survive with tantalizing hints. There have also been rumors of this element referenced in classical works through the Renaissance. The question is how to get those artifacts and works of art without tipping off my competitors to the project."

"Hence where you two come in," Chairman Kluge said to

Edward and Johann. "It is a dying custom, but young men of means still take a Grand Tour through Europe, ending in Italy, Greece, or the Ottoman Empire."

"You wanted us to pose as tourists?" Johann asked.

"Yes, your musical and artistic backgrounds will be invaluable in recognizing clues and in gaining entree to private collections." The dean poured a second cup of tea for himself. "But the original idea was for Professor McTavish to accompany you under the guise of looking for artifacts to bring back to the University for our museum. I don't know how we could include an unchaperoned female."

"I'll have Miss Smythe with me to serve as chaperone," Miss McTavish said. "And women take the tour as well. I could accompany them and pretend they are family friends protecting me and my virtue."

"I don't like all this deception," Edward said. "If you want an aetherist to play this game of 'let's pretend,' you need to find someone else."

"You are the one whose specialty is the closest to the purpose of this quest. Plus, there is no one whose research shows the brilliance yours does, and I would hate for us to have to shut it down over lack of funds," the dean said. "Or are you so eager for that appointment to Geology?"

Edward sat back with a huff, although his ego did inflate at the compliment. "No."

"Let the young lady go," Cobb said. "What's more innocent than a group of young people?" Something about the way the American looked at Miss McTavish disturbed Edward. There wasn't anything lustful or inappropriate, but rather a sense of cold calculation. It reminded Edward of the expression he felt on his own face when he was in the midst of an experimental manipulation—*let's make this adjustment and see what happens.*

But Miss McTavish isn't aether or an experimental material.

She's a female. Granted, she's a bit talky, and she needs clean gloves, but...

"So are we decided?" Chairman Kluge asked. "That Professor Bailey and Mister Bledsoe will pose as Grand Tourists and Miss McTavish and her assistant will pretend to be a young lady and her maid, also on the Tour?"

"That should be easy enough," Miss McTavish said with a look at Miss Smythe, who bit her lip.

Ugh, females. Edward didn't want that kind of complication, but he also desired to keep his job and his department.

"What say you, Professor Bailey?" the dean asked.

"Very well," Edward told them, making sure to sound very unhappy about it.

"Excellent, gentlemen and ladies," Cobb told them. "I'll have my people make the travel arrangements so we can keep as much of this out of the university gossip circle as possible. You'll be hearing from them soon. Be sure to pack and set your affairs in order. You'll depart for Europe on Friday."

Chairman Kluge looked at Edward with a huge smile. "I'll have Miss Ellis circulate a note that you're taking a research sabbatical on the continent for the summer."

"And how much do you propose to compensate us for our time and trouble?" asked Johann.

"I trust you will find my terms to be most reasonable," Cobb said.

Edward rose, trusting his friend to take care of the boring financial bits. He supposed he should go back to his office and pack a trunk of the journals and books he would need so he wouldn't get too far behind while gallivanting about Europe.

"Oh, and Professor Bailey?" Kluge asked.

"Yes, Chairman?"

"Pack light. Once you leave the main Continent, your transportation will become quite limited with regard to luggage space."

Edward didn't miss the glee with which Kluge said the words.

When he returned to his office, he found the ivy had been stripped from his window as well, and buckets of paint outside his door indicated his friends Hickory, Dickory and Dock would share a similar fate.

3

Aetherics Department, Huntington University, England, 08 June 1870

"Well, that was a strange meeting," Sophie said once the gentlemen had departed, leaving the women alone in the conference room.

Iris looked around at the soiled teacups and crumb-filled plates. She thought about picking them up, but she didn't want to set expectations that she'd clean up after them. Instead, she laid a fingertip on the spoon the American Parnaby Cobb used and focused on its held impressions. Relief and the sensation that his hidden aims had been satisfied beyond what he had dared to hope, like a just-scratched itch but more triumphant. Very strange. She squeezed her eyes shut against the soreness at the base of her skull that often followed her readings, as she thought of them.

"Yes," she said, blinking her eyes and rubbing her fingertip against her thumb to clear the impressions. "But the important thing is that they have no suspicions about us, and we will be able to go on the journey." She patted her pocket where the telegram about her father's death usually nestled and, with a shock of terror, found it to be empty.

"Sophie, did you take the telegram?"

"What? No, Miss Iris. Last I saw it, you had it."

"Oh no, oh no, oh no." Iris bent and looked under the table, hoping the paper had fallen, but it was nowhere to be found.

"Quickly, we must retrace our steps. If someone else finds it and tells Dean Hartford, we're ruined!"

They rushed into the hall, where the musician Johann Bledsoe stood. He studied his nails with a casual air, but something about him made Iris draw up short. It wasn't her usual talent to determine what a person was thinking, but if she'd been a cat, her hackles would have raised. All she could do was straighten her shoulders to alleviate the squeezing sensation that swept up her spine and made her throat muscles clench.

"Mister Bledsoe," she squeaked with a nod.

"Miss McTavish, Miss Smythe." He gave them a lazy smile, but Iris didn't miss his shrewd glance. "It's a lovely day, and I was pondering stopping by the campus commissary for a spot of tea. Would you care to join me?"

Iris did not, but his next words confirmed her foreboding: "I suspect our conversation may yield some surprising discoveries."

Sophie went pale under her mad yellow curls, and Iris was sure bright pink spots appeared in her own cheeks. "We would be delighted."

Bledsoe offered his arm. "Then allow me to escort you."

Iris didn't want to touch him, and she made him wait with his elbow at an awkward angle while she pulled on her gloves, taking extra care the seams sat just right. As they walked through the halls and down the stairs, she looked for the folded piece of paper that would save her reputation and financial state, but it was nowhere to be found.

They exited the building, which had been denuded of its ivy facade.

"A pity about the ivy," Iris said. "The little green leaves waving in the breeze gave the department such a sage air."

"Ah, yes, but it's destructive." Bledsoe gestured with his free hand. "The roots eat their way through the rocks and produce small cracks, which turn into big cracks, which can bring down an entire structure more quickly than one would expect."

"You sound like you speak from experience."

"I've seen it happen in many circumstances. Whether it's a building requiring its mortar or a musical ensemble needing a certain amount of trust and understanding, it only takes a few tendrils to bring everything crashing down."

Iris listened to his subtext and responded. "And what are these tendrils of which you speak, good sir?"

"Distrust and deception regarding motive and circumstance." They'd reached the squat stone building that housed the student dining hall with its faculty attachment. Iris stopped herself before heading into the faculty area. Yes, it was summer, but what if one of her father's colleagues happened to be in there for a mid-morning cuppa or an early lunch? She'd had her fill of lying for the day.

"Thank you for accompanying me this far," she said. "But I'm afraid I must say goodbye. I have a lot to prepare for this journey."

The musician tugged her along into the faculty wing. "We haven't finished our conversation yet, Miss McTavish. I think you'll be interested in what I have to say."

"In that case, I would be more comfortable on the student side." Perhaps one of Father's students would see her and rescue her.

"Oh no. The tea is much better in the faculty hall, as I'm sure your father told you."

Iris nodded, unable to speak while suppressing the tears

that wanted to fall. Crying would let on she hid information from him, although she suspected he knew or had found the telegram.

Sophie had disappeared somewhere between the Aetherics Department and the dining hall. Iris couldn't blame her—she'd agreed with Sophie that if she got caught, she would take the sole responsibility. However, until she knew with certainty Bledsoe had the telegram, she wasn't going to let anything slip.

A pot of tea and plate of scones with little bowls of clotted cream and plum jam appeared on the table, courtesy of the students who worked in the faculty dining hall over the summer. They were barely older than she. Would she have to take such a position if this scheme fell through? She couldn't imagine slinging scones for a living.

Bledsoe poured the tea for them and took a long sip. "Excellent, as always."

Iris thought it tasted bitter, and she added some sugar. When she looked up, she found him studying her.

"Sir, your gaze is very forward."

"I cannot help but notice you haven't removed your gloves. Are you planning on leaving so soon?"

Iris swallowed and pulled the corners of her mouth back into a patient little smile. "You are quite right. I forgot myself." She pulled them off slowly.

"Tell me, Miss McTavish," he said and took the sugar tongs from her plate with surprising gentleness before helping himself to a cube. "Do women's skirts often have hidden pockets, and when they do, do those pockets always have holes in them?"

Warm spots flared like two brands had been pressed to her cheeks. "I don't know what you're talking about." But she couldn't look him in the eye.

"I'm trying to figure out if you lied about your father so you could be included on the trip and gain fame and fortune for yourself or if your air of desperation indicates more dire circumstances."

"Now you're speaking nonsense." *Put down the sugar tongs. Put them down so I can see what you're up to.*

"As you can imagine, the task we're about to undertake is going to be quite difficult. My primary concern isn't for you, as non-chivalrous as that makes me. It's for Edward Bailey."

Now Iris looked at him. "The aetherist?"

"Yes, him. As you could tell, he can be difficult."

"What in the world could be the problem? He seemed quirky, but I didn't think he would be any trouble."

"Quirky doesn't begin to describe him. He's one of those gentlemen who likes things just so."

Iris kept her hands folded in her lap. Would he never put those tongs down? "What does that have to do with me?"

Bledsoe gestured with the tongs. "He values honesty in others above all else. You noticed the animosity between him and Chairman Kluge?"

"They seem not to like each other very much."

"Well, that's because Harry lied to Edward when he was hired. I forget about what, some small thing, but it was enough. Edward never trusted him again, and it has led to some friction in the department."

There was the mention of trust again. Iris took a scone, thankful her talent didn't extend to foodstuffs, and hoped her hand didn't tremble in an obvious way. "And so you're concerned about the expedition? What happened to him to make him that way?"

"As with most problems, his started when a woman caught his eye."

Iris straightened. "There's no need to insult me."

"There is if it makes you listen to me." Bledsoe put the tongs back in the sugar cube bowl and ran a hand through his hair, making it stand up. "He got his heart broken by a girl named

Lily. He's a simple chap in some ways—brilliant with science, but dumb when it comes to dealing with other humans, especially women."

"Then I shall be certain to give him a wide berth. He will have his job, and I will have mine. I'll make my father proud." Iris tilted her head at him like she'd seen her mother do for years when challenged. "Is there anything else?" *And do you have any proof for your allegations?*

"Is there another name you could go by?"

Iris almost dropped her scone. "Excuse me?"

"If you were Ivy, that would be fine, but Edward doesn't like flowers."

"Again, it shouldn't be any concern of his. What is your motivation in all this? Why are you going?"

"You heard Parnaby Cobb. You'll need help getting the artistic elite and their wealthy patrons to allow you into their salons, studios, and parlors to see their artifacts and paintings if you have any hope of tracking down whatever this quest is after. Do you need more sugar? You already put a cube in your tea. It will be unbearably sweet."

"Right." Iris drew her hand back from the sugar tongs. "But what is your motivation? You're a musician with plenty of patrons here."

Bledsoe returned her gaze with a startled - and perhaps guilty? - expression. "Can't a young man go on an adventure without being questioned?"

"Apparently the chances of that are the same as a young woman agreeing to help with one without being accused of deception."

He popped the end of a scone in his mouth and finished the dregs of his tea. "Remember, Miss McTavish," he said after he finished chewing, "I'll be watching you. And I'll be holding on to this." He fished the telegram from his waistcoat pocket and held it up. She clenched her fist so she wouldn't make an unladylike grab for it, as badly as she wanted to. But to do so would draw more attention to herself and her predicament; academics were such hopeless gossips. The sugar from the top of one of the scones crunched in her back teeth when she bit back a scream of frustration.

"Why not expose me now?" she asked. "Since you so obviously needed to make the point."

"Because I suspect having this information will be useful later." He stood and bowed. He disappeared before Iris could retort.

She counted backward from twenty—no, better make that thirty—to still her thrumming heart, or at least get the darn thing to stop sending clogging sensations to her throat and jolts of panic to her stomach. She slid a hand into her hidden pocket and found it, indeed, had a hole in it. When had that happened? Sophie should have been maintaining her clothes better.

Or she should have been more careful. She took a sip of the now cold tea, ignoring the invitation to see what the student who'd last handled the cup felt at the time. She picked up the tongs, but all she sensed was concern with an undercurrent of true fear.

If she didn't need the money so badly, Iris would bow out of the whole affair, but as it was, she would now have to be more careful. But about what? Not to charm the strange Edward Bailey too much? Granted, he was nice-enough looking with his chestnut hair and large blue eyes, but she'd detected his nervousness without having to read any of his possessions. Traveling with him would likely be a nightmare, but would it be more so than she anticipated?

Is Professor Bailey that unstable? Or worse, is he brilliant but truly mad?

4

G*range House, 08 June 1870*
By the time she returned home, Iris's nerves had been rubbed raw. She opened the door to find Cook in a flurry.

"Oh, Miss McTavish, I've been waiting for you. There's a gentleman caller, and I've naught but yesterday's scones for tea!"

Iris glanced at the hallway clock, and her stomach growled. Had she really spent all that time at the university? Sophie had disappeared. Iris needed to have a conversation with that girl about staying close by. She couldn't have her maid wandering off in some large city neither of them was familiar with.

Had Iris known she'd have such a frustrating day, she would not have agreed to tea with the odious Jeremy Scott, her father's least-favorite student. But Scott had insisted on meeting with her and had threatened to telegram her father if she refused. And here it was, tea time, and she must look a fright.

"I'm sure they will be fine" Iris said. "Heat them in the oven with a teacup of water and make sure the butter is softened when you bring them out." Iris hung her hat on the rack by the door.

Before Iris walked into the parlor, Sophie appeared and blocked her. "You look a fright, Miss. Let me help you change. The young man can wait a bit longer."

"I'm not looking to impress him, Sophie."

"No, but you don't want to get a reputation for being slatternly, either. It will only take a minute."

"Five minutes. Then I need to get rid of him and go lie down. My head is aching."

"Because you skipped lunch, Miss."

Iris led her up the stairs. "If you'd stayed around, I could have sent you for something."

"I'm sorry, Miss," Sophie said. Iris turned to see her maid's cheeks were pink, and an idea took root.

"Where did you go today, Sophie?"

"I needed to get some air. The dust was making me sneeze."

Iris didn't remember any sneezing, but she needed to turn her attention to her own toilette and issues.

"The brown silk, please," she said once Sophie had gotten her out of her day dress. It was a relief to be free of the sweaty, dusty thing.

"Oh, no, Miss. That will make you look pale. Here, put this one on. It will bring out your eyes."

Sophie held a gown of purple silk that Iris had always thought too fancy for daytime, but not formal enough for evening. Not that Iris cared for activities other young women did. She would always choose staying at home and reading scientific papers over going to balls and dinners. As for the opera—were they singing or screaming? She admitted to a bias against it since that was where her mother had decided on her first adulterous liaison.

"I'm not going to wear that! He'll think I'm interested."

"Well, your other day dresses have been packed, so if you

won't wear this one, it's either your traveling frock—and if you get tea on it you're traveling in this dress—or your evening gowns."

"Fine, I'll wear that one."

IRIS DESCENDED the stairs looking the part of a lady and wishing she felt poised and confident. Sophie had put Iris's hair up and rouged her cheeks—so she wouldn't look sick, goodness why was she so pale?—and Iris frowned at the thought that she might look like she wanted to appear desirable.

"You look lovely," Lord Jeremy Scott said and bowed over her extended hand, which was, as usual, ensconced in one of her nice kid gloves.

Bollocks. "Thank you. I appreciate your patience. I apologize for my delay, but I was held up at the University." She sat on the hard chaise, and he settled back in her father's favorite armchair. She blinked against the pressure at the corners of her eyes—the young man looked wrong there. The sensation of something in the center of her chest cracking like a stepped-on potsherd drove home the fact that Irvin McTavish, archaeologist and father extraordinaire, would never sit there again.

Don't cry in front of him, don't cry.

"I'm sorry, have I come at a bad time?" Lord Jeremy asked.

"No, I'm sorry, I was momentarily overcome. I didn't eat lunch."

Sophie brought in the tea service and set it on the low table between them.

"That must have been quite the meeting," he said. "To have kept you from eating. I can't remember the last time I missed a meal." He patted his stomach, which even at his relatively young age, showed a paunch.

Exasperation chased away the grief, at least for the

moment. Iris ignored the invitation to elaborate on what the meeting was and with whom and instead entertained herself with the image of him growing rounder as he aged. "Yes, it was, and you are privileged if you have never had to delay eating for something more important."

His eyebrows drew together, and a flush came to his cheeks, telling her he was at least clever enough to sense her barb. She reminded herself to be careful—as irritating as he could be, he was a member of the gentry and could cause trouble for her.

"But I am pleased I didn't inconvenience you too much," she added and took a sip of tea to wash the bitterness of the words from her tongue. Lies upon lies upon lies...

"Not at all. In fact, I'm pleased we will run late. Would you like to accompany me to dinner and the opera tonight? It's the student summer production, but I hear there is a magnificent second-year tenor. Those who hear him now will be able to claim knowledge of him as a raw talent before he becomes famous."

"Thank you, but I'm afraid I have other plans." *Like organizing my own things for packing.*

"Ah. A pity, then."

Sophie brought in a tray of foodstuffs including the scones —which looked dry but would hopefully not crumble—and cucumber sandwiches. The cucumber was so fresh Iris smelled it, and she guessed her delay had allowed Cook pick one from the garden. *Bravo, Cook! I'm glad Father planted the cucumbers before he left.*

Jeremy waited for her to fix a small plate and helped himself to more than a few items. "I've heard your cook does marvelous things with scones," he said.

"She does," Iris agreed and held her breath as he broke one and buttered it. A few more crumbs than one would expect fell to the plate, but overall it held up well. She exhaled—the baked good disaster averted. "So what did you want to speak with me about?"

"Well, I will be finished with my degree next year, and although my brother will inherit the bulk of the estate, I do have some money coming to me."

Uh oh. Iris sipped her tea and tried to avoid making a pained expression. "I see?"

He leaned forward, and the scone on top of his plate scooted forward to the lip. Iris focused on it to avoid the earnest expression on his face.

"Yes, so I was wondering, that is, if your father will agree, I'm going to be needing a wife soon."

"For what?" Iris gave him a guileless smile.

He sputtered and turned red. Iris tried not to laugh.

"Well, for wifely things," he said. "And I thought you would be perfect for the role because of our common interests. I've seen you around the department and know you helped your father with his cataloging when he came home from trips."

"Yes, I did," Iris told him. "So you need help cataloging? What about research? Field work?"

"Oh, yes, that too, well at least the research part of it. A woman has no place in field work. And I will be sure to credit you in my footnotes for any contributions you should make. You know, if you have time around keeping house and mothering children."

Iris lowered her lashes so she wouldn't give him the glare he deserved. *Footnotes? No place in field work?*

"I imagine you would benefit from the formal connection to my father too," Iris said, unable to resist poking at him.

"Oh, indeed. I would like to have access to his library and mind when needed. I imagine he has notes he needs written up into papers."

Iris smiled at him and imagined the cucumber seed she squished between her molars was his head. Was he suggesting he could write up her father's discoveries and take partial credit for them? Journal readers and editors would think a second author contributed more than what he suggested.

"I'm serious about forwarding my career in archeology. And about you," he added quickly. He nodded so emphatically the fork dropped from his plate.

"I see." She retrieved the utensil and confirmed her suspicions—a stab of hopeful triumph and the thought fragment of the intention to use her mind and her father's resources to further his career so he wouldn't have to do too much work on his own.

"So what do you say, Miss McTavish? Will you do me the honor of becoming Lady Scott?"

"I'm afraid not," Iris said. "I have my own plans, and I cannot consider marrying you until my father returns." Which was to say, never.

"Oh." The curves of his face rearranged themselves into a fleshy frown. "I thought, being one of those rare, logic-minded women, you would be excited for the ability to help your husband with research."

"Well, we logic-minded women do tend to think for ourselves," Iris told him. She stood, and he hesitated and looked with regret at his half-full plate. Finally he set it aside and rose.

"Are you sure you will not reconsider? As I said, I can offer you a small fortune as well."

"I'm afraid you'll have to be more convincing than that," she said. "Sophie will let you out."

"This will not be our last discussion about this," he promised, the hint of a threat in his tone.

Iris lifted her chin. "If my father returns and gives you his blessing, I will marry you without a word of protest." With that, she swept out of the room and up the stairs.

range House, 09 June 1870
 G The next evening after she, Sophie and Cook had enjoyed a light meal—there was no other kind at the moment—Iris went into her father's study to see what she needed to bring with her. She and Sophie had packed most of what he'd had in his university office and had it delivered to the house, and the boxes stood under the windows, in chairs, and anywhere else they fit.

If nothing else, we can burn old papers for heat this winter. Not that Iris could stand the thought of burning her father's papers. Or selling off his prized artifacts. She walked to the shelves and ran her finger over a stone bowl held on either side by strange little beasts, possibly lions. The features of their faces had softened into vague curves, but they held some sense of their former ferocity. She cleared her mind and focused on it. Old things tended to have a fog around them because of all the people who had touched them, and although the most recent contact came through the clearest, she liked impressions from the past the best. Sometimes she got images of life long ago showing how the object was used—this one was for a ceremony in a dark, smoky temple—or what the object once had been, in the case of potsherds and fragments. Although they'd never talked directly about it, Iris suspected she and her father shared the talent. Otherwise, how could he have made such brilliant deductions that proved true every single time based on so little initial information?

What needs to come with me? She didn't expect the objects to move by some sort of magical force, but nothing suggested itself to her with a nudge. No, wait, that wasn't quite right. Something called to her. It wasn't a sound, although it pressed on her ears in waves, like the ripples on the water after a stone is thrown into a pond. The sensation danced across her mind with the delicacy of a feather and the ponderous insistence of a funeral bell.

Iris turned to her left to a shelf between the windows. She didn't expect anything important to be there. Common sense said that the most significant items would be on or within easy reach of the desk, but she found a lump of black rock. Her father had talked about volcanic stones found at sites where no volcano had been because ancient peoples believed them of divine origin and carted them there. She picked it up and dropped it when a jolt of panic made her stifle a scream.

Danger, danger, danger!

She sank to her knees and wrapped her arms around her stomach, rocking to keep from sobbing out loud and bringing Cook or Sophie to her side. What would she say? That a rock made her cry?

There is something very wrong with that thing. She gulped a few deep breaths to clear the stifling sense of threat and doom around the rock, and her rational mind reasserted itself. *Why did he have it in here?*

She picked it up again, this time attempting to block the sensations, and brought it over to the desk, where she could examine it in the lamplight. A lump of dull, black stone with striations over the surface regular enough to have been carved by ancient hands, it felt less dense than a stone that size should feel, and she guessed it might be hollow. She remembered accompanying her father to a lecture he'd given with one of his geological colleagues on such stones. The volcano eggs, as they were called, had crystals in the middle of them, which led to legends of them having been the eggs of dragons or other mythical creatures.

The object warmed to her touch. Iris put it on the desk and flexed her fingers to clear the sense of dread it inspired. *Why would it put forth emotions without giving any images or thoughts? Could it be blocking something inside?* She reached for it, then drew her hand back. *I can't do this right now.*

She lit all the lamps in the office and told herself she needed the light to see, not to dispel the eerie feeling of impending threat the volcano egg gave her. She piled books and objects on the desk, attempting to figure out what she needed, but concentration eluded her. The volcano egg's force poked at the edge of her consciousness with the persistence of a street urchin begging for a shilling to buy his dinner, and Iris found herself with a dull headache. The situation horrified as well as intrigued her. She'd never come upon an object that called to her with the strength to force her to read it. Finally, she gave up and cradled it in her palms. This time it didn't put off dread but rather urgency as if its original emanations were some sort of scream to get her attention.

"What do you want to tell me?" she asked and focused on that question in her mind. She turned the volcano egg over in her hand, and her thumbnail traced one of the deeper striations. It gave, and she worked her nails further into the crack until the stone popped in half, revealing a center of small crystals so red and sharp Iris checked her own fingertips to make sure she hadn't cut herself. A sense of the air around her sighing accompanied the egg's opening, and some primitive part of her told her to freeze and listen.

A small gold box covered with strange symbols sat inside the stone. Iris pried it out. This object gave off dread, betrayal and fear, but the only image she got from it was of a pair of gloved hands tearing open a packet of powder, which was poured into a drink. She tried to see if the gold box, which was the size and shape of a flattened cigar, could be opened, but it was impossible with her fingers as sore as they were from prying apart its hiding place. It was either stuck or had some sort of catch she couldn't find. She slipped it into her pocket after checking to ensure there were no holes, closed the stone, and placed the volcano egg on the shelf where she found it.

She looked at the books on the shelves with renewed interest in finding something that would give her a key to deciphering the box's symbols, but she shook her head to clear the sense of waking from a vivid dream where reality blurred with imagination. *Pack first. Play with the box later.*

Iris returned to her sorting and organizing, but a thunk against the window drew her attention and set her heart thrumming. The curtains were drawn, so she was sure no one could see in. Still, she paused, her senses on high alert.

Another thud and a series of scratches made her race for the fireplace poker and brandish it toward the windows. Like most gentlemen of the age, her father had inherited guns and pistols, but they were in the sitting room, not his office, and she wasn't sure she would know how to shoot one. She counted a hundred breaths before she dared move, and she doused the lights. After her eyes adjusted to the darkness, she peeked through the curtains. No intruder or creature could be seen, but a circle with a box inside had been etched on the glass pane.

Iris suspected she and her father might share a special talent, but it hadn't occurred to her that others might also be able to sense objects. Now it became apparent they could, and someone knew she'd found the box. As for who and what they wanted with it—or her—she didn't know.

Iris slept with the fire poker and one of her father's ancient swords in the bed beside her.

6

H aywood House, *10 June 1870*
Edward woke with a sense of dread and looked at the clock beside his bed, which the early morning light illuminated. It told him it was five thirty, and he rolled over, relieved he had another two hours to sleep. He'd been having an awful dream of having to pack his things for a journey he didn't want to take, and a woman whose dark blue eyes bored into him and gave him the feeling she could read the tale of his failures with Lily. Thankfully he could look forward to a productive day at the office with his new aether isolation device, and—

A pounding on his door roused him.

"Come on, Edward, it's time to get up," Johann Bledsoe, who must have risen earlier, called. "The train leaves in an hour."

The memories of the past few days rushed in with the inexorable force of a large engine. Edward's reality wasn't a quiet, productive summer free of teaching responsibilities and clumsy students. It was a horrifying journey including women and the possibility of him losing his position and indeed his beloved Aetherics department if he didn't go.

Edward rolled out of bed and dressed without assistance. He was sure the servants were busy packing last-minute things, whatever that might include, and he didn't want to call for anyone. He suspected these would be his last few moments of quiet for a while.

He packed a couple of books, the last two he deemed necessary, in his valise before someone knocked on his door for his personal trunk. He allowed the two burly servants to take it but held on to his own travel case so at least he would have his books and important notes with him. He saw a stack of folded papers on the desk. On the front, printed in neat child's scrawl, was "On the Habits of Earthworms." Right, his niece Mary's initial foray into scientific observation. Fond amusement almost made him smile at the memory of when she'd presented it to him at his brother's house.

"I put it in a journal for you, Uncle," she'd said. "It'th on worms."

"And did you follow the experimental protocol we discussed the last time I was here, of *careful* observation at regular intervals?"

"Yeth, Uncle," she said.

"She did very well," her mother, the Duchess had added. "And she hopes you will give her work the serious consideration it deserves."

He'd heard the note of warning, and no one wanted to cross the Duchess. Plus, he loved his niece, the only scientist he knew with a lisp. He grabbed the "journal." Even if he never made it back from this accursed journey, Mary's report would make a useful bookmark.

Johann breakfasted in the dining room of the Duke of Waltham's town house, where Edward lived in one of the extra bedrooms. The musician looked chipper in spite of having been out the previous night for a "farewell tour of the pubs" with his favorite actress.

"What time did you go to bed?" Edward asked, prepared to remark on his friend's profligate lifestyle. Not that Johann deserved it, but Edward wanted to scold someone for something, and he wasn't going to take his irritability out on his brother's servants, who did their best for the family.

"Haven't been yet," Johann said around a mouthful of eggs. "The train is for sleeping. Bloody boring."

"Are you still drunk?" Edward asked with a horrifying premonition that his friend might vomit in the middle of their journey.

Johann gestured to his plate, which in spite of his working on breakfast for a while, held a large amount of food. "That's what all this absorbent material is for."

"Right." Edward sat at the table and buttered his toast. A servant poured a cup of tea for him without allowing Edward to put cream in his cup first, but he didn't say anything. He would have to deal with all sorts of privations soon enough—might as well get used to it now. He put a whole sugar cube in the tea as well.

"Getting ready to rough it, eh?" Johann asked.

Edward glared at him, and his butter knife went through his toast. He dropped it on the plate and checked his fingers for injury.

"Your brother thinks this will be good for you."

"He would." He put jam on one of his asymmetrical toast fragments and ate it in misery alternating with sips of his too-sweet tea.

No matter how much he sulked or tried to do anticipatory penance for his sins of pickiness, Edward couldn't revert everything to the way it once was or delay their departure forever. Even his brother came to see them off.

"Where is Miss McTavish?" Johann asked and checked his pocket watch. "We weren't supposed to pick her up, were we?"

GRANGE HOUSE, *10 June 1870*

On the day of the journey, Iris woke to a very quiet house and the sense something had gone terribly wrong. Concern she'd forgotten something important had made her toss and turn until exhaustion claimed her. But a different kind of anxiety had awoken her this time. Careful not to injure herself on the sword or fireplace poker she'd placed in the bed, she rolled over and out to check everything one more time.

In the dim room, she touched her trunk, valise and reticule in turn, then moved toward her maid Sophie's luggage. Instead of leather-covered wood, air met Iris's questing hand, and she hurriedly lit a lamp to reveal that Sophie's trunk was gone. She ran into Sophie's room, a small bedroom off Iris's, and found it to be empty of Sophie and all of her things. Iris's sleep-fogged mind told her Sophie had been taken by whatever had made the strange symbol on the office window.

"Sophie?" Iris called. "Sophie, where are you?"

She dashed down the stairs and found Cook in the kitchen. Her eyes were red from crying.

"Cook, where is Sophie? She's been kidnapped with all her things." As she said it, Iris knew how silly it sounded, and her brain put together Sophie's strange absences and distant looks of the past weeks.

"Yes, Miss, but not in the way you think." Cook gestured to a letter on the table. Iris picked up the folded sheet of vellum with trembling fingers and sensed regret and fear but also joy and excitement.

The emotions must be intense for a material as flimsy as paper to hold them.

DEAR MISS IRIS,

I am sorry to leave you like this, but I can't bear to go on a jour-ney. I've been seeing the Scotts' footman and was hoping you'd accept Lord Jeremy's suit so we could be together, but since you're deter-mined to go on your adventure rather than being sensible and marrying him, I had to take matters into my own hands. With Lord Jeremy's help, we've run off to Scotland to be married. I will see you when you return and would be happy to resume my position as your lady's maid.

 Best, Sophie

ACCEPT *her back after she's run off like that? Hardly. Cheeky wench!* Iris's cheeks burned, and she crumpled the vellum. What was she going to do now? She couldn't go on the journey without her maid, her chaperon. What would become of her reputation?

"Miss, begging your pardon for bothering you at such a time because I know how much Miss Sophie meant to you, and I'll miss her too," Cook said. "But I need to buy eggs today since our chickens aren't laying, and I need money for the market."

"Of course," Iris said, the reality of her situation crashing down around her. "The hens seem to know when something is amiss."

"Yes, Miss. Are you still going on your journey?" Cook shot her a concerned glance, but unlike Sophie had never voiced her opinion of Iris's actions.

"I need a moment to think."

Iris went into the office, where she fetched the key for her late father's strongbox, and she opened it and counted the money remaining. Even if they were down to a household of two—and Iris would need another maid if she were to maintain the appearance of her social class—she needed to bring in an income. She closed her eyes and thought about her options— stay and accept Lord Jeremy's offer of marriage or go on the journey by herself. The thought of his shocked look when she turned him down and the idea of looking across the breakfast table at him every morning made her stomach turn. But he wanted more than just Iris... Thinking about how he would desecrate her father's study and steal his work made up her mind.

I cannot marry him. The thought asserted itself with unarguable certainty. *There's no other option. I'll go on the journey unchaperoned. If I return with my reputation ruined, it will be with enough income that Cook and I can go somewhere and start over. And if I don't return...*

She refused to consider the possibility.

A line from Sophie's letter came to mind—*with Lord Scott's help.* What if the maid had revealed the plan for the journey to her lover's employer?

The grind of wheels on the stones outside made up her mind. Iris grabbed enough money for two months of household expenses for Cook, some for herself for the journey—in case of emergencies—and slam the lid of the box. She locked it, hid it and the key and ran into the kitchen. Three loud booms echoed through the house, but Iris couldn't tell whether it was the front or side door.

"Cook, go to the door and see who it is," she called. "If it is Lord Scott, please tell him I am not at home. If it is a porter for my trunk, send him in."

"Yes, Miss."

Iris dashed upstairs and finished her toilette. She attempted to pin her hair up and hoped her buttons in the back weren't askew, but there was little she could do about either. Her fingers trembled too much.

Cook appeared in the doorway followed by a tall young man whose eyes took in everything about the bedroom including Iris herself. The look he gave her made her stand straighter and lift her chin to show she wouldn't be intimidated. Instead of bowing or looking away, his lips peeled back into the sort of smile one expected to see on the patron of a naughty peep show.

"These your things, Miss?" he asked, his tone respectful unlike his expression.

"Y-yes," Iris said. The whole situation seemed ill put-together, so she asked, "And who are you?"

"Name's Lamar. I work for Mister Cobb. Your train's in fifteen minutes. We better get a move on."

Once again, the sound of the knocker on the front door echoed through the house. Iris went to her window, where she saw the familiar lines of the Scott coach with its matched four chestnut geldings in front of the house. *Bollocks!* She couldn't remember what the itinerary had said about who would pick her up, but Lamar seemed close enough.

"Yes, we should. Take the trunk down, and I'll meet you by the back gate. Don't argue, just do it."

He complied, again looking more amused than anything else. What did he find so funny?

She embraced Cook, who grasped her upper arms.

"Oh, right." Iris pressed the household money into her hands. "This should be enough to take care of you for a couple of months."

"I don't like the feel of this, Miss." Cook's face, which looked like it had been fashioned by a pastry chef to resemble the holiday dough-dolls children received on Christmas morning, fell in lines of concern. "You're going to go off with that strange gentleman?"

"It's either that or be forced to marry Jeremy Scott. He's lazy but clever, and I have no doubt he will trap me in a compromising situation such that I will have to wed him or suffer my reputation ruined." And doom herself to a life of misery. Regardless of what her mother had said, Iris couldn't consign herself to that fate. Not without a fight.

She pecked Cook on the cheek, grabbed her reticule, traveling hat, and valise, and rushed down the stairs. "Wait five minutes and then answer the door!" she called over her shoulder. "Stall them so they won't follow me. If he catches me, he'll make me miss the train."

"Yes, Miss." Cook huffed down the stairs behind her. "I've fresh scones. That's always good for stopping a man."

Especially that one. Iris smiled, rushed through the kitchen, and into the garden. Her trunk was loaded onto an open carriage, where Lamar sat behind... Not horses, but a long cylinder that puffed out plumes of white steam.

"An open steamcoach," Iris sighed. She would have been more excited—only the wealthiest had smaller vehicles good for racing as well as driving, and she hadn't had the chance to ride in one—but she wasn't sure it could outrun the Scott team. No matter, it was better than waiting to face her doom. She tossed her valise and reticule onto the seat and climbed in before the driver could get down to hand her up. He handed back a set of goggles instead. She tried to tie her hat on while he drove away but found herself having to hold on to the side of the carriage for balance with one hand and grabbing her things with the other.

"Can you take it easier?" she asked. "I'm about to lose everything."

A whinny behind her told her that they had been spotted.

"On the other hand, hurry," she said.

"Doing the best I can, Miss. The train in front of us is more important to me than the coach behind us." He shot her a look of mixed amusement and irritation. "You were supposed to be the easy one to fetch. Those gentlemen have no idea what they're getting into with you, do they?"

Iris spared another glance behind her, where she swore the Scott coach was catching up with them. How far away was the train station? She'd often gone with her mother and the footman when they had one to drop her father off before his expeditions, but this man was taking a different route. A hard bump made her lose her grip and bang her elbow when she grabbed again for the side.

"Careful," she hissed around the pain that radiated to her collarbone. She got a hold on the carriage door handle, her fingers tingling. "Do you know where you're going?"

"I'm taking the smaller streets a steamcoach can manage better than a coach and four," he said. "Don't worry, they're falling behind."

Iris looked behind her, but a sharp pain in her neck made her have to take his word for it. After what seemed to be hours when they alternated evading their pursuers and almost falling into their clutches — or so it seemed — the bulk of the train station rose in front of them. The train huffed and hissed, and Iris hoped it was settling in after stopping, not getting ready to depart without her.

7

Huntington Station, 10 June 1870
When the steamcart stopped, a shout drew Iris's attention to a group of men by the door, and a tall blond figure she recognized as Johann Bledsoe ran to the coach. She rose on shaky feet.

"You're about to miss it," he said and lifted her down without her permission. "Hurry, now."

The clattering sound of the Scott coach cut off Iris's sharp retort, and she nodded. He grabbed her things, and, followed by Lamar with the trunk, they ran through the train station and into a car, where Lamar dropped off her trunk and exited before she could thank him. She wished she'd had the chance to ask why he looked so amused.

"Is Miss Smythe right behind you?" Bledsoe asked.

"No, she has decided not to accompany me. I will have to manage without her."

"That explains your hair and dress," he said.

Iris lifted her hand to find her hair had fallen, and when she shifted her shoulders, she felt she had not, after all, buttoned her dress straight behind her. No wonder the driver

had been laughing—he'd been amused at the gradual dishevelment of her person.

"You don't have to mock me," she said.

"And with each time I meet you, I become more convinced
you're not a common criminal or liar. If you were, you would
have planned better. By the way, who was chasing you?"

"That is none of your business."

"Oh, I suspect we'll become intimately familiar with each
other's business by the time this journey is over." Then, as if to
illustrate, he offered, "By the way, if you need pins, I have some
in my pocket."

"Where did you get hairpins?" Iris asked.

"From an actress friend."

She didn't ask further.

Once she'd put her hair up, Iris settled in and studied her
two companions. Before she could get very far, a tunnel
plunged the car into blackness, and the small lamps along the
walls sputtered to life but without the gas smell Iris expected.
She stood, gathered her skirts, and climbed onto the cushioned
bench to take a closer look. If she happened to accidentally
kick Bledsoe's leg, it was the fault of the train's lurching.

"Ingenious," she said.

"What is?" Professor Bailey asked and blinked with the air
of a man emerging from a dream. He stood and steadied
himself on the compartment wall behind him.

"What are you doing?" Bledsoe hissed. His eyes had become
red-rimmed, and he kept scrubbing at his face. He reminded
Iris of a cranky child in need of a nap.

Ignoring him, Iris said, "The lamps are enclosed in glass.
One pipe brings in the gas, and another removes the fumes. I'm
not sure what the third does."

"Probably provides air to feed the flame," Bailey said. "Very
clever. A train car fire would be disastrous in a tunnel. That
arrangement ensures everything is in balance and contained."

Iris looked around. "This is not a typical railway car."

"It's Cobb's personal one," Bledsoe said without opening his eyes. "He's letting us leave Albion in style."

Iris ran her finger over the polished wood and made note of the unworn red cushions on the benches. The fastenings and accents were of gleaming brass. "I didn't notice much of it when I entered due to my hair being in my face."

"Well, perhaps you should stop talking and explore."

Iris put her hand on top of his head and not-so-gently leaned on him to stabilize herself as she stepped down from the bench.

"Would you care to join me, Professor Bailey?" she asked to tweak Bledsoe.

"No, I shall remain here." He alighted from the bench he stood upon, resumed his seat, and leaned back with a pained expression. "Too much moving about in these things makes me ill."

"Right. I shall leave the two of you to your suffering." Neither man stood when she left, so she closed the door more firmly than necessary, taking pleasure in Bledsoe's wince. Apparently he'd celebrated on his last night in town.

The compartment they sat in took up the bulk of the width of the car, so Iris found herself in a small corridor banked with windows that showed they had exited the tunnel and now moved through sheep-grazing lands. She grabbed a vertical handle for balance and gazed out at the bucolic scene of little farmhouses and fields full of animals that seemed uninterested in the train.

A motion against the unbroken blue of the sky made Iris squint, but all she could make out was some sort of bird. She shook her head at her folly, but she couldn't help but notice it flew in a line so straight as to be unnatural. Didn't birds swoop and turn? The train outpaced it, and a trickle of sweat dripped between her breasts.

Although the sitting compartment had some sort of ventilation, the corridor didn't, so Iris moved along and found the next room was a water closet—thankfully. Having taken care of her personal needs, she moved along and found a small kitchen, where a dark-haired maid set out tea service on a cart with indentations so the cups wouldn't slide about with the motion of the train.

"Can I help you, Miss?" she asked.

"No, thank you," Iris said. "Are we about to have tea? Do you know how long the journey will be?" She had glanced at the itinerary Cobb's messenger had delivered to the house, but with all the excitement over the hidden golden case—secured in her pocket—and the morning's chase to the station, the details slid from Iris's memory.

"We'll be meeting Mister Cobb's ship in Winchester, but we have to go through London first, which always slows us down. I'd say about two and a half hours, three to four if there's a delay on the tracks."

"Thank you." Indeed, when Iris walked back into the corridor, she noticed the sky had taken on a lighter hue, and a dark smudge appeared on the horizon to the south, heralding the smoke from the factories. She hoped the train car had some sort of solution to filter out the worst of the smells.

If we can succeed and find a way to harness the power of aether, it will help those poor wretches in the city who have to breathe that horrid air.

"We're about to have tea," Iris announced in as bright a tone as possible when she re-entered the passenger compartment. She had to step over Bledsoe's legs, which he'd stretched out.

Professor Bailey checked his watch. "Of course we are," he said in a tone that indicated it was not ideal.

"Is it not a good time?" Iris asked.

"It is as long as I will be able to..." He shook his head. "My usual teatime is at eight thirty in the morning. It is only eight o'clock."

A dark shape swooped down outside the window and disappeared before Iris could get a good look. It distracted her from the professor's ridiculous adherence to schedule.

"Did you see that?" she asked.

"See what?" The professor looked outside.

"Something came down out of the sky and looped past the window."

"You mean a bird?" Bledsoe didn't open his eyes. "They have those here."

"No." Iris glared at him although he couldn't see her. "It didn't move like one." She listened for the scrape of metal on glass, but the noise of the train filled her ears. And Bledsoe's resumed snoring.

Good. She glanced at Professor Bailey, who watched the compartment door with a frown. *The devil take them both. They deserve each other.*

EDWARD SHIFTED IN HIS SEAT, determined not to run to the water closet while they went through London. He'd tried after their morning tea, which came complete with the berry-lemon scones he liked, but the pressure to perform outside his usual time frame was too much for him. Now he was stuck and uncomfortable. He suspected the toilet flushed onto the tracks, and he didn't want to add to the filth and smells of the city, which crept into the compartment in spite of the ventilation system having switched to a recirculation of the air. At least that was what he could surmise from the facts that London didn't smell as bad as he remembered, and the air in their car increased in heat and humidity, indicating an extra steam engine at work somewhere. He would have to ask Cobb if he could look at it sometime because he'd never encountered a machine like that.

God bless the Americans and their ingenuity.

The train slowed to move through London, although it didn't stop at any of the stations. The smoke and fog hung thick in the air, and the residents of the city drifted through it like wraiths. From what Edward could determine, the ratio of steam carts to horse-drawn carriages was about one to three, but it was also difficult to tell from brief glimpses through the gloom.

"They look so pitifully thin," Miss McTavish said and gestured to a woman holding a child by the hand. Even with a short look, Edward saw how gaunt their faces were, how bony their wrists. Then they were gone, replaced by the smoke-stained wall of a factory, possibly the employer of both mother and child, assuming they had work at all.

Edward shifted again, this time from soul-discomfort. Of course he was aware of the conditions in the city, how the coal- and steam-driven factories burned through their workers, children and adults alike, and spit them out to a life of poverty. No one could last with twelve-hour days of intense work, and injuries that broke minds and bodies forever were common. He had the same thought everyone did—what could he do about it?—but it was uncomfortable to be faced with the result of his indifference.

"How could harnessing the power of aether help them?" Miss McTavish asked.

Edward looked up to see her dark blue eyes fixed on his face, her gloved hands folded in her lap like a good student. Dear god, her question was serious.

"What do you mean?"

"You're a scientist. Surely you don't work just to discover things. You must do so to develop things that will help people, make their lives better."

Edward looked outside at a cluster of factories all huddled

close to the rail line. Random bits of debris swirled between the train and the blackened brick walls. "I'm more of a theoretical scientist. I discover things and leave it to the engineers and inventors to transform my discoveries into practical applications."

"But don't you think about the end result?" she pressed. "Otherwise, what keeps you motivated to persist in spite of repeated failures?"

"I focus on my part, to figure out what aether is and how it can be harnessed and contained. The other chaps are the ones who build their machines around it," he said. "If I were to think too much on what they might do with it, I would lose my own direction. I'm not in it for the patents or the money."

"So you don't think about how to make it useful for everyone, or at least for those who might benefit from it," Iris said. "You're focused on things like publications and tenure, not the mother and child we saw or these poor wretches breathing in coal smoke and getting steam burns when their engines explode from being as poorly maintained and overworked as the people who use them."

Edward flinched from the disappointment in her voice. "That is not my affair," he said, but he recognized how indifferent he must sound. "If aether is found to be an alternative to coal and steam, brilliant. I won't stand in the way of those who want to invent with it."

"What if someone steals your ideas to make such an invention?"

"My ideas will be published. They can't be stolen if they're common knowledge. Science isn't subject to patent law."

Johann shifted and squinted at them. "We've finally gotten to the point where the bloody sun isn't shining in through the windows, and the two of you won't shut up," he grumbled. He looked at Iris and patted his leg. His gesture must have meant something to her Edward couldn't fathom because the formerly talkative miss pressed her lips together and looked out the window.

"We'll be quiet so you can sleep," she said.

Edward made note of the signal for his own use should she become too talkative. Or challenge him further on his failure to do anything useful with his scientific work.

8

L *ondon, 10 June 1870*
Bledsoe's reminder of her tenuous circumstances lanced through Iris, and she hoped Professor Bailey wouldn't see the tears in her eyes. She hadn't meant to wake the detestable musician—she wanted to discover if the professor had any motives more noble than saving his own job and department at the University. Seeing the residents of London always made something stir in her, a feeling she needed to *do* something to help them beyond giving the begging children a few pence, which would help for the moment but not in any lasting or meaningful way.

That mother and child.

The looks of despair on their faces caught her heart more than their pitiful thinness, which seemed to afflict all but the most wealthy in the city. Even they succumbed to the breathing sicknesses inherent in the poor air. Her father had been at a conference in London before he came home and started coughing...and never stopped.

Now she added frustration at the two men in the rail car to her sense of homesickness that grew as the kilometers between the train and her home increased, and of course her grief always simmered beneath the surface. She hadn't counted on her deception keeping her from the forms of grief—the dark clothes, the quiet days of mourning, the tearful yet insincere promises of support from family and friends—and leaving it unacknowledged made her feel unbalanced, her loss un-honored and therefore dishonored. For the first time, she could believe her father's spirit was an angry ghost.

But I'm doing this to preserve what you built for me, Papa. And to keep all your hard work from falling into the hands of lazy men like Jeremy Scott.

The train slowed and rolled into a coal yard in a deserted area. Iris thought she saw some hints of blue in the gray-brown haze above the train, but she had no desire to go outside. Then she observed something strange—the maid and the men who must be conducting and fueling the train walking around with long-handled hand-looking devices and looking on and under their cars. The men also had long-barreled steam rifles, which from the glow on the handles had been turned on and primed long enough ago to be ready for immediate use.

"What are they doing?" Professor Bailey asked.

"I don't know." Iris tried to angle herself to get a closer look at the proceedings, but she bumped her head on the window and rubbed her forehead. A thunk and other sounds above her told her someone climbed on the roof and walked across it. The crack of a steam rifle made her jump.

"Are we under attack?" Iris asked at the same time Bledsoe sat straight and asked, "What the hell...?"

More rifle shots made them all duck and cower below the window line so as not to be easy targets. Iris found her head cradled against Professor Bailey's chest, which felt broader and stronger than she had estimated.

"Miss McTavish, your hair is tickling my nose," he said.

"Stop complaining or I shall poke you with one of the pins from Bledsoe's friend."

"That would be worse," he agreed. "No telling what diseases an actress's pins harbor."

"I can hear you, you know," Bledsoe grumbled from somewhere near Iris's bustle, and she became aware of the weight of his head on her hip.

After about twenty minutes of awkward silence during which Iris heard people moving around outside and a few more shots, the train moved forward again. Something crunched under the wheels.

The maid, unencumbered by the clawed device, wheeled a lunch cart into the room, and her eyebrows raised when she caught sight of the three of them on the floor.

"Oh, I'm sorry, Miss, Professor and Maestro," she said. "What are you doing on the floor? Do you need me to return later?"

"Certainly not." Iris scrambled back onto the bench she had been sitting on, and the men did likewise. She narrowed her eyes at the maid, who looked like she tried not to laugh at them.

"What were you doing?" Iris asked. Both of the men looked at her, and she guessed they were irritated by her speaking first. It was bad enough her reputation would be at risk for traveling with the two of them unchaperoned, she didn't need to be caught in any compromising positions. Therefore, she needed an explanation to put the situation in context.

"It's the Clockmakers' Guild, Miss," the maid said. "They send little toys to crawl into Mister Cobb's and other gentlemen's trains to annoy them but also gather information. We take advantage of the stop for coal to clean 'em off."

"How do they work?" Professor Bailey asked.

"Some of 'em have cylinders in them like player cylinders, but made of wax, that they transfer information on. It's too complicated for me, but I'm sure Mister Cobb will be happy to explain on his airship. The blast from the steam rifles shuts them down, or we catch 'em with the claws and squeeze them out of shape so they can't move anymore, and the train wheels grind them into uselessness."

Iris leaned away from the fierceness in the maid's tone when she talked about the devices' destruction. She guessed the woman was more than a maid, perhaps a female guard. They did all sorts of strange things in the Americas. She wasn't sure if the dual roles of the maid made her more fascinating or frightening. Either way, she wanted to know more.

"Now, on to a more pleasant subject," the maid said. "Are you ready for lunch?"

"It's a bit early, don't you think?" Professor Bailey asked. Iris and Bledsoe both groaned.

RAIL STATION, *English Coast, 10 June 1870*

Edward hadn't been able to shake the feeling that his clothes were soiled after their little sojourn on the floor of the train car. No matter how many times he washed his hands, they felt sticky, and now he added the gritty feeling of the sand that seemed to coat everything in the station. He wanted to rub his palms on his pants to get rid of the feeling, but he would have to wash them again, and he didn't trust the washroom in this tiny station. It reminded him too much of family trips to the coast and the final, disastrous one with Lily when they were to have celebrated their engagement.

"Bad memories?" Johann asked. In spite of having slept for much of the journey, he had dark circles under his eyes.

"Perhaps," Edward replied. He tried to keep his tone light so his friend wouldn't ask further. Johann knew everything, of course. The entire town heard the story when he and Lily returned. He stopped himself from rubbing his hands on his pants but couldn't help but wonder how Miss McTavish would spin the tale of them all ending up on the floor of the train carriage. No doubt she would find fault in something he did even if she didn't complain about having her head on his chest. Truth be told, he hadn't minded so much, but he wouldn't admit that to anyone.

"I don't trust all this open air," Johann said. "A small town is better than the countryside. It's too exposed here."

The arrival of the coach forestalled more conversation. Johann stood and stretched. Edward had remained standing. He suspected the sand on the benches would stay invisible until it clung to his clothes and tried to get in every nook and cranny of his body. Miss McTavish and the maid entered, and the young archaeologist frowned like she was deep in thought.

Everything and everyone were loaded onto the carriage with great efficiency, and it rolled over the shell- and gravel-strewn path. Edward clutched the handle due to the precarious nature of the path along the bluff and the swaying of the cart in the breeze. They turned a corner, and the new angle revealed a view of the town below with the harbor and sparkling sea. And beyond the town, the white bulk of an airship stood, its canvas reflecting the luminescence of the sun like a beacon.

"A dirigible!" Edward exclaimed. "Is that what we're to travel on? Not a boat?" The itinerary had given the name of the vehicle, not the nature of it, and he hadn't dared to hope this disastrous trip would allow him to fulfill one of his lifelong dreams.

Miss McTavish faced him, and amusement turned up the corners of her eyes. "Yes, didn't you see on your itinerary?"

"I wasn't sure." Now the carriage couldn't move fast enough. He fixed it in his sight, refusing to look away in case it should lift without them. "Will we be on time?"

"Don't worry, Professor," the maid, who sat on the bench with Miss McTavish said. "That's Mister Cobb's personal airship. He's waiting for you." The two women exchanged amused glances, but Edward didn't mind if they mocked him. He ignored the exclamations over each new view and the information the maid tried to impart about the seaside town. He fixed on their destination, and when the carriage stopped at the airfield, he was the first one out.

The *Blooming Senator* loomed overhead, its balloon crowding the view of the sky and the bluffs beyond. The last time Edward had felt so small next to a massive object was when he was a child, and his father brought a new stallion named Lucifer to the stable. His brother had insisted they go see it when it arrived. From what Edward recalled, it stood seventeen hands, and as a boy of five, he didn't reach the bottom of its massive chest. The horse had never liked him, had never allowed him near it after that, and he took some satisfaction in the thought that even Lucifer would be dwarfed by the airship's mass.

"It's amazing," Miss McTavish breathed beside him, and he squelched the impulse to grab her hand and run toward it.

"Have you ever seen something so huge?"

"No. The only dirigibles I've seen were the smaller mail blimps in and over London. I've never seen one big enough for trans-Atlantic travel—they won't fit in an urban airfield. Mister Cobb must be very wealthy to afford it."

Edward glanced at her. Wariness and wonder warred for dominance in her expression, and he understood why. If Parnaby Cobb could afford a huge airship like the *Blooming Senator*, he should have been able to hire someone to go on this adventure, someone more amenable to travel than he was.

"Come now, Professor," the maid said when she appeared beside them carrying his and Miss McTavish's valises. "If you stand here gaping at it, it will leave without you as you feared."

Panic at potentially missing this opportunity replaced suspicion. He did have to save his department, after all, no matter what the motivation of the benefactor, and perhaps

Cobb had reasons for wanting everything to be subtle and secret. Edward followed her.

"She doesn't speak as a maid should," Miss McTavish said, and he wasn't sure he was meant to hear, but he responded anyway.

"Maybe she's excited for the journey as well."

"Perhaps."

Edward remembered his excitement the first time he saw the sea with its myriad demonstrations of physics, everything from how water moves to the pull of the moon. Now he experienced something similar, wonder at the miracle that allowed mankind to fly among the birds. He recalled how he and his brother had clasped hands and run toward the sea on their first trip to the shore.

This time he acted on the impulse to grab Miss McTavish's hand and pull her toward the gondola. "Come on!"

"Professor!" She grabbed her skirts and, laughing, ran beside him. He adjusted his speed to accommodate for her legs and wished maybe he hadn't been so foolish. She slowed him down, but the look on her face—delight to mirror his own. The thought that perhaps she would expect more such moments from him niggled at his mind, but he pushed it away. Nothing to be done for it now—they arrived together at the gangway breathless and flushed.

"Well, now, I haven't seen two young people enjoy themselves half so much *before* getting on my ship since she was launched." Parnaby Cobb's smile rivaled the brightness of the sun's rays upon their heads, and Edward's neck became warm at the thought he'd been caught acting a fool. And with a woman. He dropped Miss McTavish's hand and rubbed his own on his pants before he remembered his attire was no longer clean.

"Come, come, Professor, let me show you the laboratory," Cobb continued, either oblivious to or choosing to ignore

Edward's discomfort. "I thought you might want to take advantage of it to do some aether experiments at high altitudes."

Now all thought of Miss McTavish flew from Edward's mind. "Oh, that would be grand."

"Excellent. Marie, please take Miss McTavish to her quarters so she can freshen up after the professor's and her mad run."

Edward shot her a glance of apology, but Iris wasn't looking at him. She studied Cobb and nodded once to indicate she'd heard him. "Thank you," she murmured, but Edward knew she wasn't as meek as she appeared.

A light touch on his arm told him Cobb was waiting, and he followed the older man into the ship of his dreams.

looming Senator, 10 June, 1870

The laboratory Parnaby Cobb set up for Edward was everything he could have dreamed of for high-altitude experiments and more. His only regret was that he would have less than twenty-four hours to use it.

"Best get to work, then," Cobb told him with a pat on his shoulder.

Edward found the American to be congenial enough, but with too big a personality to tolerate for long periods of time. Thankfully the laboratory had been equipped with windows so he could see the ground fall away when they took off, and he watched, fascinated like a small boy getting his first glimpse of the ocean, as the white caps of the waves faded into the blue of the channel. The best part? His stomach seemed more amenable to this sort of travel than to the rocking of a boat. In fact, once he got all his gear organized but before he started his first procedure, he decided he wanted a little snack. Cobb had given him directions to the kitchen—*galley*, he corrected himself—and dining room, where there would always be tea and scones. His eating schedule had already been disrupted for the day, so what would be the harm in one more unscheduled snack?

He found the galley soon enough. Although the sugar cubes had been split, there wasn't any warm cream, so he moved to the office and raised his hand to knock and ask if any was available or if they would mind if he were to make some. Voices came through the door.

"...agree?" Cobb asked.

Edward paused. Who was he talking to and who was to agree?

"Yes."

Edward thought he recognized the voice of the maid Mary, or was it Marie? Who were they talking about?

"You have your orders for when they find it."

"Yes sir. Best I go regardless. The Clockworkers had all kinds of little beasties snooping around the train. We had to use the rifles."

"They're suspicious. Taft and Gunner will make a full report, I'm sure. Now come show me how much you're going to miss me."

"I told her I'd come back with something to settle her stomach. She's expecting me. I'm on trial, remember?"

"Fine, you can show me tonight."

The sound of kissing made Edward pull a face, and he moved away from the door and toward the other one that led to the galley itself. He'd warm his own cream, thank you very much. In fact, he was in the process of doing so when Marie came out of the office, her face flushed, and straightening her pinafore.

"Are you finding everything, Professor?" she asked and put a pot of water on the stove to boil.

"Yes, thank you," he said and gestured to the pot in front of him.

"Oh, I'm sorry. Mister Cobb told me you like your cream heated, and I forgot. I'll make sure to have some available for you."

"Thank you. Is Miss McTavish settled in?"

"She's got airsickness. Happens occasionally to first-time flyers. I'm making her some peppermint tea. She'll be feeling much better in a bit." She cast a glance at him through her lashes, and he recognized the female "fishing for information" look. His sister-in-law had given it to him often enough when she'd first caught his brother's eye.

"And Mister Bledsoe?" he asked to show he was interested in the welfare of *all* of his traveling companions.

"I imagine he's also snug in his cabin. Mister Taft showed him to his room."

The little bubbles that told Edward his milk had reached warm but not scalded appeared around the edges of the pan, and he turned off the heat. "I believe this will do it."

"Be careful out there. Sometimes a crosswind catches us and makes the whole thing jolt. If you heat cream again, which you shouldn't have to, but just in case, don't leave it unattended on the stove. There's nothing worse than a fire on a dirigible."

"I'll remember that." Edward took his milk out to the dining room and set it on a trivet on the sideboard. He fixed his tea with the proper ingredients in the right order and returned to the lab, where he started a burner. With his mind turned to aetherics, he forgot the conversation he overheard.

AFTER SOME INITIAL MOTION SICKNESS, Iris's stomach settled, and she made her way to the lounge. When she opened the door, music from the piano assaulted her. She pushed through the maelstrom of notes and found Johann Bledsoe at the keyboard. His face reflected the anger apparent in the music, and when he looked up, silence fell at the same time the heat spread from her stomach to her forehead in a flash.

"I'm sorry," she said. "I didn't mean to intrude. Please keep playing."

"Do you know the trouble you're causing?" Bledsoe asked and punctuated his question with a run ending in a trill. "Do you have any idea of the fire you're playing with?" Now low notes came from the instrument and swirled in a manner that put Iris in mind of a roaring blaze.

"He grabbed *my* hand," she said and planted her feet as though she stood in the middle of a whirlwind, not sure which direction would provide the next assault, either verbal or musical.

"Edward is like a child in a lot of ways. He seems insensitive but is easily hurt. That he shared a moment of delight with you shows he's getting attached."

"We've barely spoken aside from the day you forced me to help him pack, and I can't help how he responds to me. Besides, am I that awful of a person?"

"Asks the woman who is on this journey under false pretenses. Or has your father made the most miraculous of recoveries?"

Tears came to Iris's eyes, and she blinked to keep them from revealing how much his words and his sneering tone hurt. "You do not understand my circumstances."

"What is there to understand? You're helpless, can't even do your own hair, and now you're looking for someone else to take care of you."

"And you think I'm after Professor Bailey?" She walked to the large bank of windows and looked back at Bledsoe over her shoulder. "That's ridiculous—he can hardly take care of himself."

The musician's hands fell to his lap, and his shoulders

slumped. "Yes, that is exactly what I am trying to get across to you. If he is going to marry, he needs someone who is self-sufficient and—"

"I know, honest." Iris turned her gaze to the disappearing coast of England and tried to ignore the sinking feeling sliding from her chest to her stomach. She was now un-tethered in almost every sense. She'd lost her father, was in danger of losing her home, and now she was leaving the only country she'd ever known. She placed her fingertips on the glass.

"You've never seen him in a true breakdown," Bledsoe said. "I have. I fear another one will kill him."

"What happened?"

"A stupid woman thought he was the heir to the Duke's estates, not his brother. She strung him along, and when she realized her mistake, she very publicly ended their engagement."

"A sad story, but it happens."

"Ah, but it was his first heartbreak." The musician came to stand beside her at the window. "He didn't eat and sleep for days. He was always somewhat normal if a little eccentric with his scientific interests, but after that incident he decided the way to live his life was according to the order and predictability of science. Hence his strict schedule and other quirks that make him difficult to deal with. They're defensive—they keep life orderly, but they also keep people away."

"I understand." And she did. If she could bring some predictability to her life right now, she would, but she also recognized life was messy and complicated. Her mother had taught her that. "It's not like him to act impulsively."

"Not at all. If we're to succeed, he needs to remain stable."

"Fine." She turned to leave, and the golden case bumped the window through her skirt.

"Are you carrying a weapon?" Bledsoe asked.

"It's none of your business."

She expected him to challenge her, but he shook his head, the dark circles under his eyes apparent in the harsh midday sunlight.

"You do have the most interesting things in your pockets, Miss McTavish." And with that, he left her alone in the lounge.

10

S omewhere Over the English Channel, 10 June 1870
Edward started the two burners and the miniature Watts, engines that would suck the air out of containers and leave only light and aether. He reached to unpack the glass instruments, but a knock on the door interrupted him.

"Not now," he called and tried to convey his disgruntlement in the glare he shot at the person who opened the door in spite of his admonishment not to disturb him. He'd even put a *Do Not Disturb—Aetherist at Work* sign on the door.

"Sorry to interrupt," Bledsoe said. "But Cobb wants us in the conference room. He has some information for us he couldn't share at the university."

Edward sighed with his whole torso. "Can't this wait? I was just getting started."

"He timed it according to when I told him you take your afternoon tea," Johann said. "He's trying to accommodate you. Might as well return the favor."

Edward pulled out his watch and glanced at the dial. Bloody hell, Johann was right. It was teatime, and he suspected it would be the one meal this week that would occur when it should.

"Very well." He shut off the burners. No matter how hard he tried, he couldn't help but feel the weight of the hydrogen-filled balloon above them. Or the relative weightlessness. Either way, he was conscious of its high flammability.

Johann looked across the hall at the set of double doors, which led to the lounge as Edward recalled. He'd studied the schematics and layouts of the major airships at one point in his youth and recognized the design of the Senator as a classic Van de Venden, a Belgian plan. While the Germans were more efficient—they would have put the kitchen and lounge on the same level—the Belgians were more concerned with aesthetics and placed rooms for the best light exposure and views.

"So what was with the little jog across the landing field?" Johann asked. "That wasn't like you."

Heat came to Edward's chest and neck, and he adjusted his tie before the blush reached his face—he hoped. "I am aware of that. It was an impulse, nothing more. Aren't you excited to be on this grand airship? It's my first time on one."

"I've traveled on them before when I've played in Europe. It's nicer than the passenger ones, but stop trying to distract me. Are you all right? Is this trip becoming too much for you?"

Edward was happy they had to ascend the stairs in single file so Johann couldn't see the smile trying to come to his face at the memory of running with Miss McTavish across the grass. He'd felt simultaneously free and anchored with her hand in his, now that he thought about it.

"You're always encouraging me to break out of my patterns. It seemed a good opportunity to do so."

"Not with her. Remember what happened the last time you lost your head over a woman named for a flower."

"Miss McTavish is nothing like Lily Corvender. She's more clever, for one."

"And has more secrets."

The same sensation of being pricked with a green needle occurred in Edward's middle as when he'd watched Johann fixing Miss McTavish's hair. "And how would you know?"

Johann glanced over his shoulder. "Trust me, I know women. Remember, I've had more experience than you."

"Yes, a disgusting amount," Edward said. They reached the conference room, where Cobb waited for them in front of the windows. He had a large pad of paper on an easel beside him. Three chairs stood on the other side of the table, and Johann took the one on the left. Edward, for reasons he couldn't quite fathom, took the one on the opposite end. In spite of the delightful smells of tea and scones, he squirmed with an unsettled feeling, particularly since this teatime, which should have been one of his anchors, now seemed like an interruption preceded by a series of uncomfortable emotions.

Who was he kidding? All emotions were uncomfortable, but particularly when they occurred in the context of a conversation about a woman and his behavior toward her. Lily had trained him in that. Perhaps he should listen to those old lessons—whatever his fascination with Miss McTavish's intellect and ability to make him think of things he hadn't considered, she was a woman, and women were trouble, especially ones who made a rational man like him *feel* things.

IRIS WASN'T ALONE for long. Marie found her in the lounge staring out the window at the endless expanse of dark water beneath them. She faced south and wondered if she could already see a smudge of land on the horizon. Calais, perhaps? That was always where boats landed in novels if they were crossing the Channel from England. Not that she'd had time to read many. Her interests had always been in the latest archaeological and geological papers.

But a dashing hero would be nice. Not to marry, but perhaps a kiss...

"Mister Cobb would like everyone to meet in the conference room, which is off the dining room," Marie said and made the image of a raven-haired hero with a charming French accent flee from Iris's mind. "I can show you where it is."

"Thank you." *But not really.*

"How is your stomach?" Marie asked once Iris turned to follow her. The maid led the way into the narrow hallway and up a flight of stairs.

"Much better. The peppermint tea seems to have done the trick." *And getting furious at Bledsoe. Who knew anger could cure motion sickness?*

"Good. Please let me know if you need anything else. Afternoon tea service is set up in the dining room."

"What's on the other side of the hall from the lounge?"

"Oh, that's a small laboratory Mister Cobb set up for Professor Bailey to do experiments at high altitude."

"I'm sure he's very excited." The memory of his delight at running across the meadow to the airship came to mind. Yes, he would be like a child in a candy store with the ability to run his experiments here. Maybe some of the agony over picking what equipment to pack had paid off.

"I was afraid he'd be difficult to extract from the lab for the meeting. Luckily, Mister Bledsoe came along and helped me."

"The professor does seem focused on his work," Iris said and grabbed the hand rail when the gondola lurched. Her stomach tightened, but no nausea ensued.

"Don't worry, Miss. Sometimes a cross current makes her do that. As for Professor Bailey, I'm sure he will find the meeting to be as informative as his own work for the purposes of your mission."

They crossed through the dining room and into another room lined with windows. Iris stuck close to the walls in case of any more jolts. So far Iris had counted three levels not including the engineering and navigation level, which must be above them.

When they entered the conference room, Cobb gestured for Iris to sit at the table between Bledsoe and Bailey. The professor wore a pout, Bledsoe a frown. Iris wondered if Bledsoe had had a "discussion" with Professor Bailey, who her mind wanted to address as Edward in spite of no invitation having been issued to do such a thing. But if they were to travel into potentially perilous situations, shouldn't they be on familiar terms? Bledsoe tapped his index finger on the table, and Iris vowed not to ever call him Johann.

Insolent, vain man.

"Now that we're all here, we can get started," Cobb said. "First, I wanted to show you part of what you're up against." He gestured to Marie, who retrieved a mangled device of brass from a low shelf and placed it on the table. It was about the size of a human finger. Iris could barely make out a butterfly-like shape and wings. The middle oozed a yellowish waxy mess.

"Found this bugger flitting around the dining room," Cobb said. "We think it must have come aboard in someone's luggage."

"What is it?" the professor asked.

"It's a Clockwork Recorder," Cobb told him. "The Clock-work Guild is very curious as to my activities, and I fear they suspect the nature of our mission."

"How does it work?" Iris poked at the wax, which had already hardened to the consistency of soap.

"Very much like a phonograph cylinder. They have an array of small needles in them that respond to sound vibrations and etch them onto the wax cylinder. Then the device is collected and the etchings decoded with a cylinder player."

"That's brilliant," the professor said. "Is that what they were catching and destroying around the train?"

"Theoretically, yes, although obviously one got through somehow." Cobb frowned at Marie, who looked away. "Since steam relegated clockwork mechanisms to the realm of toys, the Guild has branched into spying devices, which they use to stay abreast of new ideas so they can steal them. That's why I waited for you all to be aboard the ship before I revealed the most important information about your journey to you—I didn't want to risk us being recorded and the Guild knowing what is afoot."

The look on Cobb's face left Iris with little doubt that anyone who crossed him would end up mangled and oozing like the recording butterfly, and chill bumps rose on her arms in spite of the ample heat in the room from the sunny windows. She decided to "read" something of his as soon as possible.

"So watch out for brass butterflies, got it," Bledsoe said. "What about the rest of it? I'm calling in a lot of favors and using a lot of connections to get us into the private collections and drawing rooms of Europe's upper class. What are we looking for?"

Iris shot a sideways glance at Bledsoe—no special talent needed to read his impatience. Was it sitting so near her that did it? Or was he irritable about his encounter with Edward?

Professor Bailey, she corrected herself.

"I like it that you get straight to the point, Musician," Cobb told him.

"And artist," Bledsoe grumbled.

Cobb seemed to ignore him. He flipped the cover open on the pad of paper to reveal a drawing of a coin with a bearded man on it. "What do you know about Pythagoras?"

∾

THE NAME of his favorite mathematician—and yes, he'd been mocked for having a favorite mathematician—caught Edward's attention, and he couldn't help but sound like an eager student. "He died in the fifth century BC. Had a mystical bent as well as a mathematical mind. A lot of it overlapped, although I don't believe in the spiritual fluff." He glanced sideways at Miss McTavish and saw she also leaned forward with an interested light in her eyes.

"It's not as fluffy as one would think," Cobb said. "Think of his philosophy—that one can only know the true substance, the basic matter of the world, through placing limits on it. This is a principle of your beloved mathematics, professor—basic shapes are defined by their boundaries—and extended to physics, aether as what exists in the void or the space between things."

"So are we looking for evidence of the void or the limits?" Miss McTavish asked.

"Hold on." Cobb flipped another page, which showed interlinked spheres. "The Pythagoreans also spoke of the notion of harmony, the 'music of the spheres'—and notice I've moved on from the great man himself. In other words, for the world to work, the boundaries and void must interact in a harmonious, or mathematically sound way."

"Right, I've been working on that," Edward said. "I've not yet found a frequency that will allow the aether to be stable and contained for long periods of time, much less harnessed."

"But the Pythagoreans might have figured out something. Legend has it that they were hunted and destroyed—burned alive in one of their own temples—because of their political involvements. However, rumors have always abounded that they were driven underground for a different reason, because they found a way to harness the power of this void. They asserted it wasn't dangerous because they didn't have the technology to use it. The powers of the day tried to destroy them for all the usual reasons such as not wanting it to fall into their enemies' hands and concern about the secrecy surrounding it."

"So are we looking for a device, then?" Bledsoe asked.

"No," Edward said, making the connection. "We're looking for a formula or frequency, something that will guide me in making the aether stable and distilling it into an element more simple but also more stable than hydrogen so it can somehow be used in industry as a power source."

"Yes!" Cobb clapped his hands. "Very good, Professor. I knew you were the right one to bring along."

"So what is the purpose of Miss McTavish?" Bledsoe asked, looking bored. "It seems that Edward can look at things and figure them out for himself."

"As you recall, it was to have been Professor McTavish," Cobb told him. "And I chose him because of his knowledge of Classical Greek art and sculpture. Also because he had an interest in Renaissance art. I believe the neo-Pythagoreans hid clues for their future members in art from the second century on so the secret would not be lost, just split into pieces until a clever person put it together at the right time for the devices of the day to be able to use it."

"And aether energy would be cleaner than coal," Miss McTavish said. "And less harmful to workers."

"Potential risks will of course be assessed before it's put to use," Cobb agreed. "But first we need to figure out how to harness its power."

"Don't worry, Master Bledsoe," Miss McTavish continued. "I studied alongside my father and have read all his papers, published and unpublished, so I am familiar with the necessary subjects. Renaissance artists were fascinated by Classical art and sculpture, so they might have included clues without recognizing it."

"Precisely." Now Cobb turned his broad white smile to Miss McTavish. "You are indeed a clever woman, Miss. Once you accomplish this task, I shall be sure to work out a position at any university you like."

"I need to finish, well start, my degree," she murmured, but Edward saw the joy in her eyes, the same he felt when he made a brilliant breakthrough.

Perhaps we're not so different after all.

"Now let me tell you about what to look for." Parnaby flipped another page, Marie poured tea, and Edward settled in for a lecture he didn't have to give. Normally the lack of control would have bothered him, but he found himself looking forward to the information, which he knew his brain would take in, catalog, and retrieve when needed.

A golden spark from outside the window caught his attention, but before his eyes could focus on it, it was gone.

A mere trick of the light, the glare from the sun catching a piece of brass in here and reflecting in the window.

But he had to force himself to pay attention rather than determine what caused the illusion.

IRIS SAT between the irascible Bledsoe and the excited Professor Bailey and tried to keep her mind on what Cobb said to them. To all of them. She felt the sting of Bledsoe's questioning her purpose on the trip as keenly as Bailey's shared enthusiasm for the theories of Pythagoras. Now Cobb talked about the art and sculpture of the Archaic period, during which Pythagoras lived, and the one after, the Classical period. Then he skipped to the Hellenistic age, when the neo-Pythagoreans lived. She knew much of the history and current archaeological discoveries due to her father's work, but the influx of information overwhelmed her. This was certainly different from Miss Cornwall's School for Young Ladies, where the lectures had been on the proper way to pour tea and needlework. Iris liked this situation much better.

"Should I be taking notes?" she asked at one point.

"Don't you already know this?" Bledsoe asked, not looking at her.

"Most of it is a review, yes, but it's a lot of information, and I thought one of us should be."

"Aren't you afraid you'd lose them?" he asked with a glance that was accompanied by a slight arch of one eyebrow. She wanted to scratch that eyebrow off his face but tamped down her unladylike anger.

"No, I'd be more afraid of someone stealing them," she shot back.

"And that's why you were not given the means to take notes," Cobb said. "I trust your quick minds will retain what is necessary, and the information will be triggered by recognition. I don't want any indication of what we're looking for to fall into the wrong hands."

"I understand," Iris said with a glare at Bledsoe. "And we need to trust each other with our respective areas of expertise."

"Quite so," Cobb told them. "Now, if I may continue? Or would you like to discuss the art of the Hellenistic period for us? As I recall, your father was consulted in particular about these works."

"I'd be happy to." She switched places with Cobb, who settled in between the two younger men and looked at her with expectation and something else Iris couldn't define. She looked out of the window to collect herself and saw they now floated over land, fields dotted by forests and farmhouses. Not being over the open water comforted her somewhat—if they crashed, at least someone would know.

Iris shook her head to dislodge the morbid thoughts and flipped to the next page on the easel, where she found a drawing of a statue of a goddess. "Let's start with sculpture."

But before she could continue, the gondola shook. The easel fell, and Iris grabbed on to the table, which was bolted to the floor, to maintain her balance.

She glanced over her shoulder to see a swarm of brass butterflies surrounding a smaller airship. Behind the glass window, two creatures with bug eyes—no, men wearing goggles—stared back at her.

11

F rance, *10 June 1870*
    "The Clockwork Guild!" Parnaby stood, knocking his chair over, and pulled a weapon from the holster at his belt. "Quick, into the dining room!"

They rushed out of the conference room and closed the door on the sounds of the Senator's crew engaging the Clockwork pirates, smashing glass and shouts.

Cobb unholstered another weapon and handed it to Edward.

Edward, who had been looking forward to seeing what Miss McTavish knew and whose brain was trying to adjust to the change of circumstances, looked at the gun. His rational mind took in all the information, surmised they were indeed under attack, and stuffed the anxious part into his chest, where his heart thrummed against the buttons at his breast.

Information, get information.

"Is that a steam pistol?" he asked.

"No, it's a Derringer. Haven't you handled a gun before?"

"When I've had to," Edward admitted. He'd never been one for hunting or the other weapon-toting activities of the upper class, but his father and brother always tried to drag him along, and he had gone to satisfy social expectations until he could excuse himself.

"Here, I'll take it," Johann said, and Cobb handed the weapon to him.

"Good, I'm glad there's another man on board with some sense," Cobb snapped.

Edward frowned at the American's sudden change of demeanor toward him. He thought Cobb liked him, but he wondered if the man's earlier flattery was all a ruse. On the other hand, people did strange things under duress. He should know.

"Take Miss McTavish and wait in the escape compartment until this is over," Cobb told him.

"What about Marie?" Miss McTavish asked.

"She can take care of herself."

In fact, Marie had opened a cabinet along the wall and pulled out one of the steam rifles. She watched the gauge on the butt to confirm it built pressure. "Go on, Miss. Let the Professor take care of you."

Edward chose to ignore the dubious look Miss McTavish gave him. She glanced at Johann and shrugged, a gesture Edward found to be stranger. What was going on between the two of them? Would she prefer the musician to protect her?

"Come on," he said. "I've memorized the schematics for this airship model. The escape compartments are below."

Iris followed the professor out of the dining room. She'd never handled a gun, but she wished Cobb had asked her, if only to show Professor Bailey and Maestro Bledsoe he didn't think she was a helpless woman along for the ride. She also wished she'd gotten to finish her lecture so she could show them what she knew, even if she'd been unprepared. She at least had the foresight to grab the pad of paper off the easel.

Professor Bailey stopped by the laboratory door and raised his hand, his ear to the door. "I think the fighting is all above. I'm going to get my equipment and valise."

"Good idea. Mine is in my room below." She turned to leave but didn't want to go alone—who knew what clockwork horrors prowled around the airship?

"We should stay together," the professor said, and Iris turned back.

"Then hurry."

She found herself clutching the pad of paper while he put on his goggles and carefully dismantled the equipment. Couldn't he move faster? He'd packed everything except the copper globe when a dark shape crashed through the window. She shrieked, held the pad of paper as a shield, and backed into the wall. She peered over the papers to see the professor swing hard, sending the intruder and globe back through the window and off the end of the line.

"My chamber!" he cried and reached toward the space where an empty rope swung in the breeze.

"Don't be a fool," Iris gasped around the bitter cold air that came through the window and tried to freeze her lungs. She grabbed his arm and tugged him out of the room. He clutched his partially open valise with his other hand. Once in the corridor, she tried to get a look at him to see if he bled, and something warm seeped through her glove. However, the gas lights, which had the same structure as those on the train, had gone out, and they were in darkness.

THE ESCAPE COMPARTMENTS were at the back of the ship under

Miss McTavish's room, so she managed to grab her bag and stuff a few things from her trunk in it. She left the mostly shredded pad of papers there. This time Edward watched with a mix of unease and admiration at the economy of her movements and decisiveness. His face and hands burned, but he couldn't look at them for fear of seeing he was more injured than he felt.

Miss McTavish wet a towel and gestured for him to lead the way.

The escape compartments were four-person boxes with two parachutes that would unfurl once the box was released from the bottom of the airship. From what Edward could recall, they worked most of the time. His stomach dropped in anticipation of that first lurch into free fall—he wanted to perform aetherics and physics experiments, not be one.

Once they settled in and opened the shades to let some light in, Miss McTavish took out a pair of tweezers.

"You have glass shards in your skin," she said in a matter-of-fact tone Edward didn't feel her statement warranted.

"Good grief, woman, does nothing ruffle you?"

She looked away, and he thought light sparkled off something wet on her face. "A few things do."

"I apologize, I didn't mean to pry. I am in your capable hands."

It took him a few tries to figure out whether he needed to watch her careful ministrations or look through the crack in the blinds to see how the fighting fared. He still couldn't accept they were under attack—why, if the Clockwork Guild wanted the information they were after, would they try to kill them? It didn't make sense. Was the Guild after Cobb?

"There," Miss McTavish said, removing the last of the shards. As she went, she bandaged his hands, so now he felt like the mummy he'd seen a picture of. "I'm afraid I can't do much for your face, but at least the cuts are clean. We need to get you to a doctor. You might need stitches in a few of them, but you're lucky you were wearing your goggles."

"Stitches." Edward slumped back, dizzy. "This is not how I envisioned this journey going." Then he remembered the manners his mother drilled into him. "But I thank you, Miss McTavish. You have saved me from grave injury, if not from death. I would not have been able to attend to my own injuries."

"You're welcome," she said. After a few seconds, she murmured, "And call me Iris."

"I'm Edward." He leaned his head back against the bulwark and tried to make it stop spinning, but he felt every sway of the ship. A lurch brought his eyes open, and at first he panicked at the dark figure who had dropped into the compartment with them. He reached for his valise. He'd sacrifice the glass globe to protect himself and Miss McTavish—Iris, why did she have to have a flower name?—but his bandaged hands couldn't manage the zipper.

"What in blazes happened to the two of you?" Johann said and put his violin case on one of the pillows. "Edward, you look like a mummy, and Miss McTavish, you're covered in blood."

Edward and Iris exchanged guilty glances. "We didn't come straight here," he admitted. "We gathered some things first."

"Idiots," Johann growled. "Cobb's men have the upper hand, but the airship is losing altitude. The captain has recommended we depart before we get too low for the parachute to open. If they survive, they'll find us and pick us up."

"You got your violin," Edward argued.

"Because it was right there in the lounge. I grabbed it on the way out." He moved aside, and Marie dropped in beside him.

"Let's go, mates," she said. Her eyes sparkled, and she held the steam rifle. She reached above them, closed and secured the hatch, and pulled the release lever. They dropped into the void below.

12

I ris clutches Edward's arm as they fall. They wait for the lurch that will tell them the parachute has deployed, but each second ticks by without the jerk that will no doubt be painful, particularly since their velocity increases. The towel she used to dab his wounds floats between her and Bledsoe like a bloody surrender flag to gravity and its inevitable effects.

"I need to pull the emergency cords!" Marie shouts. She, too, floats, and her hands scrabble for something on the ceiling. Or is it the floor? Then she pulls, Iris's neck snaps back, and everything goes black...

Iris clutches Edward's arm and blinks away from the light in her eyes. Where is it coming from? The blinds in the escape compartment are closed, aren't they? She tries to move her head but can't. What is this? Is she paralyzed?

SOMEWHERE IN THE North of France, 11 June 1870

"Hold her, Patrick." The voice managed to be soothing in spite of its flat accent.

Another American? Did we float that far afield?

"I'm trying, but it's not easy with her latched on to my jacket." Now this voice was Irish, another young man, and Iris's awareness turned to her fingers, which were indeed clutched around brawny arms inside a rough cloth. She let go, but now large hands closed around her upper arms.

"Easy there, lass," the Irishman said.

Iris managed to pry her eyes open. The light that tried to spear them disappeared. She found herself looking at two faces, one caramel brown with wavy black hair and soft gray eyes, and as if in intentional contrast, another with green eyes and flaming red hair and beard. Their ages matched their voices, probably about the same as Edward and his friend.

"Who are you?" she demanded. She struggled to sit, but the redheaded man held her pinned to the straw mattress. "Where am I? Why are you holding me down? Unhand me immediately."

"He'll let you go if you promise not to thrash around," the darker of the two said. "I'm Doctor Chadwick Radcliffe. This is my friend Patrick O'Connell."

"I suppose I should be relieved you're a doctor, but how do I know you're telling me the truth?" Iris narrowed her eyes at him. "You're American, he's Irish, and as far as I can recall, we're in France. None of this makes any sense."

"Will you or won't you cooperate?" Doctor Radcliffe asked. "I can't stay long with you. One of your companions looks like he went through a glass window. I started with you because you have blood on your dress, and I feared you might have injuries I couldn't see."

"Edward." Iris tried to rise again but struggled against the restraint. "All right, I promise to stay calm. Please release me."

The Irishman, whose large hands might as well have been made of iron, let her go, and he helped her to a sitting position. Her fingers confirmed she lay on a straw-filled mattress, and worse, her bodice had been unlaced and her skirt untied. She clutched her clothing around her. *Dear god, I hope my virginity is intact.* She shifted her weight and couldn't detect anything but an urge to urinate, nothing like the sensations her mother's ring had produced. A shadow moved in the corner of the room, and Iris was relieved to see Marie.

The two men who regarded her didn't seem to her to be rapists, although she wasn't sure what one would look like. "My traveling companions?" she asked. "Is everyone...?" She couldn't finish the words. Grief swelled from the place it typically hid, and the men across from her blurred into a distorted image of light and dark. *Hope and despair.*

"Your maid is unhurt, as is the musician. We've already talked to him. As for the other one, I have to wait and see. He has not yet woken, and I don't have all the amenities of a hospital to do a full exam."

His questioning look invited Iris to elaborate, but she didn't accept the invitation. "Can I see him?" she asked.

"In a moment. Your maid can help you reassemble yourself. I apologize, but your well-being was my concern. Please believe that."

Iris nodded. He asked her a few more questions, mostly about headache, blurred vision, and other signs she might have a head injury, but soon seemed satisfied she was generally unharmed.

While the doctor gathered his things, she looked around and found she was reclined on a bed in a room with wooden walls. The furnishings told her it must be some sort of inn, and she hoped there was a water closet ensuite. Seeing her valise relieved her, as did feeling in her pocket for the gold case and finding it there. She guessed she wouldn't be lucky enough for Bledsoe to have lost her telegram in the crash.

Once the doctor and his companion left, Marie rushed to the side of the bed and drew up short. "Oh, Miss McTavish, I'm so happy you're unharmed!"

Iris wondered if Marie had thought about embracing her. *That would have been awkward.* "What happened?" Iris maneuvered to sit on the side of the bed and paused to allow the room to stop tilting.

"I got the parachute to deploy on one side of the compartment, but the other one didn't open when it should. You and the professor knocked together and were on the side that hit first with us atop you—we couldn't help it. And we hit hard."

Iris tested her limbs and found she could move everything, but not comfortably. "I feel sore all over."

"Not surprising. You might have some bruised ribs and other things."

Marie helped Iris to stand and use the water closet. Afterward, Iris walked to the dresser and leaned with her hands supporting her while Marie reassembled her clothing around her. She sat on the bed while Marie did her hair.

"What happened to the airship?" she asked.

A warm droplet plopped on Iris's head. "I don't know." Marie paused in her brushing to sniffle and wipe her cheeks. "It might have gone down. When the Clockworks attacked, the captain turned the ship back out over the water because the Guild's vehicles don't have the range the airship does. It's standard procedure. But everything happened so fast."

"We're lucky we didn't hit the water." Iris suppressed a shudder at the thought of landing unconscious in the English Channel. It didn't matter she wouldn't have known she was drowning—it would have happened, and she would have missed out on...what? She didn't want to marry—her mother had taught her by inadvertent example how that wasn't a good option.

I would have missed out on the chance to be a great archaeologist like my father.

With her hair and clothing arranged somewhat—there was nothing she could do about the bloodstains on her jacket and skirt, and her two other dresses shared the airship's dubious fate—Iris leaned on Marie and followed her into the hall. She saw they were, indeed, in an inn.

"I have some money," she whispered, "but I don't know if I can pay for all of us to stay here."

"Not to worry," Marie murmured back. "I'll take care of it. Mister Cobb set me up in England in case something happened and we got separated."

They walked to the room next door, where they found Doctor Radcliffe and Mister O'Connell standing by Edward's bed. The cuts stood out against his face, which appeared extra pale beneath the bandage on his head, and he moaned.

"Perhaps you can help calm him, Miss?" the doctor asked.

"I'll try." Iris sat beside Edward and took one of his bandaged hands. "Edward? It's me, Iris. I helped you with your hands and face, remember?"

"No, no flowers," he murmured and turned his head. "Flowers are trouble. I want ivy."

"Is Ivy another one of his, er, friends?" asked the Irishman.

"No," Iris said in her best *don't be inappropriate* tone. "It's the plant. It's hard to explain. He's...quirky."

"My copper globe," Edward mumbled. "Out the window, hanging like a red moon."

Doctor Radcliffe coughed, and Iris suspected he hid a laugh. "And apparently he's somewhat poetic."

"Hardly," she said. "He's a scientist." She pressed her lips together and sucked them between her teeth before she said anymore. These gentlemen had helped her, but she didn't trust them.

Edward sighed, turned on his side, and let out a snore.

"We should let him rest," Iris said and stood.

"Yes, ma'am," Doctor Radcliffe said with a smile.

"I like a woman who can take charge," Mister O'Connell agreed and followed Iris, Marie, and the doctor out of the room.

They met Johann Bledsoe in the hallway. He had a bandage over one eyebrow and walked with a slight limp but otherwise appeared unharmed.

"How is he?" he asked. "Any changes?"

"This young lady got him to speak some," Doctor Radcliffe said, "but it was mostly gibberish. I hope it's from his injured body, not a fractured mind."

The glare Iris had prepared for Bledsoe turned into a look of worry they exchanged.

"Does he have a history of neurosis?" the doctor asked. Iris glanced at Bledsoe, who shook his head. "Look," the doctor continued, "I understand you don't know me, and the circumstances are unusual, but if you want me to care for him, I need to know about him."

A short bald man wearing an apron approached them from the stairs at the end of the hall. "*Est-ce que l'homme est dangereux?*"

"No, he's not dangerous," Marie said. "He's hurt and resting."

"*Oui, mademoiselle. Le dîner est servi.*"

"He says dinner's ready," Marie told Iris.

"I had basic French at school," Iris told her and felt like a snob. Which made her acknowledge the upper class assumptions behind her next thought, which was how did an American maid know French?

"He understands English but doesn't speak it very much," Marie continued, apparently undeterred. "His wife, who normally handles their English-speaking guests, is laid up with a back injury. Doctor Radcliffe has been taking care of her in exchange for room and board for him and Mister O'Connell."

"You've gathered a lot of information in a few hours."

"Oh no, Miss," Marie said. "You were unconscious for a day. It's now Saturday evening."

"Saturday?" Iris didn't want to think about that now. What

condition must Edward be in if he was asleep after so long? What if he had some sort of infection from his wounds? Shouldn't the doctor be doing more?

Iris decided she didn't want to get all her information secondhand from Marie, whom she didn't trust, either. Cobb had given her money? Had Iris accepting the maid into her service been assumed? She moved ahead, happy that the stiffness seemed to subside, and caught Doctor Radcliffe as he descended the stairs.

"What brings you and Mister O'Connell to France? We are in France, right?" Iris thought she'd asked Marie, but she couldn't remember.

"Yes, we're in the northern part of the country, not too far from the Channel," he said. "As for why we're here, we're stuck. We were returning from visiting a friend in Vienna when we got sidetracked by the fighting along the French-German border and had to go through the Netherlands."

"Then the bastards robbed us. Pardon, Miss," Mister O'Connell said. "Hence why we're stuck here. Thankfully the Missus needed the doctor."

"What about your friend in Vienna?" Iris asked. "Surely you could write him, and he could send you some money."

"Ah, the war has disrupted the tube system here," Radcliffe said, but he didn't meet Iris's eyes before he gestured for her to precede her into the dining room.

Of course he has something to hide. They all do. She wondered about the nature of the friend in Vienna or if there was one.

They entered a comfortable dining room, where the innkeeper and a maid served them a simple country dinner of roast chicken, vegetables and crusty white bread Iris had to stop herself from eating most of. She found herself to be quite hungry, which made sense after her long nap.

Too exhausted to contribute much to the conversation, which all seemed to be about the fuss on the French-Prussian border, Iris watched Marie, who ate with the guests in spite of her obvious service status, and who exchanged frequent looks with the innkeeper. What sort of strange place was France? Iris wondered how Marie was "paying" for their rooms, and the thought made her lose interest in the sorbet that had been served for dessert. As soon as she was able, she excused herself and slipped back upstairs.

Iris paused in front of Edward's door. The invitation to call her by her first name had slipped out in the escape capsule, and he perhaps had been in too much pain to recognize he'd reciprocated. It made for an awkward situation. Should she pretend it never happened? They were neither affianced nor closely related, but he had saved her from grave injury or worse at the hands of the clockwork guildsman. And they had shared some intimate moments when she pulled the glass shards from his skin and bandaged his wounds. They'd each trusted the other with their lives, which was more than many married couples Iris knew.

With a sigh and glance to make sure she was alone, she darted into Edward's room.

13

Somewhere in the North of France, 11 June 1870

The first thing Edward noticed was how he hurt all over. He tried to curl away from the blows that must be falling from the schoolboys, who had never understood his interest in science over sport, but the smallest movement made him hurt more, so he made himself take stock of his situation. He lay on something soft, but the contents of the mattress pricked him if he pinched the cloth hard enough. Someone had loosened his tie. No, no, it had been removed along with most of his clothing. Now the familiar burn of anxiety flooded through him, and he tried to sit.

"It's fine," a female voice said, and a weight on his chest pinned him to the bed. "Will you open your eyes? I can douse the candle if you like."

The voice. It sounded familiar, and he shied away from it. Was Lily here to torment him further? He thought she'd humiliated him enough at the seashore, but now, back in Huntington Village, he knew she waited to embarrass him further—scared Edward who wouldn't ride a horse on the sand with her. Funny how that happened after she found out he was the second son, contrary to her assumptions. She'd been much more patient with him and his anxieties before that.

No, that wasn't right. His mind attempted to make sense of the jumble of memories. He'd been at the shore, yes, but not at the beach. No, there had been a large creature—an aircraft. There had been an aircraft and a battle and a fall, and oh, his favorite small copper globe had gone out the window with a thug. And the escape compartment, and the shattering of the wooden walls around him along with the life and routines he had so carefully constructed to protect himself from circumstances like these.

That meant the woman in the room with him wasn't Lily. It was... "Iris?" He had to employ all his forehead muscles to drag his eyelids open and found he lay in a rustic room dimly lit by a candle that didn't have a shade over it. And sitting on the bed with him was a light-haired fairy. In the dim flickering light, her eyes looked deep purple. Her hand rested on his chest, but he found it more comforting than restrictive.

"Yes, good, you remember." But she didn't sound too certain. "How are you feeling...Edward?"

"Like I've been beaten by a horde of large schoolboys with clubs," he said. "Where are we? Are Johann and Marie...?"

"Everyone's fine. You and I took the worst of it, you most of all. You cushioned my fall."

Now the light in her eyes spread with the refraction of her tears.

"Don't cry. I'm fine, I think."

She didn't confirm or deny his assessment, and he tried not to squirm—was something seriously wrong with him?

"Are you hungry?"

"What time is—" He realized what a stupid question it was. What did it matter if it was time to eat? He was hungry. "Yes. Yes, I'm very hungry."

Iris stood, and the place her hand had rested now felt cold with its absence. "I'll inform Doctor Radcliffe."

"Who?"

"I'm not entirely sure who he is," she said. "Another man with secrets."

And with that cryptic answer, she disappeared. Edward took the opportunity to test his limbs and run his fingers over his face. He came to the conclusion his sensations had merit, but no lasting injuries, he hoped. The cuts on his face presented some concern, but as he never planned to engage in the social ritual of marriage and have to accommodate someone else in his routines, he was less worried about disfigurement than the possibility of internal harm. He would ask this Radcliffe person when he appeared. What had the man done or said to bewilder Iris? She seemed a very sensible young woman.

A dark figure appeared at the door, and Edward squinted at the light of a lamp. "Doctor Radcliffe?" he asked.

The man's face didn't turn much lighter in the lamplight. "You presume correctly," he said in a flat American accent. He ran his hands over Edward's limbs, pausing when Edward flinched, and tenderly probed those areas. Next he took a stethoscope out of his pocket and used it to listen to Edward's heart and breathing.

"Nothing broken, but I'm hearing a slight wheeze in your left lung," he said. "You seem to be breathing fine, so I'll recommend resting for a week."

"But we have a mission to complete," Edward said, then suspected he should have kept his mouth shut.

The doctor nodded. "I'm sure it's very important, but you won't accomplish anything if you can't breathe."

Edward recognized that tone—Radcliffe was humoring him —but before he could say anything, Johann came through the door followed by a redheaded chap with a tray, from which savory odors emanated.

"Help him to sit, gently," the doctor said.

Edward tried not to tense as the other men helped him to a sitting position and sucked at his teeth as Johann assisted him to and from the water closet. When he returned to the bed, his impulse was to curl into a ball in shame at being so helpless and out of control of his fate, but that meant he wouldn't be able to eat the lovely smelling broth in the bowl. Even better, there was a crusty piece of bread beside it. He lifted the spoon and noticed the others watching him.

"What?"

"Just making sure you can swallow it," Radcliffe said. "It was impossible to examine you for some internal injuries."

Edward put the spoon down. "I can't eat with you watching me. Shoo. Go away. If I need you, I'll call."

"Don't be difficult," Johann told him. "We're trying to make sure you're fine."

"I am fine," he said. "Now step into the hall, all of you."

They didn't move.

"Fine, the doctor can stay."

With shrugs, the other two left. Edward lifted some broth to his lips, aware more than anything of the doctor's gray eyes watching him. Unlike Iris's purple eyes, Radcliffe's gray ones seemed to gather the light in, swallow it, and spit it back in sparks. Edward hardly tasted the broth until the man stood and placed the ends of the stethoscope in his ears.

"If you wouldn't mind pausing, let me see if your digestion is moving as it should."

"I can be the judge of that. I can assure you that until this insane journey, it was running like—" He didn't want to say *clockwork*. That word had a negative connotation now, and using it to describe his stomach would make him feel like his digestive tract was going to try to kill him. "It was running smoothly and on a better schedule than most trains," he finished.

The doctor lifted the tray from Edward's lap and listened to his abdomen in several places. "All sounds like it should. You must have taken very good care of yourself before your crash."

"I did." Edward said nothing else. He waited for the doctor to replace the tray and finished his dinner and the watered-down wine that came with it.

"Any trouble with the wine? Any burning?"

"No, all is well. I'm very tired." Edward was barely aware of the others coming in, taking the tray, and helping him lie on his back. The room faded into a strange dream about clockwork stomachs and brass spiders.

IRIS MET the doctor and Bledsoe in the hall. The Irishman gave her a nod and carried Edward's dinner tray toward the stairs.

"Is he all right?" she asked.

"He's fine," Doctor Radcliffe said. "I put a little laudanum in his soup so he would sleep without pain."

"He's not going to appreciate that," Johann told him. "He hates losing control over any aspect of his life."

"I gathered. You two seem to know a lot about him. Why don't you fill me in?"

"No need," Johann said. "We'll be on our way tomorrow. There's a timetable we're supposed to keep to."

Iris found her own astonished expression mirrored on the doctor's face. "You can't mean it," she said. "He's gravely hurt, and our employer put *us* in danger, remember? I'm sure he would understand if we took a few days to let him rest."

Bledsoe pulled her aside. "I wasn't supposed to reveal this," he murmured, "but Cobb gave me a more detailed itinerary than the two of you. We have a very important meeting in Paris in two days, and we need to leave tomorrow if we're to get there in time. We can't miss this window—the Marquis is leaving on Tuesday for the French seashore, and he has one of the city's biggest private collections of Classical art and the Renaissance art it inspired."

"But what about Edward? We can't leave him here." Iris bit her lip. "I mean the professor."

"Edward, huh? I didn't realize the two of you were on a first name basis."

Iris drew herself up. "Surviving a life-or-death situation tends to do that."

"Yet you don't call me Johann."

"Fine, Johann." She crossed her arms and felt she'd swallowed something slimy. "But you may continue to call me Miss McTavish."

"You're an infuriating young woman, but you shall not distract me from the matter at hand. I'll arrange transport, the most gentle conveyance possible. He can rest in Paris while you and I visit the nobility. Your eyes are more important for this stage of the journey than his, Iris."

Her name on his lips made her draw back as if he'd slapped her. "Very well," she said. "But I wish we could bring the doctor with us. I don't trust him, but the fewer who know about Edward's incapacitation, the better. And Radcliffe and his friend are stuck here. We owe them for helping with Edward."

"That's a brilliant idea. I'll see what I can do."

Iris watched Bledsoe—she wasn't going to call him Johann again anytime soon—walk down the hall, his hands in his pockets, and she wished she hadn't asked him for anything, even if it was for Edward's sake.

"What was that about?" Radcliffe asked. He'd been fiddling with his pocket watch and standing a discreet distance away.

"We're trying to determine how to get Professor Bailey to

Paris," she said. "Would you be interested in coming with us to help me care for him?"

A sigh lifted his shoulders. "I would love to get out of this little town, but I'm afraid I have a responsibility to Madame Gastron."

Johann turned at the top of the stairs and gave Iris a rakish smile. Now she really worried what he was about to do.

Iris woke the next morning to shouted French. She got the gist of the yelling, but a lot of the words were ones she hadn't learned in Miss Cornwall's French classes, probably for good reason. She identified two of the shouters as Monsieur Gastron and Johann, and the third a woman who didn't sound familiar.

Marie burst through the bedroom door. "Best get up now, Miss McTavish," she said. "Your friend the Maestro revealed Madame Gastron wasn't as hurt as she made out to be and was faking it because she liked the looks of Doctor Radcliffe. Now the Monsieur is kicking us all out."

"What happened?"

Marie's cheeks pinked, and she looked down. "Best you focus on getting ready, Miss. We leave as soon as you are."

"And the professor?"

"Doctor Radcliffe is with him now."

Iris shook her head at the sheer ridiculousness of it all— were they in some French novel where the drama was always overblown?

The cessation of the shouting left a ringing in her ears, and she flinched at the slam of a door downstairs. Marie helped her with her various tying and buttoning, and the maid pulled Iris's hair back into a quick chignon. Iris remained alert to any sound outside the room, and the thump of a man's footsteps up the stairs and down the hall followed by a knock on the door made her shoulders tighten and her breath catch. Was she to be the target of yelling now? She didn't do anything wrong. Well, not recently.

The Irishman Mister O'Connell stood there. "I'm to help you with your bag, Miss," he said. "Are ye ready?"

"Yes. And the Professor?"

"I'm to load him next. The doctor is getting him up."

Am I ever to leave a place at my own leisure again? Iris followed him out, down the stairs, through the front hall, and to the front of the inn, where a coach waited for them. Bledsoe paced back and forth in front of it. Iris couldn't stand any more emotional turmoil, so she said, "I'm impressed you managed to find a conveyance for us, Bledsoe."

"A Frenchman always has rivals. His neighbor across the street was going into Paris today for some supplies that have become scarce around here due to the fighting, and he was happy to make the trip more profitable."

O'Connell and Radcliffe emerged with Edward supported between them.

"I'm perfectly capable of walking," he groused.

"Faster this way," O'Connell grunted and loaded the petulant professor into the carriage.

Iris hesitated, but Bledsoe motioned for her to follow Edward in. "Since you're on a first-name basis with him, you get to play nurse." The smile on his face indicated he would enjoy watching Iris's struggles.

"Very well." She entered the coach and settled beside Edward on the forward facing padded bench.

"Is there tea?" Edward asked. "I always have tea when I wake."

"Sadly, no." A dull ache settled in Iris's forehead, and it worsened when the others climbed in and caused the stuffy air in the carriage to warm. Opening the windows helped somewhat but let the dust in, and the doctor said it would be worse for Edward to breathe dusty air than stale.

Soon Bledsoe, who had sat beside Iris on the other side from Edward, was asleep, and she looked for something she could sneak a glove off to "read" to find out what had happened that morning. But Bledsoe didn't hold anything, and even if she could pinch a bit of fabric without him waking, she'd never had much luck with clothing. Her talent seemed to work best on objects that had more lasting properties, and fabric was too flimsy and ethereal. Buttons were held for a moment and didn't store many impressions.

A glance across the coach at their companions—Marie sat between Radcliffe and O'Connell—revealed that the doctor looked out of the window with a pensive expression, Marie with a melancholy one, and O'Connell with amusement. Iris guessed O'Connell would tell her what had transpired that morning. He acted the gentleman, but she surmised he had a good sense of humor, and if he found the morning's events funny, he would want to share. With that decided, she had to pay attention to Edward, who picked at her sleeve and asked for water. Then he couldn't get comfortable, and his shifting around made her have to practically sit on Bledsoe, who of course found her discomfort hilarious in spite of it keeping him awake.

Iris found there were many, many miles between the little French village where they'd landed and Paris.

14

Ôtel *Auberge, Paris, 12 June 1870*

According to the original itinerary, the travelers were to have had their own rooms, but with the addition to their number plus Edward's condition, they divided themselves among the three hotel chambers Cobb's agent had reserved for them. Iris and Marie took one, which was fine and not fine with Iris. She was relieved to have a maid again but had been looking forward to some quiet after their long, arduous journey. Once the carriage wheels bumped over the cobblestones of Paris, Marie started talking about what a wonderful city Paris was and simply would not be quiet.

"Perhaps you could draw me a bath," Iris requested when they reached her room. She'd stopped paying attention to Marie's narrative, something about a theatre nearby, long before they checked in. The hotel had both hot and cold running water and a large claw-foot tub in the *salle de bain* as well as a shallow bowl with a spigot and drain Iris was afraid to ask about. She knew she was hot and tired from the morning's journey and suspected she smelled less than sweet since her last bath had been the night before they set out on this horrid adventure, and she'd been wearing the same bloody—and she was happy to take the opportunity to use both literal and swearing senses of the word—clothes since her trunk went down with the airship.

That was what they had been able to surmise—that the airship had gone down because Cobb hadn't made any attempts to contact them, and there were no messages waiting at the hotel. Of course, as Marie informed them, they were to have as little communication as possible with Cobb once they reached French soil in order not to tip off the French Clockwork Guild to their presence.

However, a whirring noise caught Iris's attention while she waited for Marie to finish preparing her bath, and she saw one of the little clockwork butterflies flitting overhead. She wanted to get a closer look at an intact one and prevent it from reporting back to its makers, so she moved beneath it and took one of the cases off the pillows. It followed her, and she took her shoes and stockings off and stood on the tall bed.

"Come here, you little bitty pretty," she crooned. The little brass creature quivered and flitted nearer her, its wings a blur. Iris reached out and captured it with the pillowcase, but it continued to fly with surprising strength, and she found herself holding on to the bedpost with one hand, the pillowcase with the clockwork spy in another. Marie found her like that shortly thereafter.

"Should've figured you'd try to catch one," Marie said. "We all do, but it's a good thing it thinks it can escape. Otherwise your ears would be splitting—they have a pressure valve that makes them scream to get away like some bugs. Hold it there."

"Trying," Iris said through gritted teeth. She now hung off the bed with one leg hooked around the bedpost and wondered how much more her arms could take.

Marie took the metal top off a glass container with a clawed pewter bottom and opened a spigot behind the tea and coffee station. She poured steaming hot water into the carafe and put in a tea bag.

"This is hardly the time for tea, Marie."

"It's not for you, Miss. It's for the clockwork. Hold it still, please."

Iris didn't dignify Marie's comment with a response. As if she had any control over the whirring thing, and she did want tea once this ordeal was over. Marie held the carafe under the clockwork, and steam enveloped the flying end of the pillow-case. The tug grew less as the clockwork wound down, and Iris rolled her shoulder back and forth to loosen the muscles. Finally, Marie held the now soaked end of the pillowcase containing the clockwork in her hand, and Iris let go, sinking down on the bed. She stretched both hands, her fingers tight and sore. Now that she thought about it, all of her was tight and sore.

"Is it dead?" she asked. "And why the tea, not just water?"

"Professor Bailey would have a better explanation for it, Miss, but I'll do my best. There are things called alkaloids in most substances, and the ones in the tea break down the stuff that allows the clockwork mechanisms to fly with minimal rubbing of their parts."

Iris knew some basic science from her time in school, the one class she'd had. "You mean it breaks down the lubricant that allows the clockworks to fly with minimal friction and therefore go longer on the same amount of winding?"

"Yes, Miss, that's it." Marie smiled at her. "So it's not dead, just stuck, but it hasn't had any sudden force, so it won't break the part that makes it scream."

"Excellent. Please bring it to Professor Bailey for him to examine. He'll need something to occupy himself while he heals."

"And then a bath for you, Miss." Marie's wrinkled nose told Iris all she needed to know. "And while you do that, I'll work on finding you some more clothes. I believe there was an appointment for you with a *modiste* this afternoon, but you may have missed it. Either way, first you must bathe."

Iris didn't argue.

EDWARD MADE it to his room on his own two feet—barely—with Doctor Radcliffe supporting him on one side and Johann on the other. It seemed that whenever one part of him felt better, another started aching or stinging or stabbing and joined the chorus of discomfort. He exhaled when the bed took over supporting his body and floated for a moment in relief before the chorus, now a smaller ensemble, started again. Johann would be proud of his musical analogy, he thought, but before he could tell his friend, he drifted off to sleep.

But not for too long—a crash outside woke him. The hotel room windows stood open to the early summer breeze, and they were high enough to pull in few city smells. The noise below told him they stayed in the middle of a metropolis. *The air is something, I suppose.* Although he knew he would watch the window for signs of one of those little clockwork butterflies, at least when he was awake. The memory of him shoving the pirate out of the window with his beloved copper globe popped into his mind, and he shook his head to dislodge it.

"Are you hurting?" Radcliffe asked. He sat by the window with a newspaper open on the marble-topped table in front of him and a cup of tea beside him on the windowsill.

"Somewhat," Edward admitted. In a brief moment with the two of them that morning, Johann had cautioned Edward not to alert the doctor—who showed a strong interest in affairs of the mind—to his anxiety and previous breakdown, so he wasn't going to admit to his mental anguish at the loss of his materials. The maid Marie had cleared the shattered glass globe shards from his valise, so all he had left of his travel aether isolator were the connections and stoppers. The burner also had to be discarded after it bent and spilled its fuel.

Doctor Radcliffe examined him and said, "As far as I can tell, you're healing slowly, but it would help if we could get a look inside."

"Not surgery," Edward said. "The risk is too great."

"No, no, I have some colleagues here in Paris who are doing work on ways to look inside the human body without cutting anything open. With your consent, I'll get in touch with them, see if I can get us an appointment."

"Very well." Edward shifted, and his left hip sang a sharp solo. Yes, his mind must be injured if he was thinking in musical, not scientific terms.

The maid Marie entered with a pillowcase, one end of which sagged and dripped. "I have a present for the Professor from Miss McTavish," she said, her dimples evident.

"Oh, a present!" Edward struggled to sit, and the doctor helped him. "What could it be?"

Marie deposited the bundle in his hands, and he unrolled the pillowcase to reveal one of the clockwork butterflies. It looked smaller now that it wasn't moving, and he examined the delicate parts, all fashioned of brass, some of which greened in places where it had been nicked or scratched. *Oh, thank you, Iris! This is just the thing.*

"Marie, is my magnifier intact?" he asked.

"Yes, Professor. You wrapped it very well. Shall I fetch it?"

"Please do. I've been wanting to see one of these up close and whole."

Marie handed him his magnifying glass and asked. "Perhaps you would be more comfortable at the table so you can see the creature in the light? Would that be all right, Doctor?"

They helped Edward to the table and propped him up with pillows. He noticed the fatigue from moving that short distance but also that he felt stronger than the day before. *I shall study this device and see if I can make it useful for us.*

By teatime, Edward shifted positions every few minutes due to aching.

"You need to rest," Radcliffe told him and gently pried the clockwork, from which Edward had managed to detach the wings, from Edward's hands. He thought he'd isolated the winding mechanism.

"I don't need to," Edward told him, but he said the last word through a yawn. A new sharp pain in his arm made him look down to see Radcliffe injecting him with something, and he tried to jerk away, but the doctor held him firm.

"It's to help the pain, and you need to sleep."

Edward thought he said, "But I want to choose when I sleep —it's not time for a nap." But he wasn't sure his statement made it out loud before he was sucked into a dream about flying brass horses galloping after the airship as it plummeted to the hungry sea below.

"Did he like it?" Iris asked Marie when she entered. Iris, clean from a warm bath with an extra change of water, stood in her shift, which at least had been rinsed at the inn, and held the soiled dress away from her.

"He was very excited," Marie told her and took the dress from her. "You don't want to wear this, do you?"

"Of course not." Iris squelched the feeling of panic at letting go of the gown and reminded herself the little gold case was no longer sewn in the pocket but hidden in a secret compartment in her valise. She rubbed her fingers together, but the action didn't clear the feeling of griminess from them.

"I sent for a gown from the theatre. It's on the risqué side for daytime, but I also have a shawl for you, and it was the only one in your size. You need something to wear to the *modiste*."

"So I didn't miss the appointment with her?"

"You did, but she agreed for you to come to her shop as a favor. We've used her before for last-minute costumes, so she's pretty agreeable. Plus she doesn't make much money on Sundays."

Iris tried to remember who the "we" was, probably someone mentioned as part of Marie's ramblings as they drove into town in the oven-like carriage. She hoped the Gastrons' neighbor charged Bledsoe extra for their miserable conveyance.

Marie helped her into the corset, petticoats and light green dress, which instead of having a high collar, exposed what felt like a scandalous amount of chest with its square neckline. She'd never seen her breasts plump like that. Thank goodness Marie pinned a lace shawl around her shoulders, and it provided some discretion. Otherwise men taller than she—and that was almost all of them—would have quite the view. Iris studied the brooch, which held a large peridot inside a stylized "C".

"Is this yours?" she asked. "Wouldn't you rather hold on to it? It looks valuable."

"Not really, Miss," Marie said. "Now let's put your hair up."

Coiffed and dressed, Iris barely recognized herself. She hardly looked the image of the field archaeologist she wanted to be, but she doubted she'd be brave enough to walk around Paris in men's clothing like one of her idols Jane Dieulafoy, famous for both her archaeological discoveries and scandalous sartorial choices.

What's the harm in play acting a little?

While Marie changed into a dark blue day dress and removed her maid's cap, Iris took the opportunity to read the brooch. Disgust flashed through her, as did that feeling between her legs she remembered from her mother's ring, but no images.

"It's best I not look like your maid," Marie said and straightened her stylish hat atop her dark curls. It had silk birds and blue ribbons that matched her dress.

"Why?" Iris asked and went into the *salle de bain* to wash her hands at the sink. She scrubbed until her fingers turned red but couldn't clear the slimy feeling from them.

"I'd rather not say, Miss."

More and more secrets. But Iris said nothing, only allowed Marie to pin a small straw hat swallowed by green and cream-colored silk flowers on her head. She pushed Marie's hands away—goodness, what was she going to do if she couldn't bear for her own maid to touch her?—and tied her own chin ribbons before putting on her gloves. Marie gave her a look of mingled sadness and resignation.

Iris and Marie passed Patrick O'Connell in the hotel lobby, where he played two men in cards while others looked on askance. Iris, desirous of not being alone with Marie, remembered her intention to ask Patrick what had transpired in the inn that morning and smiled at him.

He rose and threw his cards on the table. "I've taken enough of your money for today, gents."

"We will find out how you are cheating, you devil's beard," one of them sneered.

Patrick put on his hat, turned to the two women, and asked, "Are you ladies heading out? That Bledsoe chap warned me not to let you go without a chaperone."

"I grew up in this part of Paris," Marie said. "We'll be fine."

Iris looked at Marie, who indeed seemed to bloom under the admiring glances of the men around them.

Will I ever get there? And at what cost?

"Regardless, I'll be joining you."

"That's fine with me," Iris told him. He held his arm out,

and she took it. They walked through the revolving door and into the sunlight. Iris had been too tired, hot and miserable on the way into the hotel to notice much, but now she had to struggle not to stop and look around at everything. Marie wouldn't slow when Iris entreated her to.

"Best keep moving and not say much," Patrick murmured to her. "We're being followed, and the English and Americans aren't well-liked here."

15

P aris, 12 June 1870

Marie led Iris and O'Connell down the main boulevard past the front of the hotel with its sandstone-
colored walls and crystal windows in which every pane was
beveled. They walked past shops tempting Sunday afternoon
strollers with brightly colored displays, and French spoken too
fast to understand wrapped Iris in a shawl of whispers
threaded together with the hissing of steamcarts and punctuated by the clopping hooves of horse-drawn coaches. The soft
odors of steam and perfume warred with the acrid smells of
coal and sweat, all of it over the freshness of the summer breeze
and almost-baked scent of sunshine-warmed brick.

But Iris couldn't enjoy it because she sensed someone
watching her. When she glanced behind her, she saw a famil-
iar-looking young man, but he disappeared into the crowd so
quickly she couldn't place him.

They turned onto a side street so narrow Iris wouldn't have
noticed it otherwise. The light-colored brick and wide stone
gave way to cobblestones and the weathered gray walls of a
medieval neighborhood. Iris blinked to clear her vision from

the after-images of the wide, sunny boulevard. The darkness of the stone emphasized the gloom, and the close walls concentrated the formerly pleasant breeze into a gusty chill.

"Is this safe?" Iris whispered and pulled the fichu higher around her shoulders. Noises seemed muted in the false dusk. *If the air were still, I could believe this was a tomb.*

"No one will bother me here," Marie said. Now she walked beside Iris with Patrick behind them. "This is an old neighborhood, one of the few that escaped the reforms of Monsieur Haussman. Is our shadow gone, Mister O'Connell?"

"Aye, although it won't surprise me if he's waiting for us when we return to civilization."

"There are many exits to this area, including underground. I will find one for us. And appearances can be deceiving—in spite of the architecture, this neighborhood has its modern conveniences, and we are safer here than we were on the main Rue. Ah, here we are." She stopped at a wooden door set in a wall. It appeared to be the same as all the other doors in the area without a house number to distinguish it, and gaslight flickered in the small windows.

Marie knocked in a complicated pattern on the door, and it opened wide enough to admit them.

Are we here for dresses or for a secret society meeting?

Iris didn't voice her thoughts, however, for fear of being left. This was certainly the strangest shopping trip she'd ever been on, but somehow also the most enjoyable.

A young woman about Iris's age greeted Marie with kisses on each cheek and spoke French to her. "*Fantastique.* What a surprise!" She switched to English. "Madame will be so 'appy to see you."

"Is she here?" Marie lowered her voice and used rapid-fire French that Iris could barely follow. "And don't call me that. I don't do that anymore."

"Ah, and what character are you today?"

Marie sighed with French flair. "Someone for Cobb."

The young woman nodded and turned her attention to Iris. "Ah," she said in a thick French accent, "you dressed her in the Juliet. That's suitable."

"Yes," Marie turned to Iris with a smile that made her next words an insult. "She does have the look of a virginal heroine, does she not?"

O'Connell coughed to hide a laugh.

"Oh, and this is our escort, Mister O'Connell."

"And will you need clothing for both of them?"

"For her and me. We lost ours in an airship incident."

The shopgirl wrote something on a pad of paper and went behind a narrow desk. "Madame is at the theatre. She is bringing samples to your mother and hoped to 'ave returned before you came. I'll send her a message to see how she would like me to start."

The sound of a drawer opening and closing was followed by a whoosh and thunk.

"Is that the pneumatic tube system?" Iris asked. Her fingers itched to test it out. Of course she knew Paris had such a thing —installed with the new sewers, which must run under the neighborhood—but she wanted to see and try it.

"Thank you, Claudia." Marie stripped her gloves. "Do you mind if I make something to drink? I suspect these two have never had Spanish coffee. Meanwhile, you can start. The budget is generous, as it always is with *Monsieur* Cobb." Her mouth twisted around the title.

When Claudia went into the back of the shop, Iris noted, "Your accent has become more French since being here. And Mister O'Connell's Irish brogue is thicker."

Marie didn't look up from where she boiled water on a small burner behind the desk. "I can't help it—it always happens when I'm in Paris, especially in this part of the city. It's just as well. As Mister O'Connell mentioned, the English and Americans aren't loved here."

"Yes, would you tell me why?" Iris asked. "I'm embarrassed to say that I've not kept up with world events as I should have with my mother's death and my father's illness and work to preoccupy me."

"Well, you know the States are at war with each other," O'Connell said. "The Northern ones thought they had the Southern ones beat, but France jumped in. They wanted the cotton in the South for their mills here to compete with what England is importing from India. Plus a fight with England was too tempting."

"So the war between the states is a proxy war between England and France," Iris said.

"Aye, but the French people don't care much this time around. They're more concerned with how it's draining their treasury even if they do get good quality cotton for their clothing and the supply has allowed their manufacturing to keep pace with England's."

"What it means for you, Miss McTavish, is that you need to say as little as possible and not draw attention to yourself," Marie said. "The French will always take a tourist's money but will easily take offense, and the people have been in a mobbing mood. They say the Empire is in trouble again and the Prussians pushing at the border."

Another whoosh and thunk made Iris bite her tongue over the retort she wanted to make, that she could handle herself, but she also had to remember she was in a tomb-like neighborhood in a strange city where she barely spoke the language, and it was potentially dangerous.

And I thought France was safe.

Claudia returned with her arms full of dresses. "I am afraid this is all I have. Did I hear the tube?"

"Yes, it sounds like you got a response."

Claudia opened the drawer, extracted the message tube, and shook out the roll of paper. "Ah, Mademoiselle Marie, I am sorry, but your mother wants you to come to the theatre, and Madame says I am not to help you until you visit your poor *mère* and bring the English stranger with you for dinner. She will fit you both there."

Marie said a word that sounded like *mère*—French for mother—but Iris was pretty sure it meant something else entirely. "You directed the message to Madame, right?"

"Yes, of course, but you know 'ow your mother works. She knew you were in the city as soon as you left the carriage. She has eyes and ears everywhere."

"Well, Miss McTavish, you're about to get an education," Marie said. "My mother is one of the most feared women in Paris, and for good reason."

"Lovely." But Iris couldn't miss that Marie paled a couple of shades under her rouge, and that, above all, troubled her. What sort of woman could intimidate the indomitable maid?

"Can we take the tunnel, Claudia, or are the corps working on the sewers?"

"They should be clear. *Au revoir*, or should I say *adieu*?"

Marie laughed and kissed the girl on both cheeks. "If you're going to invoke gods, find me some good ones. We're going to need all the help we can get. I had hoped to avoid this, but I should have known it was impossible."

"You will be fine. Remember, you are *Fantastique*. You can handle anything."

"We'll see. Would you send a message to Doctor Radcliffe at the Hôtel Auberge that we will not be joining him, the professor and the maestro for dinner?"

"You do keep the most interesting company." Claudia led Marie, Patrick and Iris through the shop and opened a trap door underneath the dressing room. The gas lights provided intriguing glimpses of rich fabrics and trimmings, but Iris barely got a look before Patrick handed her down into a narrow staircase that creaked under her walking shoes. She had to tuck her skirts, which were more voluminous than she was accustomed to, around her so they wouldn't brush the walls and put her other hand over her nose and mouth against the smell.

"So this is what you meant when you said you knew ways out of the neighborhood," Patrick whispered when they were all in a large egg-shaped tunnel. His tone was admiring, and Iris once again felt how useless she was in all of this. Sure, she had wished for adventure, but she'd always imagined herself leading it, not being a passive follower. And all this in the service of acquiring dresses—how ridiculous. They should be looking for clues as Cobb was paying them for, not going on a quest for silk and lace through a sewer, of all places, and having to be careful to avoid walking into the stream of filth that flowed down a shallow gutter in the bottom. Pipes ran along the sides and top of the passage. Streams of dirty water emerged intermittently from them, and Marie showed Iris and O'Connell how to listen for incoming showers. Thus conversation was forestalled in favor of clothing preservation, although Iris was sure her attire and hair would reek for days after this. Plus, her right hip, sore from their tumble from the sky, twinged with each step along the uneven surface.

Intermittent grates above them illuminated the tan stone interspersed with brick where the tunnels had been shored up. Their footsteps echoed along the path, and the whole place had an air of violated sacredness. Iris wondered how much of Paris's history had been carted away without anyone realizing it. Or had they taken care to sift through the dirt and find clues to their own past? Not likely, at least from what she'd heard about Haussman and his henchmen, whose attitude was that of improvement as quickly as possible and thoughtful exploration be damned. She recalled something about how some of these passages were leftovers from limestone quarries dating back to

Roman times, and her fingers itched to touch the walls, to search for echoes of past objects crying out for discovery. But propriety and good sense kept her from taking her gloves off down there or removing her hand from her face. Besides, what would Marie and Mister O'Connell think?

After what seemed like hours and a gradual descent during which they had to hold on to each other in the dark, they stopped at a stone staircase, and Marie indicated that she would lead the way up it. The smell of the sewers retreated in a blast of comparatively fresh air carrying the smells of old wood and candle smoke. They emerged into a store-room filled with set pieces and props that appeared to have some sort of organization to them but not one Iris could fathom. After her daydreams of Roman coins and tools, the two-dimensional wooden bushes and swords seemed an insulting reminder of what she had become—a liar and faker—and she again felt that this must not all be real, that she would soon awaken from this nightmare of sewers and false skies.

"Here we are," Marie said, "at the *Théâtre Bohème*." She pulled a perfume bottle off a shelf with others and spritzed herself all over with it. "Lemon-orange water," she explained. "It helps freshen up some of the sewer smell. *Ma mère* isn't a fan of that mode of travel."

Iris and Patrick allowed themselves to be sprayed in turn, and Iris admitted it helped somewhat. With that done, Marie straightened her spine, put her shoulders back, and gestured for them to follow her toward the stairs.

"Come, one doesn't keep one of the most powerful women in Paris waiting."

16

H ôtel *Auberge, Sunday 12 June 1870*
     "Tube for you, *Monsieur*."
     "Thank you."

The hushed voices roused Edward from his fragmented dreams. *Where am I?* He expected to open his eyes to his room at Haywood House, where he had taken a brief nap after returning from the University and a successful day of running experiments...

And no, late afternoon sunlight streamed through the holes in the lace curtains over the window, but they weren't his curtains, and that wasn't English sunlight, which no matter how close it got to midsummer, never looked that bright in the late afternoon. He tried to roll away from the wrong curtains and strange light, and his body reminded him he'd been the bottom man in a pile in an airship escape compartment crash, and he could only make it to his back. His groan brought Chadwick Radcliffe the deceitful doctor to his side.

"Did you have a good nap?" the doctor asked as though he hadn't injected Edward with a substance against his will.

Edward glared at him.

Radcliffe ran a hand through his dark hair. "I'm sorry. You were so focused and intent on dissecting the clockwork you didn't hear me when I tried to get your attention, and I could tell you were pushing yourself too hard."

"You need to talk to Johann," Edward told him. "He's good at getting my attention whether I want him to have it or not."

"Or to Miss McTavish?"

Edward turned his face away. He wasn't going to talk about his mixed feelings toward the young woman with anyone, least of all someone who wielded mind-fogging pharmaceutical means. He couldn't help but smile at the thought of Iris—she'd known studying the clockwork would be the perfect thing to entertain him, after all—and he hoped she would be back in time for dinner. The French ate late, didn't they?

"Is he sulking?" Johann walked to the side of the bed Edward tried to turn to. "Come on, Edward. We need you up and healthy for this adventure."

"Like that's under my control."

"The mind is a powerful thing," Radcliffe said, his voice resigned. "It can block the body from doing certain things and motivate it to do others."

"You sound as though you speak from experience," Edward told him. He struggled to sit, and the two men helped prop him up with the pillows. He thought he hurt less.

The doctor took a seat by the window, and Edward relaxed at the knowledge he wasn't going to get stuck again, at least not for the foreseeable future. He glanced at Johann, whose normal neutral to insolent expression had been replaced by one of concern and...fear? He'd never known his friend to fear anything. When Johann's gaze met Edward's, the musician smoothed his expression so quickly Edward wondered if he'd seen what he thought. Edward found himself picking at a knot on the blanket, and he squirmed.

"Do you need something?" Johann asked.

"No. Well, yes. I'll take care of it."

They allowed him to go to the water closet alone, although he was panting by the time he got there and had to rest before attempting to cross the room back to the bed. Radcliffe listened to his chest again.

"I don't like how that left lung sounds," he told Edward. "It could be internal bruising, but it doesn't make sense considering where your other injuries are."

"And how would you know?" asked Johann. "Aside from the fact you're a doctor, but I've met some quacks."

"I'm a *military* doctor," Radcliffe told them. "I was the balloon corps physician for a year, so I've treated men after nasty landings before. Your friend's injuries don't fit the usual pattern."

"And what brings you to Europe?" Edward asked, tired of talking about his physical state. He recalled Iris talking about the doctor, but his memories of the inn were hazy at best. Probably because the doctor medicated him without asking.

"I was visiting a friend in Vienna along with Mister O'Connell, and our return trip was diverted with the fighting along the French/Prussian border." He shrugged. "Then we were robbed, forcing us to rely on others to get us back to the States."

"And your friend couldn't help you? Communication isn't totally suspended," Johann said.

"My friend isn't able to help us."

"But surely—"

"The topic is closed, Maestro. Unfortunately, my friend's position isn't such that she..." He trailed off, his cheeks darkening.

Johann's mouth twisted into a smile of solidarity Edward recognized but once again couldn't take part in. "Ah, now I understand. Don't worry, I've gone out of my way for a woman before, and it never ends well. Might as well stick with what's in front of you."

"And sometimes that doesn't work out, no matter how hard you try," Edward pitched in. He hated being stuck in the bed and having to crane his neck to see the others and participate in the conversation, but he wasn't going to be ignored. Even if discussing women problems bored him.

Unpredictable creatures.

"Right," Radcliffe said. "That reminds me. One of the front desk staff brought me a message from Miss St. Jean. She, Miss McTavish and Patrick will be having dinner out, so it'll be the three of us. Do you feel up to the dining room, Professor?"

Edward shifted his weight forward, but he moaned when a spasm seized his lower back. "Not tonight, but I feel I am improving."

"I'll order room service," Johann said. "And a bottle of wine or two. This is all on Cobb's dime, so we may as well enjoy it."

Edward studied Radcliffe. He had the air of a man with secrets, and Edward sensed that Radcliffe's slip indicated more than the usual affair of the heart gone wrong. Of course he defined "usual affair" as what Johann got himself into with the inherent frequent breaking off and getting back together with various women with less than stellar reputations, in other words, the dissolution and reconnection of bonds that weren't tight to begin with. Perhaps Radcliffe had experienced something more akin to Edward's tragedy, or since he was in Paris, he mused, his *tragédie du coeur*.

"What is the patient able to eat, doctor?" Johann asked.

"Perhaps you should ask the patient. He seems to have a good sense of what his stomach can and cannot handle."

"Oh, you've figured that out about him?"

"It's obvious from watching him eat."

There was that feeling of being observed and talked around again. "I'm fine to eat whatever you order as long as it's not too rich."

Johann looked at him. "We're in Paris. Butter is the national food here. Then again, you eat more cream puffs without getting sick than anyone else I know. I'll do my best." He walked out of the room, leaving Edward with the doctor.

"You may feel better with more back support," Radcliffe said. He helped Edward to sit in the chair by the window, where the partially dismantled clockwork laid on the table.

By the time Johann returned, Edward had found the winding mechanism and disassembled the whistle Marie had warned him about. He'd also observed the doctor looking out of the window with a melancholy expression on his face.

"The chef says he has had the *plaisir* of serving many a picky stomach and convalescing traveler, so he will accommodate your request," Johann told them. "And the sommelier sent these two bottles. I love the French—they feel a good wine will fix everything. Doctor, would you like to do the honors?"

"I'm not much of a wine drinker," Radcliffe said and gestured to the bottle Johann proffered. "Please."

The musician opened the first bottle and poured the straw-colored liquid into three glasses. He handed the glasses around and said, "*À votre santé*, literally and in every sense. Edward, try it. Perhaps it will relax you into healing."

Edward sipped the liquid and noticed it tasted like alcohol, but also fruity and with a flavor his mind labeled as rocky. It warmed his throat and esophagus all the way down to his stomach.

"So you don't drink much, either?" Edward asked the doctor when he finished his glass and held it out for a refill. Now the soft, warm feeling extended to his limbs and muted some of his aches and pains.

"No." Radcliffe gazed into his half-full glass. "The last time I had wine was at a party, and it didn't end well."

"Oh, that sounds like a story," Johann said. He lounged on a small couch against the wall under the other window. "Do tell."

"There's not a lot to say about it. It was supposed to have been an engagement party, but it didn't turn out that way."

"Whose engagement?" Edward asked. His cheeks felt warm, and his tongue loose. The words, "Almost had one of those myself," slipped out before he could stop them.

"Mine."

Before they could ask for further details, some of the hotel footmen arrived with a rolling table full of trays giving off incredible smells of butter and cream, but also tarragon and vegetables. They moved with clockwork precision to set the table—Edward had to move his project to the windowsill—whisk the covers off the dishes, and with a bow, disappeared.

"This looks incredible," Radcliffe said and took the seat across from Edward. Johann pulled up a third chair so he sat between them at the empty place that had been set. Edward inhaled the smells of the roast chicken, potatoes fixed with some sort of cheese and of course butter, and green beans with tarragon and other herbs. There was also more of the crusty bread he remembered from the inn.

"Wait 'til Edward is better. Then we'll get a real French feast. Now about your engagement, Doctor?"

Radcliffe helped himself to some potatoes. "It didn't work out for various reasons. What about yours, Professor?"

Edward paused in his reach for a chicken leg and thigh. "The same, I suppose. Women are too unpredictable."

"What happened?" The doctor's gray eyes fixed on Edward's face with scientific intensity.

"It's not important," Johann said. "Let's say that it too, didn't work out for various reasons."

Edward gave his friend a thankful smile. "Yes, that's all we need to say about it." And more words than he intended tumbled out. "And that's when I chose to live my life with scientific precision. It's the best thing, really. Minimize the variability and whatnot."

"And that's what you've done since your heartbreak? How has it worked?"

Johann nudged Edward's foot under the table, but here it seemed he finally had someone he could convince of the rightness of his lifestyle, so he pressed on. "It's been brilliant. Well, at least until we had to undertake this sodding adventure and go looking for some bloody clues to some bloody ancient formula." It felt good to swear, to get some of his frustration out. "I had everything regulated from the time I slept to how my body responded to when I would eat. I was never sick, and I didn't sustain any injuries. Best of all, my mind has never been clearer than when it didn't have to worry about the mundane life decisions such as mealtimes."

"I see." Radcliffe cut his beans into perfect halves, which Edward approved of. "Some of your continued pain mystifies me although much of it is to be expected from your fall. Perhaps if you were to return to your schedule, it would help your healing along."

"Oh, that would be splendid!" Edward raised his glass. "To the genius of the doctor."

Johann shook his head. "Do you think that's wise? It seems to me that one of the benefits of this trip was getting Edward to loosen up."

"Yet you objected to my impulsive moment with Miss McTavish," Edward told him. The sensation of a taut string vibrating in his chest accompanied his thought that his schedule didn't permit time for female friendship—he had deliberately designed it that way.

"You're right," Johann said. "Well, then, starting this evening you shall have your schedule back. Bedtime is nine o'clock, correct?"

"Yes."

"You had better eat up. It's eight thirty now."

"Oh. What about dessert? I imagine they have lovely cream puffs here."

"They do. I've seen them. But you need to heal, so they can wait until tomorrow. I'll also inform Miss McTavish that she is to visit you at certain times. When were your student visiting hours, again?"

Edward thought back to his life at the university, which seemed ages, not days, ago. "Eleven to eleven thirty."

"Oh, that's a pity. We're scheduled to meet the curator of Classics at the Louvre for breakfast and to peruse their collections of classical art and classically inspired works. That will probably take us through lunch, and we're attending a dinner party at the Marquis de Monceau's house in the evening."

"So you're saying I shan't see her." Edward looked down at his now-empty wine glass and couldn't ignore the little green stab through his heart at the thought of Johann spending all day with her and him not seeing her at all.

"I don't know that the schedule needs to be that strict," Radcliffe said. "And friends can be a healing force as well."

"Oh, no, Doctor. We're going to be scientific," Johann told him. "And that means changing one variable at a time. I've heard that enough from Edward to know how true it must be. He is a brilliant scientist, after all."

"Is this acceptable to you?" Radcliffe asked Edward.

"I suppose." But whereas it should have thrilled him to have some order return to his life, Edward couldn't help but feel restricted. In spite of the bit of laudanum he accepted from the doctor to help him sleep on schedule, he lay awake for quite a while listening for the ladies' return.

17

T héâtre Bohème, Paris, 12 June 1870

The first thing Iris noticed once they emerged from the storeroom was a large playbill in French but with a picture of a young woman who resembled Marie reclining on a clamshell filled with gold cushions. The word "Fantastique" spanned the top in white letters edged in gold that stood out against the dark burgundy background.

"Is that...?" Iris asked and pointed.

"Not anymore," Marie replied through clenched teeth. "I told her to get rid of those."

"But if I did, *Cherie*, 'ow would I remember you since you ran away on an airship and never visited your Mama?" The speaker emerged from the shadows, which she had blended in with due to her dark clothing and hair. Shorter than her daughter, Madame St. Jean looked as Marie would in several years, but with darker skin and world-weary eyes. She also possessed more poise and determination Iris had ever seen in a woman, and she understood Marie's reluctance to face her. Mothers had a way of playing on their daughters' insecurities, after all.

Marie kissed her mother on both cheeks and stood straight

but stiff under the slow, thorough scrutiny, which required a turn.

"You are doing well, more muscular than I remember you being. Remember, *Cherie*, a woman hides her strength. It helps to keep the men guessing."

"Yes, Mama, I remember. It hasn't mattered since I saw you last—I've been busy and have needed my strength."

"It. Always. Matters." She tapped a pearl-handled cane on the floor with each word. "If a man knows your strength, he can also learn your weaknesses. It's best to keep him focused on the weakness he thinks you have. Remember what happened with the American."

Marie flinched like the words pinched her. "Every day, Mama."

"And who are your friends? Did you need to bring them through the sewers? The front of the theatre is humble but much more attractive than the store room, *n'est-ce pas?*" She wrinkled her nose and studied Marie's face. "Ah, but you had a reason. You are in trouble."

Iris's stomach tightened when she put together the woman's insight, her appearance, and the name of the theatre, which referenced the Bohemians, or wanderers. A memory came to her of being a child and hearing of a gypsy caravan coming into town. Her mother had wanted to take her to see the dancing and the special ponies, but her father had refused to allow it.

"Some people see more than others, and our daughter is special," he'd said. Although her mother had pressed him for details, he'd remained vague and stood firm—one of the few times he did with Adelaide.

Now Iris faced the glittering black gaze of the formidable woman, who Marie introduced as, "My mother Lucille St. Jean, owner of the *Théâtre Bohème.*"

"Ah, this is the young woman who I have 'eard much about," Madame St. Jean said. "And do you bring this trouble my daughter is running from? You have a deviled air about you."

"I...I don't know." Iris thought about the young man she'd seen behind them on the boulevard, how he seemed familiar. "I assure you I mean to bring no harm to your daughter."

"Most harm brought to friends is unintentional." *Thunk* went the cane. "But you have a good heart in spite of what circumstances have forced you to do. Like my Marie."

Now Iris's look of curiosity was mirrored by Marie's. They glanced away when their gazes met.

"Come, come, Madame is waiting to help you look like a lady, not a *galopine*, a ragamuffin, in a borrowed dress. You need to fire your maid."

Iris smiled at Marie's panicked look. "I'm afraid I've been without a maid since we left England. She ran off with a neighbor's footman."

"Ah, *les jeunes filles*. They are impulsive, and their mistakes come back with a bite, no?"

Iris tried not to let on how the woman's words described her own situation too well.

"This is ladies' work," Madame St. Jean said and turned her pinpoint gaze to O'Connell. "But you are one who is good with his hands. Come, let me show you where our gas light system is faltering. Perhaps you can study it while we work on dressing the girls and let me know what is wrong. Marie, bring Mademoiselle McTavish to the *Salle d'Étoile*."

Marie led Iris down one side of the corridor while her mother brought Mister O'Connell in the opposite direction. Once Iris was sure she wouldn't be overheard, she asked, "How does she know so much?"

"Don't let her fool you," Marie said. "She likes to intimidate in spite of playing the humble theatre owner."

Iris nodded.

"Although the French are more tolerant of outsiders than

the English, she needs to stay a step ahead of the law. Through the years she's built quite a network of spies and informants, whom she pays well to keep her abreast of the comings and goings of important people, particularly in this part of the city. I'm sure she knew all about every member of our party within half an hour of our arrival at the hotel."

"Ah, that makes sense." Iris allowed herself a full exhale, or at least as much of one as she could in her corset, which felt looser. She guessed anxiety over her deception took its own slow toll.

"But don't let your guard down around her. She is able to find out things from people that no one can extract from them, and you obviously have secrets."

Lovely. Iris pressed her lips into what she hoped was a serene *I've got this under control* smile. It faded when they reached the main dressing room, signified by a faded star on the lintel. The battered door opened to a frowning portly woman who took Iris in with a look of disdain.

"Marie, couldn't you find anyone better for me to work with? This one, she is so slight it will be like dressing a boy. And what is that smell?"

"We took the underground paths here, Madame," Marie said and bussed the woman on both cheeks.

"No, it is her. She smells of sweat and fear. Could you not at least find her a new chemise?"

IRIS BARELY REMEMBERED they were to stay for dinner, so upset was she after the dress fitting, when it seemed that the dressmaker counted and measured everything down to her ribs. She'd never encountered such a critical presence as Madame Beaufort, not even Adelaide on her worst days. Iris's chemise now banished to the incinerator and a new corset fitted to plump up what little she had, she couldn't argue with the smart figure she cut in her new white accented navy blue walking dress and simple but elegant *chapeau*, which resembled a man's top hat but was smaller, decorated with flowers and set at a jaunty angle. The only argument was over her gloves.

"They are *dégoûtant*," Madame Beaufort insisted. "I would rather risk the scandal of you going out bare-handed than have you be seen in one of my dresses with those. What is that, blood?"

"I helped a friend," Iris said. She couldn't help but think that Edward, as difficult as he could be, was easier to deal with in his simple selfishness than the *modiste*, who seemed insulted Iris wouldn't take her direction and become something she wasn't.

By that time, Madame St. Jean joined them, and she cocked her head and regarded Iris with an interested expression. "I will send Marie out for *les gants*. Leave the *fille* alone."

Marie was dispatched for gloves, and Iris faced the two dragons alone.

"Now for something for evening," Madame St. Jean, who insisted Iris call her Lucille once Marie left, said. She assisted Iris out of the day dress, or tried to, but the sleeves caught on the pearl buttons of Iris's gloves.

"It will be easier to get your jacket off if you remove your gloves," Lucille told her in a gentle tone. "Do not worry. I will protect you from seeing what you do not care for. It was stupid of Marie to lend you that brooch, but she does not know what you are any more than you know what she is."

"I don't know what you mean," Iris said, but she complied. How did Lucille know about her abilities? Or was she fishing for a reaction?

A purple silk evening dress that brought out similar tones in her eyes was followed by an afternoon dress and a travel ensemble. When she was down to her shift, Iris tried not to wiggle or fold her arms over herself, but a slippery silk chemise had replaced her cotton one, which had stiffened with all it had been through. She felt exposed although she was mostly covered, and she was relieved when they allowed her to put the walking dress back on. Marie appeared with gloves, which Iris slid on her hands. Now she felt fully dressed. The two older women allowed Marie to pick dresses and outfits from a rack in the corner.

"They're already fitted to me," Marie explained with a sharp look at her mother. "I suppose it's good you didn't get rid of them."

"No, she had them remade for today's styles so they would be ready for you," Madame Beaufort said.

The *modiste's* statement left Iris to come to one of two conclusions. Either Marie had known she would be accompanying them to Paris or her mother had some sort of second sight indeed. Both possibilities made Iris uncomfortable.

"This is too much," Iris insisted when they packed everything into a trunk that Mister O'Connell brought to the front hall of the theatre, from where a coach would bring them back to the hotel after dinner. "I only need the one outfit."

"Nonsense," Lucille said. "According to the letter of credit from Monsieur Cobb, you are to be taken care of. No one can fault his *générosité*." Her tone implied there was plenty about him to find fault for.

Again, there was that added edge of resentment at the mention of Parnaby Cobb's name. It seemed others shared Iris's mistrust of the man, but as Marie's brooch had hinted, their feelings may have been founded on his actions.

The gas lamps dimmed and flared back to their original brightness. Lucille narrowed her eyes. "I suppose your Mister O'Connell is working on the system. I asked him to see if he could find a leak or something that would explain its inconsistency. With what I pay for the gas, you would think they would provide more reliable service."

"You're still having problems with that?" Marie asked.

"Yes, one of the few troubles in my life I cannot blame on an ungrateful daughter."

Marie looked to the ceiling with a sigh, and Iris studied her new gloves and wished she was back in her normal environment and life. But she also felt for Marie—Iris knew what it was like to have a demanding mother who didn't understand her and her desires. From what she could piece together, Marie had more of a taste for adventure than Lucille, or perhaps she didn't want a career as an actress.

They had dinner in Marie's mother's townhouse, which was adjacent to the theatre. Thankfully the pushy Madame Beaufort was absent, having excused herself with business back at the shop. Marie maintained an air of stiffness and discomfort that Iris felt as well, and she mostly pushed the food, some sort of beef dish with wine and served over noodles, around on her plate. It was delicious, but she was so tired she wanted to get back to the hotel and sleep for a week. The wine didn't help her feelings of fatigue, although it did give her perceptions a certain softness and blurred the edges of the halos cast by the gas laps. It also tied her tongue. Luckily Mister O'Connell managed to keep the conversation going with questions about Paris—he'd been before but not to this part—and the gas system, which seemed sophisticated once it branched off from the main delivery line.

"I'll admit it's not my area," he said, "but I've worked on a few, mostly repairing the lines, and I've never seen one like that."

"Yes," Lucille said. "It was a gift from a patron, but it has troubles. In the theatre, we use lighting for dramatic effect. The unplanned ebbs and flows have been interfering with our productions, and we have had to use other means for spot-lighting."

"Are your neighbors having the same problem?" O'Connell asked.

"No, but most of them have not been able to afford the gas or install the lamps." She gestured to the fixture on the wall, which Iris had not examined. But now she noticed it had the same three-tube structure as the ones in Cobb's train car. *I think I know who the patron is, but why would he interfere with the theatre?* She clenched a fist under the table and allowed her nails to sting her palm to sharpen her focus. *I can't go asking questions, though, because he's our patron as well, and at this point we're dependent on him, especially poor injured Edward. Perhaps the fluctuations have something to do with the system being in a building, not a moving train.* She glanced at the sideboard, where a plate of chocolate-covered cream puffs sat. *I wonder if she will allow me to bring Edward one or two.*

After dessert, Lucille sent Mister O'Connell to tell the footman they were ready for the carriage. Once he was gone, she took Iris's right hand and looked at it. Iris had, of course, taken off her gloves to eat but lacked the energy to read the silverware.

"Your hand tells me many things," Lucille said, "but not as much as it tells you."

Iris tried to draw it away from the woman, but Lucille held firm. She traced Iris's palm with a fingertip, and tingles followed in the wake of its path. She then took Marie's left hand and placed it on Iris's. Marie's hand felt cold, and she looked at her mother with a fearful expression.

"You are both young women with gifts that are *merveilleux,*" Lucille said. "Even if you do not wish to have them because they have brought you difficulties as well as joy."

Iris looked away from the woman's hard black gaze. *She can't see the memories of my mother and how I discovered her infidelity, can she?*

"Marie has tried to run away from her talent," Lucille continued. "But it follows her, and she will not have peace until she accepts it. You think you are embracing yours, Miss McTavish, but you resist. You must learn to see the bad as well as the good in people and the things you study. But above all, protect and take care of each other—I am so happy Marie has a friend who can understand her if she will allow you the chance."

Iris's head tried to keep up with the rapid-fire pace of what Lucille said, but the fatigue and wine caught her, and the room tilted. Marie caught her and placed her on the appropriately named fainting couch at the end of the room. Iris's eyes closed on their own, but she maintained some level of consciousness.

"Mama, did you have to do that?" Marie asked. She sounded like she spoke through a tube.

"Your futures were already intertwined, my dear. I ensured the bond would be strong."

"I doubt this proper mademoiselle wants to be bonded with me."

"You must not allow your past mistakes to haunt you, dear daughter."

"Even if they won't go away?"

"All things will pass when they are supposed to." Two kisses. "Now go, take her back. She will wake in the morning with a memory of a pleasant evening."

Not likely, Iris thought, but she remained still so Lucille wouldn't know she'd overheard. Mister O'Connell's heavy footsteps entered the room. The brawny Irishman picked her up amid a flock of explanations from Madame St. Jean of how these Englishwomen couldn't handle good French wine and Marie adding that it had been a long day for all of them, so she couldn't blame Iris for giving in to her fatigue. Iris felt him grunt in response. Soon the cool and dark of the hallway enveloped them.

"What did they do to you, lass?" he asked, but Iris couldn't open her eyes no matter how hard she struggled, and she fought the darkness that tried to spread from the edges of her awareness. It would be so easy to fall asleep, but some instinct told her to stay awake and as aware as possible. At least it seemed Mister O'Connell suspected something had been done to her. The light patter of Marie's footsteps descended the wooden stairs behind them and followed them down the short walk in front of the townhouse.

They emerged into a chill breeze smelling of gas from the streetlights. Another smell came to Iris, of fried fish and vinegar.

"Oy," said a voice in front of them, English and sounding like trouble. "What're you doing there with Lord Scott's fiancée?"

Iris opened her eyes to see the driver of Lord Jeremy Scott's coach accompanied by two thugs with caps drawn low over their eyes.

héâtre Bohème, Paris, 12 June 1870

"Put me down," Iris said and elbowed Patrick O'Connell in the ribs. He grunted but didn't release her immediately.

"Fine, but stay behind me. You know this gentleman?" He placed her on the ground and held her until she found her balance. She stepped in front of him and ignored his, "Hey!"

"This is hardly a gentleman, and apparently his boss didn't want to come do his own dirty work. I am not affianced to his employer, and I'm not afraid of him. In fact, I turned Lord Jeremy Scott down cold."

"Your maid said you dressed special to receive him." He spat on the ground.

"Charming. And she had no idea what was on my mind. She knew her place." *Sort of.* Was this footman the prize Sophie left Iris for? If so, they deserved each other. Iris glanced around to see where Marie stood, but she was nowhere to be seen.

Lovely, another disappearing maid.

One of Lord Scott's other men crossed his arms, and a knife glinted in the yellow light cast by the street lamps.

"Are you here to kidnap me by force?" Iris asked. "I will not go willingly, and I will not allow you to hurt my companions." Not that she had any weapon but her wits, but she'd do the best she could. Mister O'Connell had been nothing but kind to her, and Marie, well, Iris had more questions for her. Like what in Hades did it mean that they were bonded?

"I'm here to bring you home, Miss McTavish," he said. "Lord Scott found out something interesting about your da."

Iris took a quick breath to calm the flame of fear that had sprung to life in her stomach at his words. "And what would that be?"

"He said you need to come finish your conversation."

The damn tightly laced corset kept Iris from taking a full breath, and she blinked against the sensation that the gas flames around her softened and rounded. *Don't faint, don't faint.* "I've said all I intended to Lord Scott."

The two men behind the footmen moved forward, and Patrick pushed Iris out of the way. "You won't take her, you English bastards."

Four men emerged from the theatre followed by Marie. Iris thought she'd seen them earlier around the place moving props and backdrops into the storage room.

"There they are," Marie said. "English thugs come to rob the theatre and *Maman*."

"*C'est vrai?*" asked one of them and pounded one fist into the other hand. "*Allons-y.*"

At the sight of the Frenchmen coming toward them, the two English thugs melted into the shadows. The footman glared at Iris. "You think this is over, Miss, but we'll be watching you. And if you come home, it'll be on Lord Scott's terms—he said to tell you he hired your cook and now holds the mortgage on your house."

"There isn't one," Iris said.

"There is now. Your da borrowed money against the place to

pay for his trip to France. His *last* trip." With that comment, he turned on his heel and disappeared down the alley. Iris sagged against O'Connell and felt like she may truly be in danger of fainting this time.

Marie spoke with one of the Frenchmen in whispers, and he nodded.

"Pierre will drive us back to the hotel in *Maman's* coach. It was stupid of me to refuse her offer earlier."

"Thank you," Iris said to Pierre. He nodded and held up a finger—one moment. He returned driving a coach out of the portico on the side of the theatre.

"So you're engaged?" Marie asked once they sat in the coach.

"No," Iris told her. "Marriage isn't my path, I fear." She clasped her hands together. The blessed things wouldn't stop shaking, and they had the strangest tingling sensation like she'd been sleeping on them. "However, Lord Scott disagreed with my decision."

"Some men won't take no for an answer," Marie told her.

"Those men don't deserve to have a woman. Ever," O'Connell put in. "It's a good thing I was there, but it was Miss St. Jean's quick thinking that saved us. From now on, you don't go out without at least two of us gentlemen with you."

The notion made Iris feel smothered, especially since Edward was laid up, and she found his company the most tolerable, if exhausting, of all of them. Mister O'Connell was fine, but she didn't feel she had much in common with him, and she hardly knew Radcliffe. As for Maestro Bledsoe—she would be forced into his presence enough over the next few days. Worse, she would need to pretend to like him.

"Don't be ridiculous," she said. "I won't go anywhere unescorted, and from now on will avoid deserted alleys and being out after dark." A large yawn stretched her jaw and made it pop. "I feel I should sleep for days."

They made it to the hotel unmolested, and O'Connell wouldn't let any of the porters handle the trunk with Iris's and Marie's new clothing in it. He delivered it and them to their room, then tipped his hat good night.

"He's a good sort," Marie said after the door closed behind him.

"Yes." Iris stripped off her gloves and laid a hand on the trunk, but it didn't give her much information, just a sense of relief at not having failed to bring them back safely. *That's interesting.*

"I'll hang the clothes, Miss," Marie said. "Let me help you out of that dress, and I'll draw you a bath."

Surprised, Iris turned to her. The other woman's neutral facial expression and vocal tone gave the impression of only being a maid, although Iris knew she was much more. But when she tried to come up with examples of Marie acting like something else, they slipped through her mind like fish seen in murky water—a glimpse here or there, but nothing more.

Or maybe I'm exhausted.

"Thank you," she said and rubbed her fingertips along her palms. *What did Lucille mean when she said we are not so different in refusing to accept our talents?* She continued to ponder it until she reached her bed, and exhaustion sucked her from the buzz of her thoughts into a dreamless sleep.

Iris felt like she had been asleep but a few minutes when a pounding on the door woke her.

"No, of course she's not up yet. We ran into an unexpected delay yesterday evening. Mister O'Connell can give you the details."

Iris buried her head in the pillows to drown out Marie's half of the murmured conversation. She was ninety percent sure the person at the door was Johann Bledsoe or someone sent by him, and she was one hundred percent certain she didn't want to deal with him today, at least not so early. A dull ache settled across her forehead, her tongue felt dry, and she had a foggy recollection of the previous evening's activities. She needed to ask Marie something, but she couldn't recall what, and why was her right hand sore?

Then, "Monsieur, no, she is not dressed!"

Iris buried herself under the covers, and she heard the scrape of the bed curtains being drawn back. The duvet disappeared from atop her, and she found herself faced with the blazing gray-green eyes and wild blond hair of Johann Bledsoe, who didn't look amused. That was fine—Iris didn't feel amused, and she sat up so quickly he jumped back.

"What is the meaning of this?" she asked in her best Adelaide voice. She rubbed her left thumb over her right palm, which throbbed and put her in more of an ill humor. "Hasn't anyone told you not to barge into a lady's room uninvited, or is that something you musicians do on a regular basis?"

"Oho, the cat has claws this morning," he said. "And does this particular lady intend to sleep through her important appointment at the Louvre?"

"My what?" Iris recalled the itinerary and why they had rushed to Paris the day before in spite of Edward's condition. "Oh, right. How much time do we have?"

"You need to be ready in fifteen minutes." He turned on his heel, but shot over his shoulder as he crossed the threshold, "And you had better be presentable. You know the consequences of failing at this. And Marie can stay here—your reputation is safe with me, and they're looser about that in France anyhow."

Big hairy ox's bollocks, Iris swore to herself, both at the time crunch and at the unexpected disappointment that Marie wouldn't accompany them. "Can we do it, Marie?"

"Don't worry, Mademoiselle, the French are never on time. Besides, I am accustomed to quick costume changes, and we will keep your hair simple. That is what hats are for, no?"

EDWARD WOKE to the sound of pounding on the door of the room next to his, and he checked the clock: seven fifteen. In fifteen minutes, a waiter would bring tea and scones, or at least whatever the French substitute was, and he would shave and dress and start his routine, or at least an approximation of it. He rolled over.

I should be looking forward to this more. Isn't it what I've wanted all along, to have normalcy back?

What if he wanted to sleep more? He was injured, for goodness' sake.

But no, Johann entered with a grin and a breakfast tray, which he set on the table by the window.

"You look insufferably smug," Edward grumbled.

"I had no idea I'd enjoy wake up duty so much." Johann opened the curtains. The room brightened and emphasized Edward's sense of wrongness about the whole situation. This wasn't his room at his—fine, his *brother's* house. He wouldn't be going to the University. He was going to be stuck in this hotel room all day. Again.

"Who else have you been waking?" Not that he cared. He needed some way to get out of this room, perhaps explore. Walking would be good for him.

"Miss McTavish is rather grumpy in the morning, if you were curious. As for you, Doctor Radcliffe will be in momentarily, but I'm to help you dress. We have to hurry so I can give the impression of being put out waiting for our archaeologist."

Edward swung his legs over the side of the bed. "Why do you insist on trying to irritate her? She's along because of her ailing father. I'm sure she would much rather be home."

"I'm not so sure about that. She came in ridiculously late last night, so she must have been up to something fun. From the looks of her, she'll no doubt need to move slowly this morning."

"Right. Help me dress, and you can go keep her out of trouble." Edward's lower back echoed the twinge of curiosity in his chest as to Iris's activities. Where had she gone? Who had she met?

"You're in luck. The tailor I spoke with yesterday had this ready for you." Johann pulled a suit from the closet and helped Edward dress in that and a shirt but no waistcoat or cravat. "Since you're not going out for at least another day, I told him not to worry about bringing the accessories until later today. At least this way you're mostly decent."

"But what if Miss McTavish visits?" Edward pulled his collar closed. "I feel naked."

"She's not going to, remember? Your social interaction hours will be while she and I are out visiting stuffy exhibits and boring museum curators."

"Oh." Edward sat at the table and dropped his hands to his lap. In the light of day, the working of his throat muscles with no comforting stricture made him feel exposed, vulnerable. He poured some milk in his teacup so he wouldn't have to meet Johann's eyes. No sense in allowing his friend to see his disappointment and distress because he couldn't explain it himself. Here he was, allowed to spend the day as he'd been wanting and not having to bother with things that society said he needed, but restlessness possessed him.

"The doctor will be in soon. Do you need me to help with your breakfast dishes? Those lids are heavy."

"I'm not as much of an invalid as everyone thinks." Edward hoped his hand didn't shake too much as he poured his tea— the French made thick carafes. "I'm feeling much better."

"Right." Johann took the pot from Edward's trembling hand and poured the tea to a third of an inch below the rim of the cup. "Don't push yourself too hard. Radcliffe's a good doctor even if..."

Edward put a quarter teaspoon, or his best estimate, of sugar in his tea. "Even if...?"

"Well, don't you think it's suspicious, them ending up in the same little town we did? A doctor stuck without funds? He seems too smart to be caught out like that. Especially since people like him need to be more careful anyway."

"Perhaps people *are* less likely to help him because of his exotic skin tone," Edward agreed. "He is rather...dark."

"Right, so he's not going to find aid around every corner like someone like Miss McTavish." Johann ran his fingers through his hair, giving his blond curls more of a rakish appearance. "But he's given us no cause to think less of him."

"So stop suspecting him of something. And go. You don't want to keep Miss McTavish waiting."

Edward smiled at Johann's grumbling as his friend left the room. He wished he knew what his friend had against the young miss other than that she seemed much less worldly than Johann's usual female companions. Perhaps her innocence perturbed his friend. As for him, he liked her guilelessness. Perhaps she was a female person he could begin to trust.

19

Hôtel Auberge, *Monday 13 June 1870*

Twenty minutes later, Iris gazed at herself in the mirror and admitted she looked quite smart in her new day suit, and Marie had laced her corset to to an almost stifling degree, but she could mostly breathe comfortably. She sauntered down to the lobby, where Johann raised his eyebrows and looked at his watch.

"So sorry to keep you waiting," she said with as sweet a smile as she could muster.

"I'm sure you are," he said. "Our coach will be here in five minutes."

She narrowed her eyes at him, and it was his turn to smile without sincerity, as far as she could tell. "How is the professor this morning?"

"Oh, is he no longer Edward to you?"

"Not if we are somewhere we could be overheard. I wouldn't want anyone to suspect me of any impropriety." She tried the eyelash batting thing she'd seen other young women do but feared she looked like she had dust in her eyes.

"Because you've never been guilty of that." He placed his hat on his blond curls and held his arm out. "Shall we?"

"You didn't answer my question."

"The doctor has surmised Edward may heal more quickly if he goes back on the routine he'd so carefully established for himself at Huntington Village. Thus, he is being woken and brought his morning tea, after which he will dress and work on whatever interests him until his midmorning break at ten o'clock."

Iris swallowed around the parched feeling in her throat. Tea would be the thing for both her headache and her mood. But she wasn't going to ask him for anything.

"And before you ask," he continued, "we're going to be out during the normal times he would have company, so you won't be seeing him today."

"I remember our agreement," she said and tried to appear that she was nonchalantly gazing at the bustle of traffic in front of the hotel. A closed blue steamcoach with white and gold monograms on the side stopped in front of them.

"Oh, I couldn't tell," he said and handed her into the brightly colored vehicle.

She chose to ignore his comment and asked, "Whose vehicle is this?" once they were settled inside.

"My friend, the Marquis de Monceau. He was in town for the day, so he offered us the use of his coach while he is in his meetings to prevent his driver from idling his day and salary away in the gambling halls," he told her in a quiet voice.

"I see."

"You'll meet the marquis at breakfast. He's going to introduce us to the curators of Classical art and Renaissance art at the Louvre."

They traveled down a series of wide boulevards with uniform appearance. Iris wondered if they were to be excavated in the future, would it be difficult to catalog the finds due to the lack of variability of the stone in the buildings? What would the archaeologists of the future think about their time? And would she have the opportunity to change the course of history with the discovery of a practical application for aether?

"We'll be breakfasting in the courtyard at the Palais Royale," Bledsoe said as the coach slowed. "Try not to gawk. It's quite an unusual place."

They drove through a narrow shrubbery-lined lane and into a wide courtyard surrounded by shops. Some of them looked shabby, others prosperous. It seemed a strange juxtaposition of old and new, wealthy and poor. From what Iris could tell, there wasn't any interaction between the shopkeepers and restaurateurs. Indeed, contrasted with the noise of the boulevards, the silence of the courtyard settled over them like cold dew. The steamcoach rolled to a stop in front of a small cafe, and Iris welcomed the clinking and clattering noises that invaded her ears when the coachman opened the door. For a few seconds, anyway, until her head started to hurt again.

The *maitre d'* led them to a corner table, where three men waited for them, and they all stood. Each complimented Iris and kissed the back of her hand when they were introduced, and she was almost relieved for Johann's steady if disapproving presence.

This must be how a fish in a bowl surrounded by cats feels.

He held a chair for her, and everyone settled back into their seats.

The Marquis de Monceau wore a coat of royal blue that would have seemed a century out of date had he not paired it with a tailored shirt and tie. The ensemble gave him a devil-may-care air, as did his too long wavy dark hair and chocolate brown eyes that assessed Iris more thoroughly than Madame Beaufort's tape measures had. She shifted in her seat at the feeling of being naked under his scrutiny.

"Oh, lay off the young lady, Monceau," Johann told him.

"She isn't interested in you, and she's too proper a miss for your propositions."

"You wound me, Maestro, like that cut over your eye but in my heart," the marquis said and put a hand on his chest. "I am interested in why you brought Irvin McTavish's daughter rather than the great man himself."

"My father is ill, so he sent me in his stead," Iris said.

"Ah, then *bienvenu* and please pass along our wishes for his speedy return to health."

With each repetition, it felt like it could be true, that Irvin McTavish was merely ill and waited for her to visit him in the south of France and catch him up on her adventures. A memory of Jeremy Scott's footman telling her that the odious lord now held the mortgage on her house surfaced. She folded her hands in her lap and tried to pay attention to what the other two men—obviously toadies trying to gain the Marquis's favor—said, but her heart wanted to beat through her ribcage. Now even if she did acquit herself successfully, she wouldn't have a home to go to, at least not as long as she continued to refuse young Lord Scott.

A waiter brought soft-boiled eggs, and another poured coffee into Iris's and Johann's cups.

"Would the mademoiselle prefer tea?" the Marquis asked. "Or perhaps an Italian coffee with steamed milk?"

"Tea would be wonderful," Iris said. If nothing else, she would always have tea. She selected the type she wanted from a list, and soon she had a fragrant cup steeping in front of her and a *pain au chocolat* on a plate beside it.

"And now that you have your tea," the Marquis said, "tell us why you are interested in Classical and Renaissance art. The Maestro said it had something to do with your research? Or your father's?"

Iris looked at Johann, who shrugged as if to say, "You're the one accustomed to lying."

She smiled at the Marquis and picked up her tea cup. "I'm looking into elemental symbolism in Classical art and how it was portrayed in the Renaissance."

Monsieur Anctil, the Renaissance curator, nodded so hard Iris thought his glasses would fly off. He had little tufts of curly graying dark hair over his ears and a mustache she found ridiculous. "Yes, yes," he said. "Especially in the Renaissance, in the paintings of the Greek gods. The marquis has a particularly nice Eros and Psyche."

Iris kept the smile on her face even though her dimples hurt by now. "I would love to see it," she said and hoped she didn't accidentally tip them off to the search for the Eros Element.

The *maitre d'* appeared with a message for Bledsoe. The two men conversed in whispers, but Iris was close enough to hear.

"I can't talk to him right now," Bledsoe said.

"He was very insistent, Monsieur. Said he would cause a scene if you did not meet with him."

"Very well." He stood and threw his napkin on the table. "Excuse me, gentlemen. Some urgent business from home is calling me away for a few moments."

"Anything I can help with?" the Marquis asked and shifted his weight as though to rise. Bledsoe put a hand on his shoulder.

"Not this time, my friend, but thank you. I'll only be a minute." He followed the *maitre d'* out of the restaurant. Iris turned to the remaining three and took off her gloves to eat her croissant. She made as to move the fork Bledsoe had been holding away from the edge of the table and read it. It produced an all-too-familiar bitter sensation in the back of her mouth— lying and fear of being caught. He was hiding something from her and the rest of them.

A sip of tea cleared the taste but not the residual headache, which piled on top of the one she already had. "I apologize," she said, "but I'm not feeling very well. Is there a, er, water closet for women here?"

A waiter showed her the way, and she lucked out—the room had a ventilation window, and it gave her a limited view of the wall of another building, which meant it opened onto an alley. She climbed onto the counter beside the sink and was rewarded by hearing voices.

"—can't pay you more than this," Bledsoe was saying. "It's all I've been able to gather."

"That'll barely cover my travel to chase you down for what you owe, Guv'nor," another man said. His accent said lower London. "Our beasties told us you're on Cobb's payroll. You should have access to more than that."

Iris stood on her tiptoes and strained to hear the men's voices over the clatter of the kitchen across the hall from the toilettes and the pounding of her own heart—so the Maestro had been lying to them all along.

"I'm trying not to be obvious about it, a skill you apparently lack," Bledsoe said. "We won't be paid until the end of the mission, which you are jeopardizing. Was it necessary to pull me away from an important business breakfast? And how did you learn I was to be here?"

"We have our sources. We're watching you, Maestro. I know you like your cards, but your companions wouldn't appreciate you gambling with their lives, especially that brunette. She looks like she'd snap you in two. And the Irishman likely has a temper to go with his red hair. Can't trust those brutes."

"I'll get your money to you. Leave me alone and let me work."

"You've had your warning. Cobb won't appreciate knowing the Blooming Senator's attack was our little message to you. Keep us informed as to your progress."

He did put us in danger! Iris sucked in the corners of her mouth so she wouldn't break into a vindictive smile that would tip him off when she came back to the table. She crawled off the counter, took care of business, and walked back to the table, where the Marquis stood and talked to Johann and the other two men ate what looked like piles of cooked eggs.

"I'm afraid I must excuse myself," the Marquis said with a bow when she joined them. "I am finalizing my travel plans with my agents here in the city and have much to do. I will send my coach for you this evening for the gala. It will be good to hear you play again, Maestro."

"I'm looking forward to it," Johann said. "You and your guests are always such a sophisticated audience, the pleasure is mine."

They said their goodbyes, and Iris took her seat at the table and nibbled at her *pain au chocolat*.

"My daughter likes to dip her *pain* in her cafe," Monsieur Anctil said and put something that looked like cherry jam on his croissant. "Perhaps it would work as well with *thé*?"

"I'm willing to try." Iris broke off a piece and gave its corner a quick soak in her tea. It left a residue on the top, and although she enjoyed the buttery flavor the hot liquid brought out, it didn't work otherwise. "I fear it might work better with coffee," she said.

"Ah, leave her be, Anctil," Monsieur Firmin, the curator of the Classics collections, told him. "She is a young woman, not a child, and she is kind to humor you. Besides, you know you should not be eating the preserves. They will worsen your diabetes." The wrinkles along his mouth and between his eyes told Iris his customary expression was one of disapproval, and indeed, she felt that to be the case with her. His irritable demeanor caused her to feel more comfortable since that was the typical expression her tutors had given her. She knew how to handle dour and exasperated.

The genial Monsieur Anctil, on the other hand, helped himself to another spoonful. Now he made her uneasy. No one could be that friendly, and she didn't appreciate being compared to his daughter, whom she pictured as a true child. Even Patrick O'Connell had a certain edge to him she knew not to test, and she wondered what Anctil's seed of darkness was. Every person had one, she was coming to find.

Breakfast finished, she and Bledsoe followed the two curators across the courtyard and into a small passage well-hidden behind the wall and shrubbery. Now she watched the musician and noticed how he maintained his genial conversation but examined each person they passed. Iris listened to what the men said but also for the quiet whirring of the little clockwork spy devices. Now she knew the Clockwork Guild pursued Bledsoe, she needed to be extra careful about what she said and did around him. There was no telling where the little beasties hid.

They entered the Louvre through a back door unlocked by Monsieur Firmin. "You will start with me, Mademoiselle. As I recall, you are most interested in the Archaic through Hellenistic periods?"

"Yes, that is correct," Iris said.

"I'll leave you to your pottery-gazing," Bledsoe said. "You have the practice room with the piano and violin, right, Firmin?"

Anctil stepped up. "*Bien sur!* The orchestra is not rehearsing this morning, so it is all yours. It will be an honor to hear you practice even if we do not get the pleasure of tonight's performance."

"Yes," Firmin said. "I am glad you will be visiting the Marquis before he heads to his estate on the coast for the summer, Mademoiselle. He has a fine collection of *kouros* statues you will find quite fascinating. I have been hinting he should donate them to the museum, but alas, he is quite attached to them. He told me he couldn't stand the thought of possible damage during transport between the Monceau suburb and here."

"I'm looking forward to it," Iris said. "Now tell me about your collection." She glanced over her shoulder at Bledsoe and Anctil, and she caught the Renaissance curator giving her a curious look as they walked in the opposite direction. Something about it made her fingertips tingle to read something of his.

Firmin led her into a large room where statues peered out at her from alcoves and pottery shards and reassembled pieces lay arranged on tables.

"Where would you like to begin?" he asked.

A movement at the corner of her vision startled Iris. She looked to her left and expected to see their shadows moving along the wall, but no, one of the statues lifted its hand.

20

Musée du Louvre, *13 June 1870*
It's a shadow, a mere trick of the light.

Iris tried not to appear to be one of those vapid, jumpy, "Oh, I think it's waving at me," females like the girls at Madame Cornwall's School for Young Ladies, where they'd had one—just one—trip to the London Museum of Art. Her stupid classmates, having been stirred up by an admittedly handsome street preacher at the Huntington Station, were convinced the remnants of pagan times were in some way imbued with Satan's spells and therefore out to get the Christian misses. The curator had rushed them through the tour as a result of the girls' silliness, and Iris, being the last out due to trying to get a final lingering glance at an Egyptian sarcophagus, heard him say to the docent before closing the door behind them, "Good grief, they're raising them stupid up north!" She'd fumed the whole way home and begged her parents to allow her to go to a real school, or at least to the boys' academy down the road. Of course her mother had refused, although her father later told her he thought she belonged more with the boys, anyway, in terms of interest and intellect.

At least the preacher who'd started the trouble had been "encouraged" to move on.

But no, the arm of the statue moved at the elbow and raised its hand as if to greet her. Iris simultaneously had the compulsion to look away and the desire to watch it in case it decided to move other parts and come after her. Monsieur Firmin gestured to various objects and droned on, but Iris couldn't concentrate on his words. She noticed he had stopped talking.

"Miss McTavish, you barely seem to be listening. Is something wrong? You do realize I'm taking time from my busy schedule to show you my collection."

His condescending tone, so similar to that of the London Museum curator, snapped Iris out of her fear.

"I apologize, Monsieur, but I was distracted by your statue's apparent familiarity with me. It hasn't stopped waving since we arrived."

"Oh!" He walked over to it. "It does this sometimes. She was once part of the Magna Graecia Automaton, and certain footsteps, often one light and one heavy, set her off." He stilled the statue's hand and gestured for Iris to come closer. "See? She has a hinge at the elbow and clever counterbalancing. Writings from that period tell us that when it was complete, the automaton had a twenty-minute cycle with several statues performing different movements."

Iris studied the statue and moved the arm herself. Certain aspects of the statue told Iris it was made too late to be part of the automaton, but it was designed to appear so.

Someone wanted this young woman to be remembered, but it was a risk.

The girl seemed to stare through her, her slight smile like that of a woman with sad but precious memories. The expression looked odd on such a young face. Iris decided to play along with Firmin's assumptions.

"What do you know of this statue other than that she was part of the Magna? And where are the other parts?"

"I don't have good answers for you, I fear. Legend has it that the automaton series was dismantled and brought to Rome, but a curse soon resulted in its being destroyed except for a few pieces deemed not to be threatening such as this young lady here."

"A curse," Iris murmured. "By whom?"

"You have heard of the Pythagoreans, yes?"

Iris shrugged to cover her interest. "Yes, the theorem every geometry student has to learn."

"The cult had a dark side. Rumor has it they killed the poor man who discovered there was no rational way to derive the square root of two. After the massacre at Metapontum, they went underground, where according to legend, some of them went mad and turned to occult and secret arts."

"There is a price to pay for magic, after all." Iris's fingertips itched. She wanted to read the statue of the young woman, but she couldn't take her gloves off in front of Monsieur Firmin without appearing wanton or forward. "Well," she said, "as you said, you are busy. Do you mind if I wander around in here on my own while you do what you need to do? You could come back in a half hour to take me to the main gallery."

Firmin cut his eyes to the right and left. Iris knew she guessed correctly—he didn't see the point in babysitting an English miss. "I will return in thirty minutes. Don't touch anything."

She clasped her hands in front of her and nodded with the most serious expression she could muster over her delight. As soon as his footsteps faded from the gallery, Iris stripped off her gloves and wiggled her fingers. A chorus of sensations washed over her with objects begging to be touched and read.

I have a small amount of time. What's the most important?

"Definitely you, my dear," she said to the statue in front of her. She reached for the marble girl's hand but stopped. Firmin touched that part of her, and Iris wanted older impressions. She caressed the maiden's cheek and saw a flash of a real girl with her features and dark curly hair, a tear coming from each eye. The roar of a crowd, a human scream, and an animal's howl pressed in on Iris's ears. Terror radiated from the girl, and Iris had to step back and clutch her lower back, where pain stabbed through her after the vision subsided. Now she was horrified...and more curious.

"What happened to you?" she whispered. She placed a hand on the girl's shoulder and noted the stone felt warmer. Iris hadn't touched the statue there yet, so the increase in temperature couldn't have come from her own body heat. Now the floor shifted beneath her, and her feet stood on cold stone. Iris followed someone's gaze up the side of a temple to a high window. The sensation that accompanied this vision was the crushing sense of despair at the thought of an impossible to escape situation.

Iris tried to make note of the delicate stuccoes, mostly of couples. *Psyche and Eros.* The words came to her mind, *The price of love is deception.*

Now a chill came over Iris, and she blinked to see the white walls and soulless eyes of the statues in the Classics Gallery at the Louvre. Her walking boots pinched her feet, but she preferred them to shackles, and she bent to rub one ankle. She followed the compulsion to move to the other side of the room from the girl, but the suspicion that she'd gotten into something way over her head followed her.

Approaching footsteps made her pull on her gloves over trembling fingers, and a glance at the clock told her that the half hour had passed. This most of all perturbed her—where had the time gone? Where had *she* gone? Her visions had always been *of* someone, not vividly from their viewpoint since that one where she'd gotten caught up in her mother's puerile fantasy.

"Ah, there you are, Mademoiselle!" It was the genial Monsieur Anctil. "*Allons-y.* I have much to show you in the Renaissance wing."

EDWARD GAZED OUT THE WINDOW, the now completely dismantled clockwork butterfly in front of him. He thought he'd isolated all the different parts, but for some reason, he couldn't figure out how to get it back together. Actually, he knew the reason. He was an aetherist, not a tinkerer. If he was going to be stuck in this hotel room and acting according to his usual routine, he could at least have the chance to run some experiments to see whether anything changed being this much closer to the Equator. Part of him mourned the equipment he lost in the airship crash, particularly the beloved copper sphere he'd sacrificed to defending himself and Iris against the Clockwork Guildsman.

Iris... He supposed she was at the Louvre by now with Johann exploring the treasures there.

A knock on the door startled him before he could follow that line of thought any further.

"Come in," he called. He glanced at the clock—*Oh, right, time for midmorning tea.*

The Irishman Patrick O'Connell entered carrying a tea tray. "The chef said he wasn't going to waste his good butter on scones, so he sent croissants up instead." He looked around for a place to set the tray. "Where do you want this?"

"Oh, you might as well put it here." Edward swept the remains of the clockwork to one side of the table. "I'm stuck as to what to do with this anyway."

O'Connell set the tea service in front of him. "Looks like

you got it apart without breaking anything. Now what do you want to do with it?"

Edward gestured for the other man to join him. "I can ring for more tea if you're thirsty."

"I'm fine." He remained standing. "Not sure if I'm supposed to stay. Chadwick said you're to be left alone between the hours of eight and eleven except for bringing your tea."

Edward shifted to ease the tightness in his chest that started that morning during his conversation with Johann. He wondered if it might be his lungs—wasn't the doctor concerned about something he heard in them?

"Well, I'm stuck, and sometimes I'll go to my colleagues to see if they can make suggestions to move me along." *Or to see if they need me to make suggestions, but close enough.*

O'Connell sat, and Edward reached for the handle for the tube that would relay his wishes down to the kitchen. "I can't drink alone."

"Aye, I appreciate that, Professor."

Edward wondered if he'd accidentally referenced the Irish tendency to drink too much alcohol and scrambled to change the subject so O'Connell wouldn't leave. "Oh, please call me Edward. You see, I'm hoping you'll act as a colleague and help me to understand these clockwork devices better. I'm sure I can use them somehow in my research."

"Patrick." The look he gave Edward made him feel as though he were a device being picked apart by the Irishman's brain.

A servant brought in more tea and croissants at Edward's request, and he poured, pleased to see his hand shook less than at breakfast. Of course the pot was also lighter, but he would take the improvement.

"So you're a tinkerer," Edward said.

"I prefer the term inventor," Patrick said and helped himself to a croissant. "Can't seem to resist the chocolate ones."

"Oh, and what is your training? I fear I missed out on much of the introductions since I was, well, unconscious after we landed."

"Landing isn't the most accurate term for what you did."

"What would be?"

"Try falling from the sky with the chutes opening and catching you in barely enough time for you all to not be smashed to bits. It's a miracle you survived."

"Well, yes, I suppose." Edward experienced a jolt of anxiety at the thought of what had almost transpired. *Smashed to bits? How terrifying!*

"So if your brain isn't working like you want it to, don't worry, it will. I've been hit on the head enough times to know it comes back."

"In fights?" Edward kicked himself for vocalizing another assumption based on stereotype. What must Patrick think? Edward wasn't putting forth his best enlightened self.

"Aye." Patrick held his teacup as if to toast Edward. "Mostly against university types like you who didn't want to see beyond my hair and beard to my brain. Luckily my skull is harder than theirs."

"So what professional training and education do you have?"

Patrick poured more tea to warm Edward's cup, thereby disrupting the delicate balance of cream and sugar flavors, but Edward didn't say anything. Edward had never cared about insulting others previously, but he found himself not wanting to alienate his new red-bearded colleague.

"My father was a blacksmith, and I learned from him. Then I went across to the States and learned what I could until I met Chadwick, and he convinced me to stay in one place long enough to get a degree."

"And that was...?"

"Harvard." He grinned, and Edward tried to school the shock from his facial expression.

"Harvard, that's impressive."

Patrick dismissed Edward's comment with a shrug. "It's a school like any other, and Chadwick helped pay for it. I owe him a lot, hence why I'm on this crazy trip with him. But that's his tale to tell. Let's look at the beastie you've taken apart. The best thing to do is put it back together so you can learn how they work."

"And you can help me do that?"

"If you're fine with a redheaded Irish brute for a teacher."

"Oh, most definitely." Edward took the last sip of his tea, which wasn't bad even if not perfectly sweetened, and set the cup aside. "I'm ready to learn, Professor."

"Then the first thing will be how to catch and disable them. There's another one flitting around outside the window." He picked up one of the teapots and filled it with steaming water from the faucet on the wall adjacent to Iris's room. "Watch and learn. You have to put them to sleep so they won't cry out. I heard Miss McTavish captured the one in front of you."

"Yes." A smile pushed through Edward's sour expression in spite of his efforts to keep his facial expression neutral at the mention of her name. "She's quite clever, you know."

"Aye." Patrick balanced on the settee and held the steaming spout under the butterfly. "Did you know she's engaged?"

21

Musée du Louvre, *13 June 1870*

Monsieur Anctil bowed at the waist and straightened with a grin. Iris blinked to clear the sense of disorientation from her little trip through time, and she noticed he was short for a man, about her height, and he had a bald spot between his salt-and-pepper curls. She took his proffered elbow and smiled through the tightness in her cheeks from wanting to scream at him to leave her alone, let her figure this all out before she moved to something else. Studying the past should allow her to do that, right?

"Did you learn anything interesting?" he asked.

"Perhaps. I always need some time to think about things after I see them to allow my mind make connections." As they left the gallery, the feeling the waving statue watched Iris dissipated, and she took as deep a breath as Marie's corset lacing allowed.

"That seems wise," he said. "So many people talk before thoroughly sifting through the evidence. As an archaeologist you know the importance of finding all the pieces before you make a conclusion."

"Yes, exactly." Iris thought she heard something different in his accent but dismissed it as a trick her ears played on her. She couldn't trust her senses until she felt completely anchored in this time, and the path they took through the Egyptian gallery didn't help. The sarcophagi in particular whispered to her, and she clenched the fist not on Anctil's arm in an attempt to dampen the sensations.

What had happened to her?

"Ah, the tombs will not hurt you," he said. "They are full of dead things. It's the living you need to fear."

"*Pardon*?" Iris asked. They descended a stairwell that wrapped around a pedestal with a headless winged statue on it. She pretended to admire the details in the drapery and wings while checking to see if anyone else was around. She wondered where Bledsoe had gone.

"A recent find in the Ottoman empire," Anctil said, seemingly oblivious to the strangeness of his previous words and their effect on her. "Firmin was very excited, but I find it a pity we now have to go so far abroad when we could make our own discoveries here at home. There are rooms full of the junk found during the rebuilding and renovations no one has bothered to sort through. I'm sure there are many Roman artifacts from their original construction of the sewers and many items that could shed more light on medieval life."

"I thought something similar." Now they crossed a courtyard, and the sun on Iris's face cleared the residual cobwebs of her strange experience from her mind, which turned to analyzing the situation. Something strange had happened to her. Anctil appeared immediately after and made an odd comment, which he passed over. The likelihood of his accosting her—minimal since she observed workmen and cleaners at irregular intervals, and she suspected some of them might be part of Lucille's city-wide network of spies. Anctil had information. She would have to play the role of slightly intelligent but not too clever archaeologist to get it from him.

"The emperor has been preparing to start a school." But before she could ask what kind, he said, "Ah, here we are." He held open a large wooden door carved with floral patterns, their sharp edges rounded by time and exposure.

Iris walked in and blinked at the brightness of the colors and gleam of the jewels and gems in their glass cases. One cabinet in particular drew her closer. It contained several little cases similar to the one she found in the volcano egg.

"What are these?" she asked. "They're beautiful."

"Ah, but also deadly, Mademoiselle. You have found the poison cases used by courtesans and female assassins in the Renaissance." He pulled a key from his pocket, unlocked the case, and opened the lid. A rosy hue came to his cheeks pinked as he said, "Their unusual shapes are so they could be hidden on a woman's body, sometimes inside certain crevices, although that was risky. Some of the poisons were ingestible, and others could be absorbed through the skin, and in such small amounts, they had to be potent. You can imagine the disaster should the containers open accidentally, so most of them had a trick to gaining access to them."

Iris's cheeks heated as well. Could she really be here having a conversation about things that could be hidden on, or worse *in*, a woman's body with a *foreign man*? "I see the concern. How did they work?"

"The devices were such that natural and certain other motions of the, eh, person wouldn't be enough to pop them ajar." His face reddened more, and Iris wondered if he'd made some sort of innuendo. "So there were often two actions required. This one, for example." He picked up a jeweled ebony comb, the part that showed thicker than one would expect, but Iris imagined it would not stand out in a tall curly hairstyle. She guessed he chose one that went outside, not—*blush*—

inside a woman's body, but that wouldn't help her solve the mystery of the one she found.

"That's beautiful, but what about this one?" She pointed to a gold one almost identical to the one in her valise.

Now his flush reached to the top of his head. "Ah, yes, Mademoiselle, that one is for the most vicious of courtesans for whom a poison ring or other jewelry would be too obvious. Only four or five of these particular devices are in existence, all having rumored connections to the infamous House of Borgia."

"How do you open it?" Iris asked. She acknowledged the part of her brain that screamed that having this conversation could ruin her reputation. The desire to know, both for her own curiosity and for the purposes of increasing her overall historical education beyond the whitewashed version from school, immolated the lattice of caution so carefully installed over the years by her mother and other sources of Victorian propriety.

Apparently Anctil also decided to go full steam ahead in spite of his growing redness, now almost purpleness. "As you can see, it's somewhat flat so as to fit more comfortably under a breast—Madame de Venile was particularly well-endowed—or in other intimate places. It required a twist to a specific point to reveal the contents for sprinkling and a pull at another to open it completely."

He moved the two halves, and they clicked along.

"It seems noisy for a murderous device."

"That is because it has not been lubricated." The poor man looked about to explode, Iris was sure of it from the color he turned and the way his hands trembled. "It was much more quiet when the original goldsmith assembled it."

"How do you know where to twist it?"

"The Italian mistress's hands were sensitive enough to feel where the points were, but in case they couldn't for some reason, the craftsmen put clues on the outside." He gestured for Iris to follow him to where sunlight shone through a window.

"See the marks? They are more than mere scratches or carving. They are signals in the language of the poisoner."

"I see." Iris ran a gloved finger over the surface, which had been decorated in the pattern of a feather, perfect for the shape of the deadly little gold box. "What is it a feather from?"

Anctil put a hand on his chest, and Iris thought she could hear his rapid heartbeat. "Ah, and the archaeologist's mind comes forward. I would suspect a phoenix or some other mythical creature symbolizing death and rebirth, for every death one causes results in a change in oneself."

"Typically not for the better, I would imagine."

Now Anctil breathed heavily, and he clasped Iris's wrist. His fingers pressed points of pain through her glove. "Mademoiselle, you must listen to me very carefully."

Iris tried to jerk away, but he held fast and gazed at her with dilated pupils. "Monsieur, what's wrong? Are you ill?"

"Not in the way you might think. You must be *très très* cautious, for you tread a dangerous path." He reached into a pocket and pulled out a piece of paper with a crude drawing and an address.

Iris fell through time again, but in her memory, to the night she'd found the gold poison case in her father's study. The symbol on the paper, a square inside a circle, resembled the one that had been etched on the window. Now Iris recognized them as both potential Pythagorean shapes symbolizing a combination of earthly and heavenly—or this life and afterlife —paths.

"The cult of Pythagoras is alive, Mademoiselle McTavish, and they do not want their secrets to be disturbed."

He let go of her wrist, his eyes rolled back in his head, and he collapsed to the ground. The case fell from his fingers, and a gold flash drew Iris's gaze outside, where a clockwork butterfly flitted against the window.

JOHANN BLEDSOE HEARD a discordant note to the one he played
and put the violin down to examine the strings of his bow. But
the sound, more a scream, continued. Before his mind regis-
tered his actions, he placed the violin on the chair and sprinted
down the hall and across the courtyard in the direction it had
come from. He recognized the double doors to the Renaissance
art wing.

Iris! What has that girl gotten herself into now?

He found out when he pushed through the doors and found a
crowd of workers and Monsieur Firmin around Monsieur Anctil,
who lay on the floor, his skin a ghastly shade of gray. Johann
discovered Iris at the back of the crowd by the window, which she
had cracked open. Wet tracks down her cheeks and her trembling
chin identified her as the source of the sound that had interrupted his practice. She clutched his arm when he approached.

"Are you all right?" he asked.

The look she gave him from beneath her wet lashes didn't
say damsel in distress. Rather, it was the cool expression of a
master schemer, and he had to simultaneously respect her and
remind himself she couldn't be trusted.

"What did you do to him?" he hissed. "You can't go burning
my bridges all through Europe. Anctil is a decent sort."

"*Was* a decent sort, you mean," she shot back. "And I didn't
do it. He was holding this." She opened the palm of her other
hand and showed him a small gold case, the shape suggestive
of something a virginal English girl shouldn't know about. He
reached for it, but she stopped him.

"I suspect it has poison on it or that Anctil was given something slower-acting at breakfast. Possibly something that was
meant for me. Either way, he was kind." Now tears welled in
her eyes, and he knew they were real.

Johann wanted to marvel at the crack in her typically solid composure, but there were other problems at hand. He dug a handkerchief from his pocket and gave it to her to wrap the container in. "Make sure you don't have any holes in your pockets or reticule."

"Of course," she replied with a huff that told him his barb hit home.

Yes, I'm a cad. She's obviously upset, and I had to tease her. "And you're going to have to be careful with those gloves."

"It's this one, and it's kid skin, so whatever is on it should wipe off. However, I want to bring it and the case to Doctor Radcliffe before I do. Perhaps he has some way to determine what was used."

"So you want to carry a priceless Renaissance artifact out of the museum in the name of knowledge?" He shook his head. "You are cut from a different cloth." *And that's something Edward would do. Dammit, she* is *perfect for him.*

"Yes, and then I want you to accompany me to..." She rattled off an address that sounded familiar.

"That's L'Hôpital des Enfants," he said. "Why there?"

She gestured toward Monsieur Firmin, who approached them. "I'll tell you later."

"He is gone," he said. "The museum doctor has pronounced him dead. The gendarme would like a word with the young lady."

"I will accompany her to the interview," Johann said.

"That is not necessary." Iris stood straighter. "If you would allow me another brief word with the maestro, I will come momentarily."

"Of course." He inclined his head and walked away.

"I can't take this now. What if they search my reticule in the office?"

"Well, I'm not taking it. Your glove will have to do for the poison sample." He frowned—his favorite mistress had given him that handkerchief, which he couldn't take back now.

Oh, well, easy come, easy go. Like the woman who gave it to me.

"Oh, and one of the clockwork devices followed us," she whispered. "It was flitting outside. You must find it and capture it. I don't want our conversation getting back to your friends in the Guild."

"They're not my—" Her words struck him. How did she know about his troubles? "Fine, but be careful what you say."

"You know I'm good at monitoring my words."

"All too well."

"Excellent. Now go. Find it, and I will meet you after I speak with the gendarme."

Johann watched her walk away and imagined a rod of steel instead of a backbone. His handkerchief fluttered to the floor behind her, and a chink in the case told him she'd dropped the poison holder into it.

His handkerchief was easy enough to retrieve, and he was careful to hold it by the corners. He couldn't help but be impressed at how Iris strategized the situation.

If she were a man, she would be formidable.

A whirring noise caught his attention, the device flitting outside the window. He glanced around to ensure no one saw him, swung a leg over the sill, and stepped outside.

Iris sat with her right hand curled tightly around her left one in her lap. The museum guard had been joined by a young but dour-looking man, who wore a dark suit and introduced himself as Inspector Davidson. She answered their questions with enough information to be truthful but not enough to give away anything about her and the others' quest. She wished she knew where Anctil had been poisoned or if that had been the cause of his death.

Death, death, death... It seemed determined to follow her, and she pushed the thought away that she had somehow attracted it after that last argument with her mother before she became ill.

No, I'm not going to think about that now. Those memories will make me look guilty.

"Mademoiselle?" The head of museum security sniffed so hard his entire moustache jumped.

Iris put an automatic polite smile on her face, her best weapon as a woman in a man's world. "*Je suis desolée*, Monsieur. It has been a trying day. Poor Monsieur Anctil..." She wiped at her eye with her right hand.

"I believe that will suffice," the detective, who sounded like he'd gone abroad to study English, said. His clipped tone belied his youthful appearance but matched his aristocratic demeanor.

He seems too handsome to be a detective. And I am too distraught to think straight.

"Obviously the Mademoiselle can't tell us much in her current state." He handed her a card, which she took and put in her reticule. "If you think of anything else, please contact me."

She stood and curtsied, and they let her go. She met Johann outside the front of the museum, where he waited with Monceau's steamcoach. He held his right hand at an angle away from his body, and water dripped from his sleeve.

"Did you get it without attracting attention?" she asked. She glanced around for signs of Jeremy Scott's men—somehow she doubted they were far away. With all those people watching them—and now she had to add the Pythagoreans and possibly the dandy detective to the list—she wondered how they were to discover anything and keep it a secret.

He lifted her into the carriage, and she was sure to give him her right hand. "Yes. I managed to knock it into a fountain, and the water muffled the sound of the capture alarm."

"That explains your sleeve."

"Indeed. I look forward to Edward and Mister O'Connell figuring out how to play the cylinder so I can hear the conversation you desperately want to hide."

Iris's cheeks warmed. "I do not mind you listening to it, truly, for I have a favor to ask you related to it. But I'm glad you captured the clockwork spy device. It will be something else to keep Edward occupied during his convalescence." She wanted to ask if they would return to the hotel during his allowed visiting hours, but she didn't want to push it. Although she possessed a secret of his now, she had something bigger to ask for. "Since we're done at the Louvre early, perhaps we can visit the address poor Monsieur Anctil gave me. You said it was a hospital?"

Bledsoe squeezed the end of his sleeve, and water dripped on the floor of the steamcoach. It didn't add much to the already humid atmosphere. He gave her a skeptical look. "Perhaps you should go back to the hotel and rest. You just witnessed a man's death, after all. Or are you unhappy he did so where you could see him and therefore you can't pretend he's alive?"

"That's not fair. Now the world has lost two of its brilliant minds in archaeology and history." She gazed out of the window to quell the desire to slap him, especially not with her possibly poisoned with her left glove. As much as he infuriated her, she didn't want to have anyone's death on her hands, not Edward's best friend's. And having death literally on her hand caused power and a sense of entrapment to war in her chest. She returned her gaze to the musician, who studied her with a crease between his blond brows.

"What?" she asked.

"I've encountered many women in my time—"

"Don't be crude."

"—but I've never met one who could switch her emotions off and on like you. Not even the best of the actresses, who admittedly never made it as far as treading the boards in London. But I could always tell what they're feeling no matter how hard they tried to hide it."

"What are you saying about me? That I have no feelings?"

"No, but that you have a strange ability to shut them away. A man died in front of you." He gestured to the floor in front of her as though Anctil's body lay there. "At your feet! And here you sit, cool and hard as one of those marble statues you're so fascinated with, and you want to follow some vague clue—from a man who died giving it to you, no less—that may put you in more danger, which you're not worried about in the least." He stopped and ran a finger under his collar. Iris's stomach wanted to bust through her corset to take enough of a breath for the response she wanted to make, but Marie had laced her in too tightly, so she had to settle for icy disdain.

This explains Adelaide's typical response when I angered her. She never allowed sensible corset lacing.

"Make no mistake, Mister Bledsoe," Iris said. "I mourn my father. You have no idea how badly I miss him and wish every day I could ask his opinion about this crazy quest and the things we're finding out." She almost said, "About ourselves," but she didn't want to give away anything about the strange events of the previous night until she'd puzzled through them herself. "I feel flawed, cracked down the middle and held together by the need to survive all humans seem to have whether they're slave girls about to be sacrificed in a temple or the most powerful philosophers or kings. I know my strength, which is to solve problems and figure out riddles given to me by the past. I cannot control my gender, but I can do what I can to keep it from hampering me. I will not apologize for not meeting your low expectations and melting into tears in your arms like your typical female companions, but I have a job to do, and you do too."

He sat back, and his mouth opened and closed like a drowning gargoyle. "That's not at all what I was saying, and I certainly have no desire for you to be in my arms. You've too many hard and flinty bits for me."

"If you're trying to insult me, you failed. I wouldn't be soft and gentle for Jeremy Scott, and I won't be for you!"

"What does that milquetoast have to do with anything? Now you're arguing like a woman."

The steamcoach stopped in front of the hotel, and the driver opened the door.

"Hopefully that will satisfy you. Now if you will excuse me," Iris told him, "I shall return to my logical self, find Doctor Radcliffe and see what he can tell me about Anctil's death, what substance may have been responsible." Her throat burned with tears at the thought of the little man's kindness to her that morning—at least compared to Bledsoe's and Firmin's harshness—but she'd be damned before she allowed Bledsoe to see her cry now. She *liked* her flinty bits. "And then I shall change gloves, find Marie, and go to L'Hôpital des Enfants and satisfy Anctil's final wish. Do be sure you don't catch cold with those wet clothes. Dead men can't pay their debts."

And with that, she swept up the stairs and nodded to the doorman, who tipped his hat at her like she was the queen. She walked into the lobby, chin tilted at a most confident angle, and searched the faces for Doctor Radcliffe. He wasn't hard to find, and she approached him with a determined stride.

When he saw her, his expression wasn't the welcoming one she expected. Instead, he stood, crossed the distance between them in two steps, and said in a low, curt tone, "We need to talk about something. You're engaged?"

22

Hôtel Auberge, 13 June 1870

What do you mean she's engaged? Edward asked again in his head. Patrick O'Connell had long ago left him to his sulking. Instead of working as his schedule dictated, Edward gazed out of the window like some idiot he'd seen in a painting. That was all they did in those French pictures, stare outside like lovelorn fools. Patrick said he didn't think Iris meant to be engaged, exactly, but there was some young man determined to marry her, and some agreement must have been made, or else why would he have sent his men after her? Plus a packet of official-looking papers arrived for her from Scott. A marriage contract, perhaps? The courier had knocked on Edward's door while Radcliffe was in assessing his condition, and Edward answered the door. The young man asked if they knew if she had left for the day, and years of teaching had taught Edward to read upside-down, so he could see Scott's name on the return address.

Iris, the beautiful, delicate Iris with more strength, determination, and cleverness than any woman he'd met. Why did he let himself get so tangled up in her charm? He replayed the events of the past week in his head, how he'd been so impressed by her cool demeanor in that initial meeting with the dean, department chair, and that American Parnaby Cobb. Of course she had a secret. Everyone had secrets, but he had hoped hers would be something innocent and girlish, not a fiancé determined to bring her back at all costs.

But his anxiety emerged. Where was she now? Was Johann watching over her? Those men could be anywhere waiting to snatch her up and whisk her back to England, where the next time he'd see her, she would be someone's wife. Perhaps she was along because she wanted to escape, not because her father was ill. But that didn't make sense. If Irvin McTavish wasn't ill, she wouldn't be alone, but why would a father risk his only daughter to a strange expedition when she could be home safely wed to a local nobleman, even if he was a second son?

A second son... Perhaps that was the root of it. In his heart, which Edward wasn't accustomed to thinking of as an actual receptacle of anything important, he knew he didn't have much to offer her. A modest aetherist faculty salary, assuming, of course, that the department survived. She deserved a season in London, suitors of much higher means than either him or Jeremy Scott, whom Edward's brother likely knew. Edward didn't follow the doings of the ton. But what if Iris preferred to be back in England with Scott but was along because of her father's wishes?

Something about the situation didn't add up. Edward drummed his fingers on the table, where the clockwork butterfly lay in the same disassembled state as previously. The door opened, and Johann came through.

"Iris has a secret," Edward said. He couldn't keep the moroseness out of his tone.

Johann's shoulders slumped. "I was afraid you'd find out."

"You knew she's engaged?" Edward stood, but pain shot

through his lower back and left hip, and he lowered himself. "How does everyone know but me?"

"Wait, what?" Johann shed his jacket and sat across from Edward, who saw his friend's right sleeve was damp. "She's engaged? To whom?"

"Lord Jeremy Scott." Now Edward was sure he would hate the lordling if he ever met him.

Johann barked a laugh. "If she is, I can assure you it's not a happy engagement. She seems to have a low opinion of him."

Now Edward's anxiety twined into the green tendril of jealousy he hoped had shriveled but seemed to be as tenacious as his beloved ivy. "She's talked of him with you? This gets worse and worse."

"In a sense. Trust me, I'm not exactly a girlish confidant." He reached into his pocket, from which he drew a clockwork butterfly. "But the contents of the cylinder in this one should be much more interesting than worrying about who's engaged to whom."

"You're trying to change the subject."

"Yes, because that young lady isn't worth worrying over. Trust me, there are others out there much better suited for you." But Johann didn't sound convinced.

"So what is Iris's secret, then?"

"Oh, her connection with Scott, of course." Johann gestured to the clockwork he'd laid on the table. "Think you can get it apart and figure out how to listen to it?"

"I'm an aetherist, not a tinkerer, but I'll do my best. Why is there another one? Why is the Clockwork Guild watching us so closely?"

"Let me worry about that." Johann stood. "I need to change and take Miss McTavish back out. A clue was dropped in her lap by an unfortunate gentleman."

"Unfortunate how?"

"He's now dead."

"How? Never mind." Edward returned his gaze to the street outside. "I am not supposed to be having visitors at this time, anyway, and you're disrupting my concentration with your talk of women with secrets and dead men."

The door shut, and Edward was once again alone with his thoughts, which went back to his secure, predictable time in Huntington Village and to his brother and family. Did they miss him? He turned his attention to the clockworks in front of him, and an idea squirmed into his brain as to what to do with them. He reached for his valise.

IRIS FOLLOWED Radcliffe into the hotel restaurant, where they were shown to a booth in a corner by the window. Gauzy curtains gave Iris a hazy view of the street outside, where men's faces melted into light-colored smudges between their dark coats and hats. None were as dark as Radcliffe, and she wondered if he felt as out of place among the self-assured Parisians as she did, no matter how confident she could appear for a moment. And now Jeremy Scott made trouble for her again. But first they had to follow social convention and order tea and croissants for a late morning snack so as not to draw suspicion. Once the waiter left, Radcliffe didn't allow Iris a moment to draw a breath to ask the questions on her mind.

"This came for you," he said and brought a packet of papers from his inside pocket. It was addressed to, "My Beloved Iris McTavish," and the return address was Lord Jeremy Scott, Hôtel de Musée, Paris.

Big hairy ox's bollocks, he's in Paris! "I can assure you, if he finds me beloved, the feeling is not reciprocated."

"So you do not have an agreement?"

"No!" She removed her gloves, careful to allow the left one to slide itself inside-out as she took it off, and untied the string.

Porous impermanent materials like textiles and paper didn't hold tight to many impressions, but she did get an overwhelming sense of disappointment and confusion.

Oh no.

"Was Edward with you when the courier brought this?" she asked. The reproachful look in his gray eyes answered her question. She swore again, this time under her breath but couldn't say anything aloud until after the waiter poured their tea and moved away.

"I assure you, Doctor Radcliffe," she said again in as even a tone as she could, "I am not engaged to Lord Scott, nor do I wish to be. I find him to be a most odious human being and wish he would cease this ridiculous pursuit."

"Whether or not his pursuit is welcome is immaterial." Radcliffe removed his gray gloves and poured cream in his tea with movements Iris admired for their precision. He didn't waste a single ounce of energy, and she could understand why her supposed engagement irritated him—it went against his plan for Edward.

"I'm so sorry it inconveniences you." She took a cube of sugar, picked up the cream pitcher, and read it. The flash of fear seemed incongruous with Radcliffe's unruffled appearance, but he watched her with those hawk's eyes of his, and she couldn't hold on to the cream longer.

"My convenience is also irrelevant," he said. "The problem is that you've upset Professor Bailey, whom you are intimate enough with to be on a first-name basis. I understand that some women are not of a nurturing kind, but you must at least wish him no harm."

"Of course I wish him no harm, and I do care for him." Iris trapped her tongue between her teeth before it made any other awkward revelations. *Where did that come from?*

"I see. The psyche is a fragile thing, and the professor's world has been turned upside-down. He seems to care for you as well, and the morning's revelation may have set his recovery back."

"How is he?" Iris asked. Now that her declaration flitted between them like one of the clockwork butterflies, she decided to ask what was on her mind.

"Still in a lot of pain, but I cannot find any physiological reason for its intensity. Admittedly, he has some bruising from the crash, but nothing to warrant his symptoms other than emotional turmoil."

"And you believe that, emotional turmoil? Could it have that much effect on the body?"

A cloud passed over the sun outside the window, and Radcliffe's face also darkened. "They are studying it in Vienna, the relationship between the mind's output and the body's experience. Have you heard of hysteria?"

A dark shadow in her peripheral vision caught Iris's attention, and she turned to see a woman in mourning dress and veil take a seat alone at a table. It was impossible to tell under the tower of dark clothing what the woman looked like or how old she was, only that she had lost someone and could wear her grief openly. And hide from prying eyes.

Iris wanted to go to her, take her hand, and tell her she understood and to take as long as needed. But she turned her attention back to Radcliffe and the table, where the croissants had appeared. The memory of Anctil's telling her they were his daughter's favorite, the glimmer of fatherly pride in his eyes, made her feel that fissure in the core of her soul, that crack from grief unexpressed. Another daughter would be crying tonight, and Iris's stomach quivered at the thought she had something to do with it. For if she and Johann hadn't gone to the museum, Anctil may still be alive.

"Miss McTavish?" Radcliffe's face folded into a frown of concern. "Are you ill?"

"I'm as well as could be expected." *...after having a man die in* *front of me and finding out my tormentor is in Paris.* But she did what young women were expected to do—she smiled and took a croissant as if everything was fine.

"You're not telling me the entire truth. As I mentioned, I know something about hysteria."

"That's a flippant term for soul-sickness, and perhaps I don't feel like talking about it, not here." She didn't mean to snap, but she'd had quite enough of men accusing her of lying, never mind that they were right. They had more important puzzles to solve. She lowered her voice so he would have to lean in to follow the thread of her tones among the tapestry of restaurant and traffic sounds. "What you could do to help me is determine what kind of poison was used earlier to kill a man."

Radcliffe paused the journey of the croissant to his mouth and returned it to the plate in front of him. "Come again?"

"I'm not repeating what I said." She handed him her gloves, the left one inside the right one. "I may have been holding the object that carried it in my left hand, but thankfully I wore my new gloves."

"And do you have the object itself? What was it?"

"Not something a lady of polite society can discuss in public. I had to abandon it at the Louvre because security wanted to question me, and I didn't want them to accuse me of thievery. I didn't trust Bledsoe to carry it out for me."

"Interesting. I'll see what I can do. What symptoms did the victim display?"

Iris tried to separate herself from the emotional details of the memory, to describe it as if she were documenting a just-opened tomb, not the journey of a man to his own grave. "He became flushed, and when he grabbed me, I could feel the heat of his hands through my gloves. Toward the end, he seemed to have trouble breathing, and his eyes got wide. Not his eyes, his pupils."

"Thank you. That gives me somewhere to start. My field is

military and battlefield medicine, but I've some experience with poisons." He glanced at the window and swallowed. "And I've become friendly with the apothecary around the corner."

Iris drew her shoulders back against the shiver of skin at the back of her neck. "Don't reveal anything to him. Your discretion is of the utmost importance in this. There are dangerous men afoot."

"I gathered. People usually don't get poisoned if there aren't."

"Don't be flippant. It's not a funny situation."

"Oh, so you are not amused?" He sipped his tea, but the crinkles around his eyes told her he hid a smile.

"I am most certainly not amused." *Wait, isn't that one of Queen Victoria's sayings? Cheeky man.*

"You're also not accustomed to death and dying. When you're in that situation on the battlefield, it's necessary to keep your sense of humor, even if it is of the gallows variety. Now," he said and placed his empty teacup on the plate in front of him. "I feel it would be best for my patient if you were to go tell him you are not engaged to Lord Scott and don't intend to be. Patrick will recognize his man if he comes sniffing around here again."

"Thank you." Iris rose. "I'm glad to be surrounded by such gentlemen."

She walked away from the table, and again the woman in the mourning outfit caught her eye. Iris nodded to her with a grim smile that she hoped said she understood. The other woman nodded once, so perhaps the message got through.

She crossed the lobby, her thoughts full of how relieved Edward would be, when she encountered Bledsoe getting off the elevator.

"Oh, good," he said. "I'm glad I found you. If you want to visit the place you mentioned earlier, we need to get going."

Iris thought quickly. "But I don't have any gloves." A sensation of pressure built in her chest not unlike that of the volcano egg on the night it called for her to discover it, and she turned to see who or what wanted her attention. Marie approached from the side door.

"Oh, there you are, Miss!" She held out a package. "I had the feeling you might need more gloves, so I found these for you."

"Perfect!" Johann helped Marie unwrap them and held them out for Iris. "Now let's go."

But I need to see Edward! However, the look on Johann's face told her she shouldn't push him, and she did need to see what Anctil was trying to tell her with the address. *I'll see Edward later. He's probably found something to work on by now.* With a resigned nod, she thanked Marie for the gloves and followed Johann to the curb, where he hailed a steamcab.

Iris glanced toward Edward's room and thought she saw the smudge of his face in the window, but from what she could see, he was in profile, so he wasn't looking outside. She raised her hand anyway, and Johann tugged her into the cab.

The jolt the steamcab gave when Marie jumped in echoed the jarring in Iris's center upon seeing her.

"What are you doing?" Iris asked, but she couldn't muster an angry tone as much as an annoyed and weary one.

"My mother will have my head—and trust me, they do that here—if I let you go off alone again. I got a message from her earlier." Marie's answers made sense. Of course Lucille wanted her to be close to Iris. In the light of day and the knowledge of whatever Lucille had tried to do to connect Iris and Marie, her motivation became clear—she wanted to know what was going on with their little expedition, particularly because it had been funded by Cobb. But Iris also sensed in Marie the same core of rebellion so familiar from her dealings with Adelaide. Could she trust Marie with her secret?

She thought fast for some way to keep Marie out of the

hospital while she and Johann, who looked about as happy to see Marie as Iris was, sought what Anctil wanted her to find there.

"So this is a children's hospital?" she asked when the steamcab pulled up to the front. The name of L'Hôpital des Enfants stretched over the arched entranceway, beyond which a long walk led to the front door between high hedges.

"No, it's named for the Holy Innocents, the children Herod killed when he was searching for the infant Jesus," Marie said. "It's supposedly a place for the helpless and those who have no one to support them, but as with most of the institutions under our beloved Emperor, it's turned into a way for him to make money, mostly off foreigners who become ill here."

They exited the cab, and it drove off. Iris squelched the urge to call it back, to go back to the hotel and Edward and stay with their original task. *No, I have to see what this place holds. A man died to bring me here.* The thought gave her an idea.

"Marie," she murmured as they walked up the lane to the front entrance of the hospital, "I'm not sure why we're here, but it might be a trap. Please remain in the lobby and look out for anything suspicious, especially any of the men from the other night. Lord Scott is in Paris."

"Yes, Miss." The maid's hazel eyes narrowed, but she didn't say anything more.

"Do we know what we're looking for?" Johann asked after they entered and looked around at the quiet hall lined with benches. No one sat there waiting to be seen or admitted, which struck Iris as strange. Had Paris been blessed with a surge of good health as well as nice weather? The admissions clerk didn't wake from his snooze behind the desk. Or maybe he was pretending not to notice them so he could continue his nap.

Either way, how odd.

"May I help you, Mademoiselle?" A woman wearing a

nurse's cap and wire spectacles approached them. Her face, although unlined, held the severity typically seen behind the wrinkles on the elderly.

"Yes, I think. May we speak privately?"

Johann raised his eyebrows and followed Iris and the nurse through the door to the left of the desk. She brought them into a small office and gestured for them to sit.

"Now I am assuming you are here because you are missing a family member and you believe he or she may have been admitted?" she asked. Her lilting French accent didn't soften her tone, which implied they had been careless, indeed, to misplace someone at *her* hospital.

"It was recommended I come," Iris said.

"Yes, it usually is." She rose and walked to a set of shelves behind them, where folders bound together with string lay. "What month did you lose contact with your family member?"

"You last heard from your father in May, right?" Johann asked. Iris nodded, playing along. Did she dare show the nurse the paper with the symbol on it? But she didn't know why Anctil had sent her here.

"We have an excellent photographer *de la mort*. It's one of the services we're able to offer families." The way the nurse glanced back at Iris told her it wasn't a free service, and if she recognized someone, they'd be given a bill.

"A photographer of death?" Iris asked. "As in, someone who photographs deceased people?"

"Yes, it is a custom we borrowed from the Americans, as barbaric as many of us feel it is. But a body only lasts so long."

"How sad," Iris murmured. But she could understand the necessity of it in this situation. If someone was sick enough, they wouldn't be able to communicate their identity, and papers often got stolen. This way the hospital could help give families an idea of what happened and also collect for their services.

"He delivered the rest of May to me today," the nurse continued, obviously accustomed to barreling through whatever shock visitors experienced. She selected the last folio on the second shelf and handed it to Johann.

Iris watched the odd events unfolding. This place, this situation took on the same flat, fake aspect as the props in Marie's mother's theatre. Indeed, what a strange role she played, but it was comforting to know she could express some of her bereaved feelings.

"Look through the photos, dear," Johann said. Iris bit her lip so she wouldn't let forth a hysterical giggle at him stepping into a part too.

She nodded and wished she could slip off her gloves. Something about the bundle of paper and photographs on the desk in front of them called to her, although in a more muted voice than the volcano egg had in her father's office. She wondered what the folder, although it was flimsy and therefore temporary, would tell her about this strange place. Instead, she focused as much through her fingertips, but the first photo in the file made all her desire to read it flee.

There, appearing to slumber peacefully in a chair in a garden abloom with spring flowers, sat Irvin McTavish.

23

L 'Hôpital des Enfants, 13 June 1870
      If Iris intended to pretend she didn't recognize any
      of the unfortunate images in the folder, to walk out of
there with her secret intact, she failed.

Seeing her father like that in a pose she'd so often found him in at home in the study or in his own beloved garden, laying with one hand on his stomach and the other curled around his favorite pipe... She wanted to cry, to scream at him to wake up, this wasn't funny, this wasn't a good prank, *Open your eyes, Papa, please!*

But none of it came out around the burning in her throat and feeling the tears she'd hidden for weeks would explode from the corners of her eyes and wash all of these ridiculous situations and people and places away.

She wished for a veil like the woman in mourning at the hotel restaurant so she could hide away from the world and have it leave her alone for a while. She supposed now she could invoke her right to mourn, now she could pretend that she had just found out and that she hadn't lied. But she knew the man beside her wouldn't let her get away with that, and she hated him for it.

"He looks very peaceful," Johann said. "You wouldn't know he'd been ill."

But Iris could tell. His skin was pale, more so than she would have expected in death, and dark half-moons sat at the base of his fingernails and under his eyes. He looked older and like he was covered in wrinkled paper rather than flesh. Something had eaten him from the inside after he'd left.

What is he doing here and not at the coast like he said? Who sent the telegram?

"So that is your father?" The nurse folded the corners of her mouth into something approaching a sympathetic expression. "My condolences for your loss. I can have Francois bring his things for you."

Iris nodded, unable to say anything. Bledsoe removed the photo from the folder and handed the rest back to the nurse, who placed the folio back on the shelves with the others before leaving the room.

"You have to pull yourself together," Bledsoe said. "It's not like this is a surprise."

"No, but this is the first time it's real." It was true. Before, she could pretend he was away on one of his expeditions and that he would be back. But now she had proof beyond the flimsy paper and printed words of a telegram announcing its grim news across the miles. Now there was a body and a true loss.

"You can't let the others know."

Iris looked at him through her tears, which distorted his face into a half-smeared image and tugged one corner of his mouth into a sneer. "What? Why?"

"Because you will be expected to leave the expedition, go back to England, and handle arrangements." His tone held an edge of desperation, and a wisp of satisfaction uncurled in her chest—he did recognize her need to be there. Then anger torched the satisfaction.

"Suddenly you're more concerned for yourself than poor Edward." She wasn't going to mention his dilemma with the Clockwork Guild again. Let him wonder what, if anything, she'd heard.

He twisted around so he faced the door. "We'll discuss this later. Someone's coming."

The door opened to reveal not the nurse, but Marie. "Mademoiselle? Is everything all right?"

Iris hoped her eyes didn't show too much of her recent emotions. "Yes, Marie. Why aren't you standing guard in the lobby?"

Marie shook her head. "I felt something was wrong. I'll go back out."

Iris wanted her to stay, but she didn't need this news getting back to Cobb. "We should be finished shortly."

Marie left, and the nurse entered with a box. "I believe these are your father's belongings."

"You can't bring them," Bledsoe said. "Not all of them. We don't have room."

Iris nodded. It would be too difficult to explain where they came from, especially to Marie. Still, there must be something for her.

"Would you excuse me?" she asked the nurse and Bledsoe. They exited, leaving her alone with the box of her father's things. She pulled out his jacket first. It smelled of his sweet pipe smoke and the faint crisp odor of fresh-turned earth that clung to him even when he wasn't gardening or on an expedition. But there was also something acrid that hadn't been there before. She felt in the pockets but didn't find anything. The same held for his pants.

When the ancients hid something precious, they often put it in the least obvious place, his voice said in her mind. She'd been ten at the time he'd told her that, and he was talking about crown jewels that a displaced monarch had put in the hollowed-out heels of his shoes.

She dug through the rest of the box, which held his small-clothes and shirts, and found his well-worn shoes. However, when she held both of them, the left one seemed lighter. She pulled back the lining of the right one and found a compartment with a small wooden tube, which she pried out. When she pulled the two halves apart, a small scroll of paper fell out. On it was written, *45 degree twist, half pull, 30 degree twist other direction.*

This is how to open the poison hider! What could he have hidden in there for me?

She rolled the little scroll and replaced it in the tube, which she stuck in her reticule. She reassembled the shoe and searched through her father's other things. She took his pocket watch and pipe, which she had seen him with so many times they seemed part of him. She couldn't imagine anyone else using them. Aware that the others waited for her, she decided to read them later.

When she stepped into the hall, the nurse, Bledsoe, and Marie waited for her in the company of a spry wrinkled man.

"Mademoiselle," Marie said. "This man approached me in the waiting area. He says he is the photographer *de la mort*, and he has a message for you from your father."

24

L'*Hôpital des Enfants, 13 June 1870*

"You have a message for me?" Iris asked. She glanced at Marie, who now knew an incorrect but damaging version of her secret, but she'd have to deal with the maid later. Now all she wanted to do was hear whatever he had to say and go back to the hotel and open the poison hiding contraption to see what it held.

"Oui, Mademoiselle." He twisted his cap in his hands, and he reminded her of the urchin who had brought the invitation to the meeting that had started this all. *Or perhaps it started before then.* She filed the insight away for later pondering.

"I need my office back," the nurse said. She eyed the photographer with the look of someone who watched an insect crawl across the floor but didn't want to put the effort forth to squash it.

"Is there somewhere else we could talk privately?" Bledsoe asked. When Iris opened her mouth to object, he said, "I cannot allow you to go unchaperoned with a strange man, my dear."

"Of course."

"The garden is typically deserted this time of day because the hospital residents are eating lunch," the photographer said. "I'll show you."

Iris refrained from asking whether that was when he did his work, and she hoped he hadn't set up one of his clients in the garden to be photographed after they talked.

"Your father was fascinated by what I do," he said once they were settled at a table under some fruit trees. "He said future generations would wonder about our customs when they saw them, why we took pictures of our dead, but he said it wasn't that different from tomb decorations, only that those were for the dead and my creations are for the living."

"And the message?" Iris asked. In spite of the warm breeze that made spots of sunlight dance through the leaves, something about the little man left her feeling cold, and she wanted to end the interview as soon as possible.

"He said you would eventually come to Paris, and he had a friend who would steer you here. He made me repeat this over and over and promise to tell no one but you." He glanced at Bledsoe and Marie, who moved away a discreet distance, and lowered his voice. "He said to tell you that the dead will dance if given the right music, and that the keepers will kill to prevent the gardener from coaxing the rose's petals open."

"Was he already ill?" Iris asked. It sounded like gibberish, but creepy gibberish, and talking to him gave her the sensation of a thousand invisible ants crawling over her skin.

"Oh yes. But you knew that, didn't you? He came here to die, to end the story, but you followed him too soon, so it must continue." He leapt from the chair and stalked away, muttering about the story continuing, and wouldn't it have a pretty ending now with lots of people for him to take pictures of?

Iris brushed at her arms to clear the odd sensation he left her with and to give her hands something to do. Now she really needed to get back to the hotel, but she also had to address the problem at hand.

"Marie," she said. The maid came to her side, and they walked out of the garden onto the road, where Bledsoe set about finding a cab for them.

"I'm very sorry for your loss," Marie said. "It must have come as quite a shock." Her eyes, the color of the greenish-brown moss that grows on trees deep in the woods, softened, and Iris had a sense of complete sympathy. She guessed Marie, no matter the relationship with her mother, would miss Lucille terribly if the strange old woman were to die.

"Thank you," she said. "And as much as I would like to be able to mourn properly, we can't let word of this spread. At least not yet."

Marie nodded with an air of utter practicality. "I understand. You need the money from this expedition more now, I imagine. Especially if what we found out last night is true."

"Yes." The sense of responsibility and need for independence tightened the imaginary cord twisting around her heart. "Now that Jeremy Scott holds the mortgage on Grange House, it's imperative I make myself financially stable so I don't have to marry him."

"Lucille is using her contacts in England to verify that man's claims. She is rather attached to you now."

Iris suppressed a shudder at the fuzzy memory of something being done to her, sweaty palm pressed to cool one. "I'm not sure how I feel about her."

Marie laughed. "You're not the only one. She is a complex woman. By the way, if you want to keep the secret about your father, it is best you ask her directly. I suspect she will know within the hour."

"How?" But the nurse had seemed eager to get them out of her office. Did she have tube access in there? Did Lucille have the nurse under her power somehow? It wouldn't be a surprise. "Then let's stop by the theatre on the way back."

"Now you're learning how things work here."

MARIE HADN'T WANTED to go to the theatre the night before, and she sure as hell didn't now, but the sooner Iris learned how to play the game, the better for all of them. Lucille had only failed at one thing in her life—protecting her daughter from Parnaby Cobb. Marie had long ago acknowledged the role of her youthful stubbornness in that occurrence, and she always attempted to make it up to her mother when she could.

Thinking too much about these conflicting loyalties, and now her strange affinity for Iris and her emotions, made Marie's head hurt. She focused more on what she needed to do now, which was to shepherd Iris through the process, keep Bledsoe out of the way, and get them all back to the Hôtel Auberge in time for a late lunch so Iris could rest and prepare for the Monceau gala that night. She hoped Lucille would cooperate.

The cab pulled up to the theatre. "So this is the Théâtre Bohème," Bledsoe said. He alighted from the steamcab and helped the ladies out. "I've heard much about it."

"And we've heard much about you," Marie said. "Don't get any ideas. This isn't a recreational stop."

"So you're Madame St. Jean's daughter. I didn't put the last names together until yesterday evening. What are you doing working as a maid?"

Marie stalked up the walk of the residence next to the theatre and shot back over her shoulder before ascending the steps, "What I need to do to keep everything running smoothly."

As she suspected, her mother was in her townhouse, not

the theatre. That happened the day after a ritual, particularly if more than one other person was involved. Simple curses? No problem. Binding spells? Definitely more effort, especially if one of the participants wasn't willing.

Lucille opened the door wearing a day dress. "You brought guests," she said. It wasn't a question or a challenge, simply a statement as if she'd been expecting them. Marie guessed the nurse sent a message updating Lucille.

"Yes, we thought we should speak with you."

Lucille gestured for them to follow her, and they passed through the front hall and ascended the stairs to the parlor adjacent to the dining room.

Iris looked around warily before making eye contact with Lucille. Anger sparked in her dark blue eyes, but she held her tongue, thank goodness. Then Bledsoe walked in. Marie grabbed his arm. "You wait outside."

"But I haven't had the chance to make the acquaintance of the lovely and famous Madame St. Jean." He smiled, and the temperature in the room increased by a couple of degrees, or so it felt, with him turning on his full charm. Marie wondered if he had some latent ability he wasn't aware of, or maybe he knew all too well the power in his smile.

"You can save your smiles for the girls, Maestro," Lucille said, but she held her hand out.

He took it and bowed over it. "It is a pleasure to finally meet you."

"Likewise. Go with Marie into the theatre. She'll show you around. I have to discuss a few things with this young lady, who's gotten herself in over her head."

Iris gave Marie a "Don't leave me!" look, but Marie shrugged. "Don't worry, she doesn't bite. At least not unless you provoke her."

"Insolent girl," Lucille said. "Now go. You did right bringing her here."

Marie pulled Bledsoe not too gently into the hallway. She knew he was strong enough to resist, but he didn't. Once in the gloom of the hallway, he took his hand from hers.

"Will she be all right?" he asked.

The concern in his voice startled Marie but also vindicated the suspicion that had sprouted in the cab. Was it possible that the enmity between him and Iris was growing into a different kind of passion? The Professor wouldn't be happy with that, and in her opinion, he seemed the best match for the young archaeologist, at least with regard to preferences and morals. Bledsoe, Marie had heard, was a consummate rake. Evidence to the point: he had his hand on her bottom.

"The hallway isn't that dark, Maestro. There's no need to feel your way around."

"So you pull me in here but don't want to do anything? That hardly seems fair."

Marie turned to face him and put her hands flat against his chest. With a shove, she said, "Don't use me to distract yourself. I can see what's going on."

He didn't move forward, but the lift of his eyebrows was obvious in the gloom. "And what would that be?"

"You're attracted to Mademoiselle Iris, but you don't want to move in on her because she's about to have an understanding with your friend Edward."

"Oh, is she? Has she said something to you?"

"No, but that's obvious too. You men are dense." She turned and stalked down the hall. He followed her, his footsteps hesitant and then more confident. "Good," she said. "If you want a tour, follow me. But not too closely."

"Yes, Mademoiselle. Your wish is my command."

The low purr in his voice made the spot where he'd put his hand tingle, and she wondered again if he had some sort of extra ability, something to explain why people flocked to his concerts and women to his bed. From what her mother had told her, that would be unusual enough for a man, but she didn't doubt it was possible. Anything was possible, and every rule had an exception.

Now she hoped she would be the exception to his charm. *Time to turn on the shrew and hope he doesn't take it as a challenge to tame me.*

She took on the scowl from one of her favorite roles and said, "Hurry up. I don't have all day."

IRIS AND LUCILLE squared off in spite of the overtone of the visit being pleasantly social. The thought crossed Iris's mind that life was much easier when all she had to do was figure out how to maintain her household and avoid unwanted marriage proposals. This world of manipulative theatre owners and death photographers with cryptic messages seemed needlessly complicated.

Lucille spoke first. "Have a seat, Mademoiselle." It wasn't a request.

Iris perched at the edge of the chaise where she'd lain the night before when Lucille had done whatever she did to link her and Marie. Iris sensed Marie was somewhere near and that her emotional state was as conflicted as her own.

"So you have something to report?" Lucille asked and sat across from Iris on a fringed armchair in a ridiculous dark pink color. "And don't scowl at me like that, Mademoiselle. You do not like having to tell me, this I can see, but I can also help you."

"I'm here as a courtesy. How could you possibly help me?" Iris asked. "I mean, I appreciate the clothing, but this adds another layer of complexity to an already impossible situation."

"And what is impossible about it, *ma petite*? That you want more from your life than you can achieve due to your sex? That you counted on your father to help you navigate around the obstacles society will put in your way so you wouldn't have to sacrifice what so many before you have?"

Lucille's words brought to mind the courtesans who had carried the poison in secret places on their bodies in the little containers Anctil had shown Iris. This was the second such uncomfortable conversation. She wasn't interested in that part of life—coupling made people stupid and selfish, but she wasn't going to use any attractiveness she might have to manipulate anyone else.

"It's hard because every time I think I get closer to an answer, I have to deal with some pointless requirement by someone who thinks they know better than I what's best for me. I wish people would leave me alone to figure all this out." She knew that wasn't completely true, but she did want to let Lucille know she was unhappy with this... Well, whatever it was. Lucille wasn't her mother. She'd already had one of those, and it hadn't worked out well.

"Ah, but the best problem-solving happens with others. Isn't that why there are such things as universities? Because people think better together?"

"Not me." That, at least, Iris could say with certainty.

"And you are so sure, I can see this. But there are things you would not have known had it not been for others. Even if you have a quick mind, you need information from others to put it all together."

"All right, I'll give you that." Iris wished she could sit back, but the corset wouldn't let her. "But I don't see why I should have to report to you. My affairs are none of your business."

"They are now because they involve my daughter." Lucille stood and paced the narrow avenue between the dining table and the back of the chair she'd been sitting in. "You truly do not know what you are up against."

"If this is information I need, please enlighten me."

"Your father has died, which you knew, but instead of being in a place on the coast, it was in a hospital here in Paris. Another man has died, this one right in front of you. Yet you insist on staying in the realm of puzzles, not human lives, which means yours is in grave danger. And along with yours, my daughter's."

The objects in Iris's purse called to her to read them, but she refused to do so in front of Lucille. "If you have the information already, why did you need to speak with me? I could be figuring out this problem and bringing us closer to a solution rather than wasting my time here. Unless there's something else I need to know."

Lucille threw up her hands with stage-ready flair. "The important question, which you need to consider, is whether searching for a solution is the best course of action. Perhaps you should return to England and resume your life there. To continue this path is madness, and as I said, you endanger others, not just yourself."

Iris recalled her unintentional reading of Marie's brooch, the peridot one with the stylized C. "Is this about me or about thwarting Parnaby Cobb? Whatever he did to or with your daughter is not my concern."

"If you, too, are caught in his net, it is your concern. He will be a kind benefactor as long as you cooperate, but if you do not... Believe me, Mademoiselle, he is pulling your strings, and I am your most powerful ally against him."

"Then tell me what you can do to help me!" Now Iris stood. "I've had enough riddles and hints and secrets to last a lifetime. If you have something for me, give it to me. If not, don't confuse an already convoluted situation. No, I don't like it that we're dependent on Cobb, but you don't seem to understand that I'm doing what I need to survive."

"I sense you will need my help before another day passes. All I ask in return is that you remember that others' lives are at stake. There are many kinds of survival and many more ways of dying. You walk where the dead dance with the living and try to pull them across."

"Another riddle." Iris sighed emphatically. "I will do my best to take care of Marie, but keep in mind she is more than capable."

"She is more vulnerable than you think. That is why I had to ensure you would stay close—she is strong where you are weak and vice versa."

"Right." Iris suppressed another sigh. *At least Marie has a parent who cares for her, whereas I am dreadfully alone.* "Well, I appreciate any help you can give me, but I should be going. Big night tonight."

"Yes, do not go without Marie. Remember servants are invisible and often overhear valuable information."

Finally, a helpful tidbit! Iris smiled and curtsied. "I will do what I can. I'm afraid our itinerary is up to Maestro Bledsoe."

Lucille smiled with the grin of a woman who knew more than most when it came to the male species. "Most men are easy to manipulate. I have faith you can arrange it."

Iris walked out of the apartment and exhaled with relief once she reached the sunny street outside. The stifling feeling of the marital trap Jeremy Scott laid for her increased with the sense something bigger than she led and pushed her to an end she didn't understand. She'd thought the expedition would give her the means to live independently, but would it instead keep her stuck in a cat-and-mouse game with only glimpses of the predatory feline? Lucille's words confirmed her intuition about Cobb—that he worked from less than honorable motives.

But we won't know until we get to the end of this journey.

A flash of gold caught Iris's attention, and she spied a clock-work bug climbing down from Lucille's window. She checked the angle of the sun and reached into her reticule for a mirror. She didn't know if it would be enough to melt the wax cylinder, but perhaps the heat from the reflection would be enough to at least warp whatever information had been collected. She ducked behind a parked carriage and managed to aim a bright spot at the thing when it crawled into a sunny place. She hoped the already bright sunlight on the gray stone masked her intervention. It stopped and quivered. Iris counted to twenty before it fell from the building and into the hands of a waiting street urchin, a rag picker Iris hadn't noticed.

Servants are often invisible. So are the poor.

She watched the boy dart into an alley. Unfortunately she was not quick enough to follow him, not that she could without attracting attention.

Voices raised in argument drew her attention to the front of the theatre, where Bledsoe and Marie emerged.

"The pit is more than sufficient for the music that is needed," Marie said.

"Not if you want to have large productions."

A musician who's being blackmailed, a maid who isn't a maid and who is working for Cobb, a doctor with secrets of his own, and an Irish tinkerer who doesn't seem to know what place he wants in the world... And an injured professor who is the only one with clear motives in the whole bunch. And as much as I want to tell him about my father, the fewer of us who know about this, the better, especially since he is being given the painkillers and may say something out of turn. So that leaves these two.

Iris stepped into the sunshine to greet her erstwhile allies, but a chill passed over her at the thought of the enormity of the task ahead and the tangled threads around it.

25

Hôtel *Auberge, 13 June 1870*

Edward looked at the clockwork worm he'd fashioned. It was more of a snake with a visible head and tail, but it was close enough. His niece's treatise on what worms did, how they dug, allowed him to remake one of the wax cylinders into a coating that would allow it to navigate tight spaces. The other would continue to record sounds, including echoes. Patrick had shown him how to rework the distress calling device into a noise-emitting tool that the worm would pause and use every so often depending on how they set the winding mechanism.

"You have a knack for this," the Irishman told him as they sat and admired their work. "You're wasted with sitting in that stuffy university office all day."

"Ah, but aether will always have a beloved place in my heart," Edward told him. "Think of how we could use that power potential combined with things like this—we could have machines that do complex calculations faster than the human mind, even mine, could. Perhaps they would learn to act on their own on a grander scale than the little clockworks."

"Now you're being irrational. What would we use them for?"

Edward opened his mouth to answer, but the sound of the door to Iris's room opening and closing made him pause. This was the conversation they'd had on the train, about the purpose of science and his scientific work. Perhaps he could invent a mechanism to help him understand women. But did he want to understand her? She had, after all, kept the secret of Lord Jeremy Scott's pursuit from him. Not that he had a right to know about it, but he thought they had something approaching an agreement. But he didn't want to have understanding with women, or at least he hadn't before meeting one as intelligent as she.

"This isn't helping," he said out loud, and Patrick looked at him quizzically. "Sorry," Edward told him, "my mouth skipped a few steps my mind made. My sister-in-law says this is a partic-ular problem of mine."

"I can see that. What isn't helping?"

"Wondering about her." Edward inclined his head toward Iris's room. "I should speak to her. Would you invite her to come talk to me? If you don't mind acting as her chaperon."

"Of course." He rose, opened the door, and stepped back. "Come in, Miss McTavish."

IRIS NEARLY JUMPED BACK when the tall Irishman opened the door. She'd forgotten how brawny he was, and his bulk filled the doorway.

"I'd like to speak with Professor Bailey," she said.

"O'course." He stepped back so she could pass by. *I'm glad he's with us even if I don't know what his motives are beyond helping Doctor Radcliffe.*

Edward sat by the window, the afternoon sun picking up

the red highlights in his chestnut hair. The golden thing on the table in front of him caught her attention first, and he smiled at her.

"Miss McTavish!" He rose, and she was relieved he seemed to do so with little effort. "I'm glad you came to see me." He had shadows under his eyes, although not as deep as the day before, but tightness around his mouth told her he experienced pain. It reminded her of the expression on her father's face in the latter days of his illness when he tried to put on a good front, but she could tell he hurt. And he hadn't called her Iris.

"I came as soon as I could," she said. "I understand that there's been some question of whether I'm engaged."

Now his lips curled into a genuine smile. "And you get right to the point, one of the best things about you. Please have a seat."

She sat across the table from him. The sun warmed her left cheek and hand like a couple of kisses. *Kisses? Where did that come from?* She closed the curtain. "Don't want to get freckles on one side of my face," she said.

"Understandably. Freckles on both sides would make more sense." He settled into his chair.

O'Connell stood on the other side of the room, and Iris understood he was there as chaperon and possibly as body-guard for the injured professor. Not that Edward needed one, at least not more than she did. Her hands slicked with sweat inside the stiff kid, so she removed her gloves and stretched her fingers in the sun. The words she wanted to say, that her father was dead and that they were all in danger from all sides, blocked the ones she needed to reassure him about the non-seriousness of her intentions regarding Jeremy Scott. Even though the lordling held the mortgage on her house now and would make it impossible for her to return to Huntington Village, the situation now held a much more trivial place in her mind. But she had to address it.

"I haven't been entirely honest with you." There, that was a good start. "And I know how much you value honesty because you've been lied to before, and it hurt, and hurting you is the last thing I want to do." *Please believe me.*

"I'm glad to hear that."

"Good." Iris leaned forward, but a sunbeam smacked her across the face, so she had to sit back. "Before we left England, I received a marriage proposal from one of my father's students. He's not so much interested in me as in having access to my father and his library, all the discoveries he's not been able to publish yet." *And never will, but I can't cry about that now.* "I turned him down, but he was determined. His footman seduced my maid Sophie into marrying him, and he sent his coach after me the morning we left."

"So your adventure started before we reached the airship. That's why you looked so disheveled on the train—he must have chased you."

"Yes, and since I had to do my own hair, it wasn't up securely or well to begin with."

Iris hoped the look on Edward's face was of admiration, not horror at what must seem like wanton circumstances. It all sounded so ridiculous when said out loud. But she had no control over any of it, as she couldn't determine his reaction. Whatever he felt, he appeared to be calculating, well, something.

"Do my circumstances fit any of your physics or aetherics models?" she asked after the silence stretched for several minutes.

"No, I'm trying to calculate what we need to do to keep you safe." He gazed at her with eyes that matched the color of the summer sky outside. "This was not supposed to be a risky adventure, but we didn't have all the variables, like Lord Scott's interest in you. It hardly seems fair that you, the woman, would face more inconvenience."

His expression softened, and he took one of her hands in both of his, which enveloped hers. It occurred to her that his hands had both strength and dexterity, and the heat that came to her cheeks wasn't from the errant sunbeam that found her again. What would it be like to entrust herself to them, to him?

"I don't mind. I'm happy to be on this adventure with you even if we've had our misadventures." She leaned forward, her eyes on his lips, and a cough from across the room reminded her they had a chaperon.

Edward started like he'd forgotten too, and sat back, leaving her hands in the false-seeming warmth of the sun on the table. "Now tell me, Iris," he said. "Are there any other variables I need to be aware of?"

Meaning, have I kept anything else from you? She glanced at the bedside table, where small apothecary bottles lay along with what looked like a child's manuscript complete with scrawled writing on the cover. "Are you in pain?" she asked.

"Not enough to count as a variable in our risk equation. Doctor Radcliffe keeps it under control with laudanum, and I'm taking a smaller dose every day."

Father always refused to take laudanum for his pain. He said it made his lips too loose, and he didn't need the world to have his secrets. "I see. I have nothing else to tell you at the moment." She rose. "If you'll excuse me, I need to prepare for this evening's gala."

He rose. "Thank you for being honest with me."

Iris nodded. Her tongue hurt from biting it to keep herself from telling him everything, but her father's words plus Bledsoe's description of how Edward had spilled the intent of their mission to Radcliffe under the influence of the French wine made her only nod in reply.

∽

"You're upset, Miss," Marie said after she opened the door.

Iris entered and sat on the chaise by the window, which had the shears pulled to so the sunlight didn't pour in like in Edward's room. She squeezed her lips and eyelids shut, but tears escaped anyway. Marie sat beside her and put a hand on her shoulder. It must be her imagination, but Iris thought she felt soothing warmth coming from her maid. Whatever it was, she brought herself under control.

"Thank you," she said, although she wasn't sure what for other than calming her. *But that's impossible. Emotions can't be transmitted through touch or the air.*

"*De Rien,*" Marie said, and the French words, *It's nothing,* seemed more appropriate than the odd English response of *You're welcome.* "What happened?"

"I had to lie to Edward. I told him about Lord Jeremy, but I didn't let him know about my father. He won't be stuck in his room much longer, and I'm concerned about the effects of the pain medication."

Marie nodded. "We had a girl at the theatre who broke her leg during a performance. The doctors gave her laudanum for her pain, and everything that went through her head came out of her mouth."

"But he hates it when people lie, and he held my hand." Iris hiccupped, and it felt like a prelude to sobs, so she clenched her teeth. *I will not cry, I will not cry.*

"Oooh la la," Marie said. "And does the Professor have nice hands?"

"I believe so. They seem strong and flexible. He had something on the table beside him, but I couldn't tell exactly what it was, only that he made the clockwork butterflies into something else that looks like a snake."

Marie squeezed Iris's shoulder and laughed.

"What's funny?"

"Oh, the combination of what you said."

Iris gave her a quizzical look. "I'm missing something."

"*Bien sur.* You are a proper English miss, after all. Don't worry about it."

"I won't." Irritation and the sense of being mocked replaced distress, and Iris stood. "Now please leave me be. I have to do some things I need privacy for."

Marie rose from the chaise and curtsied, all traces of levity gone and replaced by a properly deferential manner. "I'm sorry, and yes, Miss."

Iris moved to the bed after the door closed behind Marie. Her room was smaller than Edward's, so it was difficult to find the right spot to do what she needed, something away from the window but also not near the wall between the room and the hallway in case she accidentally said something and one of the little listening devices picked it up. She tossed her reticule and valise on the bed, removed her shoes, hopped in, and crawled toward the headboard. She pulled the curtains so she sat in a little room inside the room. A check under the covers and pillows revealed no hidden recorders, and the rebellious part of her smiled at the dishevelment of the bed Marie had so carefully made. *Not that there's any reason to rebel against her.* But she resented the implication she didn't belong to the world of sophisticated women or possess necessary but secret knowledge.

Iris pulled her father's pipe and pocket watch from her reticule and the poison hiding container from her valise. She laid them out on the bed in front of her and added the photograph of her father asleep—she couldn't accept he was dead in that picture—to the mix.

Is this what we come to, a collection of small things for a great man's life?

This time she allowed the tears to flow freely, and a memory nudged the edge of her consciousness.

range House, 5 May 1864

"You're not ready yet." The door to Iris's bedroom framed Adelaide, who stood in her opera clothing, her fur shawl over her shoulders in spite of the warm weather. The way she had it draped accentuated her décolletage, and she seemed to have put more care into her cosmetics than she usually did when Iris's father was away. Irvin was due back any day now, but the last train had come, so Iris—and apparently, Adelaide—guessed he wouldn't return until the next day at the soonest.

Iris sat on her bed in her wrapper, the hated corset beside her. "I'm not going. I can't breathe in that thing."

"But don't you want to see your friends? I know Lettie was looking forward to you coming to play while I'm out." Now it was the wheedling tone that made Iris hunch her shoulders. Next would come pleading, but lately her mother had progressed to yelling and tears. Iris steeled herself—if she made it through the storm, Adelaide would allow her to stay home by herself with the servants, although at this time of night, the only ones who stuck around were the scullery maid and Sophie.

Now the muscles in Adelaide's face hardened. *Yes, we're heading for Rageville, one more stop down the line.*

"Do what you want, you impossible child," she hissed. "Fine, stay with the servants. You'll be lucky if you end up being one of them someday since you don't care about being a lady."

"I don't want to be a lady," Iris said and made sure to infuse her tone with the same contempt she heard in her mother's voice. "Unlike you, I'm too smart for that. I want to be a scholar."

Adelaide crossed the room impossibly fast and raised her hand to slap Iris across the cheek. Iris tilted her head up—she refused to flinch away from her lying, deceitful mother—and braced herself for the blow. But before Adelaide's arm descended, a strong hand caught her wrist and gently lowered it.

"Papa!" Iris wanted to run to him, but he held his seething wife, whose expression now showed fear with a hint of guilt. At Iris's cry, contempt flooded over both emotions. Her mother's face had more terrifying expressions than an array of ceremonial masks, and Iris cringed against the headboard.

"What have we talked about with regard to speaking to your mother?" Irvin McTavish's voice held a new edge.

"Always speak in a respectful manner."

"You owe her an apology, then. It's not nice to flaunt your intelligence to insult someone."

Iris's cheeks felt like they had the slow flame of the furnace in them. "I'm sorry, Mama."

"Adelaide?" Irvin asked. "Your turn. I heard all of it."

"I apologize," Iris's mother said, but her tone contradicted the words.

"Good, now come. We need to talk."

Iris waited for them to leave and followed their shadows

down the hall to the parlor, where she sat outside the door. Their voices carried through the wood, which they later found was half-rotted on the inside.

"You can't carry on like this," Irvin said. "We have a child."

"We have a useless girl who won't wear a corset even though she became a woman last month." Adelaide's tone was now weary, and Iris curled her lip.

Of course she's going to sound put upon to get his sympathy.

"We have an intelligent daughter who doesn't find the same things important as you."

Iris preened. He did understand her.

"That said," he continued, "I don't care if you want to have dalliances while I'm away. God knows I haven't been an attentive husband, and you're like a child in your need for attention. But I don't want you leaving our daughter unprotected when you go to meet your lovers."

Adelaide's startled gasp echoed Iris's own, and Iris put a hand over her mouth.

"Leave one of the footmen here in the evening when you're out. I'll pay the overtime. And please be more discreet."

Now Iris huddled against the wall, confused and hurt, both for herself and her mother. What madness was this? Her father was supposed to go in, sweep Adelaide off her feet with professions of undying devotion, and win her affections back with promises he couldn't keep. Or kill her. Both were possibilities according to the novels Iris "borrowed" from her mother's bookshelves when Adelaide was out, and passionate murder didn't fit his personality. Nor was he the willingly cuckolded type, and his giving up disappointed Iris more than she thought. Logically, she could see how the arrangement would work, but she wanted a real family.

"Did you say Iris became a woman last month?" Irvin asked.

"Yes. She started her courses a few weeks ago."

Iris jumped up and raced down the hall so she would look

like she had just descended the stairs. Her father emerged from the parlor, and his face creased in a familiar smile when he saw her. In the waning light of the hallway, he appeared more tan than previously, his skin further dried by the sun. Iris always thought he looked older than her friends' fathers because of his job, but maybe it was also because part of him had left the youthful hope of love behind. She wondered what she could have done to stop it. Be a better daughter so Adelaide didn't get as frustrated? She tried so hard, but nothing she did seemed right, and she couldn't help getting dirty. There were so many interesting things to dig for in the garden.

"There you are," Irvin said. "I hope your mother didn't frighten you."

No, you did. But she didn't say anything, just shook her head.

"Good. Come into my office. I brought you back something you can keep for the weekend, but then I need to bring it to the University."

This got Iris's attention. She followed him into the office, where he had set his trunk and valise.

"How did you get home?" she asked. "You weren't on the last train. I waited until everyone got off and it pulled away."

He rubbed his eyes. "I'm sorry you were there so long, but at least the weather is nice. I needed to surprise your mother, so I got off at the previous station and hired a steamcart." He put his valise on his desk. It was streaked with dust, and Iris ran a finger through it and rubbed the powdery stuff between her thumb and forefinger. The stress had caused her hands to sweat, and the dirt turned into a slick paste, which she wiped on a handkerchief.

"The sands of the middle east are soft like powder," he said. "It's impossible to get off. When I think I've wiped it all away, it reappears."

The expression on his face told Iris he wasn't only talking about the sand, but she'd learned to stay quiet rather than ask for clarification and interrupt his musing. But he didn't say anything further. He rooted around in his luggage and pulled out a string and paper-wrapped object about the size of Iris's fist.

"Now remember what to do," he said.

"Don't open it like a Christmas present, but very slowly because what's inside might be fragile."

"Exactly. Good girl." He handed it to her, and she smiled at the praise. That was the difference between her and Adelaide—she'd learned to be gentle and slow and not barrel ahead.

Iris untied the string, and Irvin moved his valise so she could put the package on the desk. She unfolded and unrolled the paper as he'd shown her, with deliberation and care for whatever might be inside. At the center of it was an emerald ring, the stone large but the band small enough to fit her. She knew people in the past were smaller, but it seemed tiny even for them. She reached to touch it, but her father stopped her.

"Listen to it first," he said. "Every object has a story, as do the people who owned it. If you approach it with the attitude of wanting to hear what it says, it may tell you surprising things."

Iris nodded. She closed her eyes and pictured the ring. *Tell me your story.* A tingling sensation spread from the base of her spine to her skull and down to her fingers, which she wiggled. Her father didn't say anything, but she could tell he was right there beside her in case something went wrong. She picked up the ring and held it in her right hand. The stone added some heft, but the metal of the band was also surprisingly dense. Also startling, she could feel the triumph of the person who had rescued it from the sand in the corner of the temple they excavated, silence, and further back, the sense someone held a secret, and it was for their own survival and that of their family. At the hint of danger, Iris dropped the ring.

"What did you feel?" Irvin said.

"That it has secrets and belonged to someone in danger."

She frowned up at him. "But that doesn't make sense. How could a ring have feelings?"

The expression on his face mixed pride and fear. "Don't ever tell anyone about this special way you have of reading objects," he said. "I brought this ring to you because it belonged to a little princess who was killed, although we don't know why. Keep it with you this weekend and see if it tells you anything else."

Overwhelmed by the experience and the discovery that her parents' marriage was worse than she thought, Iris shook her head in spite of the curiosity that made her want to grab the ring, put it on, sleep with it, and find out everything it had to say. "I can't. It's too much."

"I understand. I'll keep it at the University, and you can visit it whenever you like." He wrapped it, and Iris slipped out of the office. She made it as far as the stairs before her shaking knees made her sit on the bottom step and curl around her aching middle.

"Are you all right?" her mother asked. She'd changed out of her opera clothes into her house dress.

Iris shook her head.

"Well, it is about time for you to start cramping again. Come on, I'll put you to bed and bring you a hot water bottle for your tummy." She held out her hand, and Iris took it. The look in her mother's eyes told Iris she, too, was disappointed by Irvin's surrender.

Now Iris looked at the objects in front of her. She'd forgotten that conversation or had blocked it out amid all the conflict with Adelaide and the realization her father had given up on their family. But one thing he said, one phrase, now stuck out in her mind as significant—not to leave her unprotected. Not alone, as one would say to a parent of any twelve-year-old, but unprotected. Was it possible his work had brought him and his family into danger even then? Was that why he pushed Adelaide and Iris away?

But why wait so long before telling me, before leaving these things for me to find? Her mother's words echoed in her head, that she was a girl, and girls didn't get to live in the world of excitement and danger like men did. *You were quite wrong, Mama, and now I have to know what he meant for me to discover.*

First she held Irvin's pipe. As in the museum, she got a strong image, almost a flashback, of holding it in her hand, its bowl warm, as she gazed up at the sky through the budding leaves of the trees in early spring. Then a horrible pain in her middle, and finally a clear image of the poison hiding device and counting seven scratches from the long one in the middle and twisting precisely there. She blinked and returned to the room, where the dimmed sunlight coming through the curtains seemed dark in comparison to her vision.

Seven, the Pythagorean number of virginity. The irony of it being on a courtesan's murder device didn't escape her.

Iris placed the cold pipe on the bed and picked up the pocket watch. This time she allowed the tears to slide from her eyes as the memories of all the times she'd seen her father holding it flashed through her brain. She closed her eyes and took a deep breath, willing it to tell her what it knew and trusting it would show her what was necessary.

First she—in her father's body—held the pocket watch in a classroom and looked at Lord Jeremy Scott, who gazed back with anger.

"This is not acceptable, and this isn't the last you've heard of me," Scott said before standing and storming out. Iris had the impression he'd been caught cheating on a test, and Irvin had kicked him out.

The image shifted, and now Irvin/Iris held the pocket watch

in the study at Grange House and looked at the time to make sure he wouldn't be late for his train. Ensuring the little piece of paper he hid in it didn't block the device, Irvin pushed the two parts of the poison holder together, and Iris saw it click at the third scratch from the other end of the one he'd counted to in the other vision.

Iris returned her attention to her cozy nook on the bed and listened for any of the little clockwork devices. Marie would be vigilant for them—as they all were now—but the little buggers were sneaky.

Satisfied nothing watched or listened to her, Iris picked up the courtesan's poison container. She hefted its light weight in her hand and thought about trying it under her breasts to see if it would fit but decided against it. That would be too bizarre, she thought, and what did she have to hide in it, anyway? Instead, she examined the scratches, which she'd thought the crystals in the volcano egg caused. The pattern Irvin studied jumped out at her, and she twisted the end at the seventh deep scratch forty-five degrees and pulled at the third one on the other side. The end popped off, and a small scroll of paper like the one she'd found in his shoe fell out.

The little paper tube felt so flimsy, but in spite of its non-permanent material, it emanated a sense of something weighty, a revelation she wouldn't be able to hide from once she uncovered it. It had the same air of danger that originally attracted her to the volcano egg that hid it. With trembling fingers, she unrolled it.

27

W ritten from the Grange House, 13 April 1870
       My dearest child,
       If you have found this note, it means that all my greatest hopes and all my deepest fears for you have come to pass. My hopes because it means you have manifested the gift I, too, was given, to be able to discern the secrets of objects. My fears because with this gift comes the potential to discover secrets others want to leave hidden.

You've heard the legend of the poor fisher boy who was murdered by the Pythagoreans for discovering that the square root of two is an irrational number, that is, not able to be described using simple number ratios. Although the legend itself is an exaggeration, the substance, of a cult willing to kill to keep its secrets and influence alive, is tragically true. I don't disparage Pythagoras himself—as with many religious leaders, his followers have twisted his teachings to achieve power for themselves. If you are reading this, I am dead, another of their victims. All I can say is I hope you are reading this safe in my study at home.

An opportunity will come your way, and it will be tempting. It will seem to be the key to unlocking all your hopes and wishes of *following me into this life of an interpreter of the past. Let it pass you by, child, for it is a trap to use your talents to gain power for others. As much as I wish it wasn't true for an intelligent woman, your safest course is to do as your mother always wished, to marry and have a family of your own, just not with Lord Jeremy Scott. My own desire for you is freedom and happiness, but not if it comes at the cost of your life. Some secrets are best left buried.*

Be well, my daughter.

Love, your father, Irvin McTavish

HÔTEL *AUBERGE*, 13 June 1870

A knock at the door startled Iris, and she reassembled the poison container as best she could. It hung open at one seam, but in her haste, she couldn't figure out how to make it all click together as it should. Her head reeled with confusion, and her heart ached at the thought she'd blundered into something over her head in spite of the nobility of her intentions. Why hadn't she researched the courtesan's poison hider in England? She could have taken a day to go to London, where she was sure she would've found examples in a museum. But how would she have known how to open it without the clues left by Irvin in his objects? Unless he counted on them being sent back upon his death, and he knew she would read them. And perhaps they would have been had she waited. But Cobb's offer came, and she jumped on it. Now she had one more reason not to trust the American.

No matter how she turned it over in her head, Irvin's letter didn't change the fact Iris needed funds to attend the University and run her household. She especially needed money to pay off the mortgage Lord Jeremy Scott now held on the house. No, if she wanted to have a chance at an independent life, she had to push on.

She hid the courtesan's case and pipe in the pocket of her valise and put her father's pocket watch in her own dress pocket. She lit his note with the flame of the lamp and allowed it to burn in the fireplace before answering the door.

"Are you all right, Miss?"

Iris stepped back to admit Marie. "Yes. Is it already time for me to start getting ready?"

"Yes, you've been napping for an hour and a half. I didn't want to wake you, but—oh! Is something burning?"

"It's nothing. Now please make me some tea, and we can begin."

But begin what?

BY THE TIME Marie had laced Iris into the evening corset, which plumped up what little she had to the point she thought her ribs would crack and her breasts would pop, put her hair up in an elaborate style topped with a jaunty mini-cap with feathers, and squeezed her into the light purple gown she'd gotten from Madame St. Jean, Iris barely felt like herself. She certainly didn't recognize this woman who gazed back at her from the mirror. Marie also used some cosmetics, very subtly applied, to make Iris's eyes stand out and cheeks appear higher.

"Voila," Marie said and stepped back. "You look like a fairy tale princess."

"I feel like a princess in danger of fainting. Does this thing need to be so tight?"

"If you make a good impression on the Marquis, he's more likely to let you peruse his collection. Or have you forgotten why you're going?"

"No, I remember, but I feel the pressure of this thing in my brain. No wonder my fellow women say and do such stupid things."

Marie shook her head, but she laughed. "The world would be better off with more like you, Miss. Now let me change into my formal maid attire, and we can go shock Mister Bledsoe."

Iris pretended to admire herself in the mirror while watching Marie dress. How did she do it, assume the role in which she wanted others to see her? She used the barest of cosmetics, but when finished, Marie looked dull of eye and intellect. She must be a fantastic actress, indeed.

Bledsoe met them in the lobby of the hotel, and the look he gave Iris told her Marie worked her magic.

"You look lovely," he said. "Not at all like the prudish miss I've had to endure all day."

"And you are as much of a boor as ever even if you do acquit yourself well in your formal attire." He did look dashing, she had to admit, in his white tie and tails.

"Miss McTavish!"

Iris turned her head toward the cry and saw Edward seated at a table in the hotel restaurant with Doctor Radcliffe and Patrick O'Connell. She found herself moving toward him before she recognized she'd turned in that direction.

The three men stood, and Edward clasped her hands. "You look quite lovely."

Coming from his mouth, it sounded so much more genuine than Bledsoe's compliment, and Iris knew it wouldn't be followed by an insult. "You look well yourself."

"The doctor says I can start getting out and about as long as I don't strain myself."

"Yes," Radcliffe said. "He has made rapid improvement, particularly this afternoon."

"And I have a present for you," Edward told her. "I'll give it to you tomorrow."

"I look forward to it."

Marie plucked at Iris's sleeve. "The Maestro is getting impatient. He asks that you remember he has a performance this evening, and although they cannot start without him, he doesn't want to keep our host waiting."

"Right." Iris curtsied to the gentlemen and smiled at Edward before following Marie out to the Marquis's coach.

EDWARD WATCHED Iris walk out of the lobby. Her purple silk-clad figure stood out among the blacks and darker colors of the other visitors. Like her namesake, she appeared both vibrant and delicate, and he hoped that odious Lord Jeremy Scott wasn't around. He would have to trust Johann to keep her safe, but his friend didn't have the reputation one would like for a chaperone. At least the capable Marie accompanied them.

"How are you feeling?" Radcliffe asked for the hundredth time, but this time Edward suspected the question was regarding his emotional as well as physical health.

"Tired but well." Edward picked at the salad in front of him. It had corn on it. Who put corn on a salad? Apparently the Parisians did. At least it came with that crusty bread he'd grown rather fond of, but he found himself wishing he could go to the chateau with Iris and the others.

"She looked grown-up," O'Connell said.

"Yes," Edward agreed. "She is quite a striking young lady." *But I like her better when she's puzzling out a problem or challenging me about science. Then she's really Iris.* He stood. "I'm going with them."

"You're doing what?" Radcliffe asked.

"I'm going to the gathering at the chateau tonight." He placed his napkin on the table. "There are dangerous men afoot, and the more protection Iris has, the better. Johann can hold his own, but not if he's outnumbered."

O'Connell stood and put a gentle hand on Edward's shoulder. Edward sank back into his chair under its weight.

"If you're that concerned about them, I'll tag along," the Irishman said. "Those Parisian lords don't let anyone in without an invitation, but if I'm there to help with the steamcoach, they'll think nothing of it." He strode off before Edward could protest.

"He's right," Radcliffe said. "I'm pleased with your progress, but I don't know that you're quite up for fisticuffs, or whatever you English call it."

Edward turned to him with a frown, and he saw the doctor regarded him with both amusement and respect. "But I could be ready for more physical activity soon?" Not that he ever anticipated needing to box anyone—he preferred to engage on an intellectual level, where he knew he had the advantage over most men.

"Yes." Radcliffe smiled behind the glass of wine he lifted to his lips and sipped. "Miss McTavish's visit this afternoon seems to have done wonders for you. Plus she left us with an interesting puzzle to solve."

"I like puzzles," Edward said. "Is it another clockwork?"

"Better—it's poison."

IRIS SAW the light and felt the pulsing energy from the Marquis de Monceau's estate long before the chateau itself emerged from behind the trees along the long drive. Built of white stone in a classical style, it blazed with both gas and electric light, giving the flat walls a rounded appearance depending on where the shadows fell.

"He likes a good *trompe l'oeil*," Bledsoe told her. "I'm playing Bach tonight, so he wanted to make it look like a German castle."

"Did Bach live in a German castle?" Iris asked.

"Probably not, but the Marquis has an interesting way of

thinking about things. Don't let him throw you off from what you're supposed to accomplish."

"I know my mission." Iris tried not to move much so as not to wrinkle her dress before they arrived, but she found herself restless. What was wrong with the place? It felt like something was trapped in there and wanted to escape, but it didn't know how or why.

The steamcoach pulled into the circular drive in line behind other steam-powered vehicles and the more traditional horse-drawn carriages. Some of the animals, perhaps not accustomed to the growing technology, rolled their eyes and snorted. Or maybe they sensed the same thing Iris did, that something coiled in the middle of the chateau, stirring and ready to wake and strike. The thoughts came to her mind before she could stop them with her usual ability to concentrate on solving the problem at hand.

I'm willing to face the Pythagorean Cult and the Clockwork Guild, poison and spy devices, but this might be too much.

A weight on her shoulder made Iris look at Marie, who once again somehow projected calm through her touch. "Whatever it is, Mademoiselle, you can handle it."

Iris tried to smile, and the muscles in her face relaxed so she could give Marie a genuine, albeit small, grin. "I'm glad you're here. Something is in there."

"I can feel it too."

"Whatever are the two of you talking about?" But Bledsoe fidgeted with the lock on his violin case. Their steamcoach pulled up to the front door, which was framed like a Greek temple with columns and a lintel. Iris adjusted her elbow-length purple silk gloves and focused on the weight of the amethyst bracelet around her wrist, a present from Lucille. The footman opened the door, and Iris and Marie accompanied Bledsoe into the house.

The bracelet slid away from her wrist over the slippery

glove when the marquis lifted Iris's hand to his lips. "Welcome to my home, Mademoiselle McTavish. You grace it with your beauty."

Iris searched his eyes for some sign of sincerity, but all she found was flirtatiousness. What sort of man must he be to harbor something not evil, but wild and trapped, in his home? Or perhaps his reaction to it was at the root of his flirtatiousness. If there was anything Iris learned on this strange journey, it was how people responded in less than logical ways to their emotions.

"The pleasure is mine," she said and curtseyed when he relinquished her hand.

"Allow me to finish welcoming my guests, and I shall be happy to show you my collection. Your maid can join the others in the kitchen. I'm sure my housekeeper can find something to keep her occupied."

Iris's throat itched with panic at the thought of being separated from both Marie and Bledsoe, as annoying as he was.

"Thank you, but I would prefer to keep her with me as my chaperone since Maestro Bledsoe will be occupied."

"Of course." But his smile dimmed.

They moved through the hall, down a wide flight of white marble stairs, and into the grand ballroom, which already filled with the murmur of voices and the clinking of glass, both from the champagne glasses being passed and the large chandelier overhead, which shimmered with a thousand rainbow sparks. The stage at the far end was set up for a small ensemble and faced chairs arrayed in rows. There were too many seats to count with a glance.

"How many people are attending this *small* private performance?" Iris asked Bledsoe. He emanated irritation. Had she done something offensive to their host by insisting Marie stay with her? She had to preserve her reputation, after all. Even if the French were looser about such things, one never knew when one might encounter an acquaintance unexpectedly, and rumor of a dalliance with an unmarried Marquis would skewer her credibility as a young woman of virtue. Although she found the societal rules to be annoying and unnecessary, Iris didn't want to deal with the inconvenience of being shunned, either.

"Enough," Bledsoe said. "By the way, do be sure to watch yourself with Monceau. As I said, he's a consummate flirt."

"I'm trying," she replied and plucked a shallow glass of champagne off the tray of a passing waiter. Now that she had it, she didn't know what to do with it since she didn't drink spirits, but perhaps it would help her to fit in amid the swirling, silk-clad society members. He nodded and stalked off, presumably to warm up for the performance and run through some things with the other musicians.

Marie hovered unobtrusively behind Iris, a feat since Marie topped her in height by at least half a foot. Iris pretended to sip her drink and watched the other guest's faces as they saw Marie, made some gesture of surprise at the maid being with her mistress rather than with the other servants, and then, with dull eyes, looking away and resuming whatever conversation was to be had. Iris recalled how Marie pulled on the identity like a mask. How did she do it? And could she teach Iris?

Something shifted in the room, and Iris placed her glass with empties on another waiter's tray. Marie caught her elbow so Iris wouldn't stumble to her knees.

"Did you feel that?" Iris asked.

"Yes, but no one else seems to have." The mask slipped to reveal Marie's concern.

"What do you think it's from? It feels like some sort of ancient energy."

"You're the archaeologist."

"Right, I am. Let's go find it." She didn't want to go find anything. She wanted to call the steamcoach and have it bring her back to the Hôtel Auberge, where she could see what

Edward invented and spend the evening in his eccentric but safe company.

"Don't be afraid," Marie said.

"Right. There's an ancient something here big enough to cause the entire ballroom to feel like it moved, and you're saying there's nothing to worry about." But her feet carried her toward the source of the feeling.

28

C *hâteau Monceau, 13 June 1870*
They left the ballroom and moved past servants who scurried along with single-minded purposes, one with a fresh tray of champagne, another with a tray of hors d'oeuvres. No one challenged the two women or asked where they went. It seemed that whatever the energy was, it ground people into their preferred mindsets.

Iris stopped and flattened herself against the wall. She focused on the cold, hard surface pressing through her bustle and the thin fabric over her shoulders, and her mind cleared. Her favorite mode was that of problem-solver, and from the conversation she'd overheard between Marie and Lucille, she knew Marie enjoyed being a coconspirator.

"We have to stop and think this through," Iris said. "What if it wants us to go in there?"

"It's bigger than both of us, but we need to know what it is, so what choice do we have?" Marie asked, but she blinked and the foggy look on her face cleared. "But you're right. It's clever and is drawing us right to it."

"Right." Iris pushed herself away from the wall and almost into a server with a tray of canapés. He looked at her, startled.

"You shouldn't be in this hallway, Mademoiselle. The women's powder room is on the other side of the ballroom."

"*Merci*, but the Marquis wanted me to take a look at his collection of ancient artifacts and Renaissance art," Iris told him with her most beguiling smile. "Perhaps you could direct me to where they are?"

The look the man gave her made Iris have new sympathy for how the chicken in the coop felt as it was selected for that night's dinner. "I'm sure the marquis would prefer to show you himself."

"Oh, but we would be so very grateful if you could tell us." Marie stepped past Iris and gave the man a smile with no sweetness and all spice. He drew himself up with attempted haughtiness, but the tray trembled. Now Iris wanted to look away from what seemed to be headed toward a very private moment.

"It's down this corridor and through the family hall," he said, and sweat rolled down his bald head.

"*Merci*," Marie purred.

He nodded and walked away quickly enough for his footsteps to echo in the corridor but slowly enough that the tray maintained its horizontal alignment.

Iris turned toward Marie. "Well done, Fantastique," she said.

"Don't call me that. Come on, if we're going to wander into the lion's den, I'd prefer it to be with one predator. Don't tell me you didn't see how that man looked at you. The marquis has some interesting plans for you, it seems."

"Right."

They followed the man's directions and walked into another room as large as the ballroom, but with books lining the walls. The dim light revealed the presence of statues, and the smells of dust and old paper made Iris breathe deeply—*this is a place I could belong.* But the skin across the backs of her hands tightened, and her fingertips tingled. Marie went around to the lamps and turned them to full brightness, and Iris caught her breath.

At least a dozen *kouros* and *kore* statues like the one that had waved to her at the Louvre stood in various alcoves and on the balcony above her. A large painting of Eros, the son of the goddess of love, and Psyche, the woman who dared to fall in love with him, hung over the fireplace. They clasped each other in a tight embrace. The artist had rendered Eros's feather wings and Psyche's butterfly ones with great care, almost more so than the two people.

Marie walked to one of the male statues and poked him in the lower abdomen. "These Greek boys are a bit skinny for my taste," she said.

Iris tried to smile, but she couldn't shake the feeling of being watched from all sides. *What sort of place is this?*

The plaintive sound of a violin warming up in a minor key made Iris jump. The simple scales moved through the air and caressed her ears like a dying lover's touch, and she wanted to lean into it. She opened her eyes, which she hadn't realized she closed, to see the statues moving their arms. Her thoughts raced ahead of her rising panic.

It's like the museum statue, they must be part of some larger piece.

"Oh, getting fresh, are we?" Marie leaned into the statue she'd teased, and his arms moved in and out from their hinges on the elbows, tapping her bustle. "Cheeky!"

"Marie, be careful." Iris held on to the back of a chair to steady herself against the sensation of the room moving around her and the floor beneath her. She couldn't see anything, but the air pressed on her eardrums. She wanted to analyze it, to figure it out, but it defied explanation.

Marie stepped back, but the statue clasped her to it. "Um, Iris?"

The doors slammed shut, and the locks clicked into place.

Iris ran to Marie and reached for the statue, but she paused. It emanated some sort of power she could feel through her gloves. What if touching it put her in some sort of trance like the statue at the museum had, and she was unable to defend herself from whatever trapped them in the room?

Now the music went into more complicated passages—Bach—and the statues turned their heads toward Iris. She knew their half smiles, called Archaic smiles due to the time period, were more due to the style of sculpture, but their attitude of vague amusement added to their sinister air.

"Uh oh," she said.

"What have you done, Mademoiselle?" a voice from the balcony above them asked.

Iris looked up to see the Marquis gazing down at them. Or maybe down the front of her dress. She resisted the urge to hunch her shoulders or cross her arms over her chest—there was no reason to let him know how uncomfortable she was.

"Is this your game?" she asked. "Bring young ladies into the room to see your collection, then catch them when they swoon in fear over the statues' movements?"

"I do no such thing. This is the first time I have seen them act like this. They perform the movements from the great automaton of—"

"Yes, I know, Magna Graecia," Iris said. Her hand reached for the statue holding Marie almost of its own volition, and she kept having to pull it back.

"Yes, clever girl." The Marquis descended the stairs. "But do you know where in Magna Graecia?"

Iris watched him warily. "No."

"Several years ago, a cache was found in Metapontum."

"Metapontum? Where the cult of Pythagoras was destroyed?"

"The very same. Those who discovered these statues said they were most likely part of a temple display, but the temple wasn't found." Now he stood beside Iris. She found his speech to be at odds with his foppish appearance.

"Iris," Marie held her hand out. "Please get me away from this thing."

"Perhaps if we each took an arm?" The Marquis gestured to the statue that held Marie. "We can gently pry it apart, and your maid can escape."

Marie mumbled a word outside of the finishing school French canon and said, "I don't care if you rip its arms off. Get me out of here."

"Oh, we cannot damage such a valuable artifact, Mademoiselle," the Marquis told her. "I care deeply for my statues and would not risk them for anything."

Iris hesitated. "I can't touch it." *If I do, I'll be sucked into the past, and all will be lost.*

"Yes, you can." Marie grasped her wrist. "I'll hold on to you, keep you here."

Iris's mouth dropped open. "What do you mean?" *How do you know?*

"No time. Please do it quickly. It's tightening its hold on me, and my back will break."

Iris gulped a deep breath and placed her hands on one of the statue's arms while Monceau grabbed the other one. Marie held Iris's wrist, and Iris focused on the feeling of the other woman's fingers digging into her own flesh, but she fell into the past anyway.

~

THE SMELL of stone and dirt permeated the air, and Iris

coughed. Or the body Iris inhabited did, but the dust that clogged her lungs wouldn't be expelled, not right away. She held on to the same statue she'd been holding at the chateau moments ago, but this time she held it steady while another worker made slight adjustments to its position according to the angle of the sun.

This was the same temple she'd seen as the slave girl, but earlier in its construction. The dust swirled in the shafts of sunlight coming through open spots where windows would be, and painters and sculptors worked on the friezes and other decorations. A melodic language, a mix of French, Spanish and Italian, eddied around her, and she picked up a few words. One of them was Roma, and it was accompanied by a gesture and facial expression that told her that must be where they were. The position of the windows meant this place was underground, and she searched her memory but could not recall anything in her father's journals about a below-ground temple, although there were speculations of one in Rome.

Stinging pain across her back returned her attention to what she was doing, and she hoped her attempts to orient herself hadn't caused a slave to be punished. How much did she affect the past when she visited? She held fast to the statue, which didn't give her any impressions, perhaps because she was already in one?

Her partner, an older man, nodded, and she let go and stepped back into the present.

~

Now Marie clasped Iris's wrist in a stone grip that threatened to crush the bone.

"Let go," Iris said and opened her eyes to see the statue leering at her with a smile wider than it should have. Stone dust swirled in her peripheral vision in time to the music coming from the ballroom.

Now she felt a tug at her waist, and Marie said, "It let me go, but it grabbed you so fast, I didn't see it, Mademoiselle."

Iris tried to pull her wrist out of the statue's hand, but it held firm. So did her presence in the past, which overlaid her view of the present such that the temple workers moved like transparent ghosts about their tasks.

"What do you want of me?" she asked the statue.

The words echoed in her mind. *"For our secrets to remain hidden, lest you bring destruction upon the world."*

"What kind of destruction?"

"The death of the free will granted to every man at the hands of the forces of chaos that birthed Aether and Eros. Chaos awaits."

"Big words coming from a statue installed in the temple of a violent cult by slaves." She leaned over and felt around for something, clasping a hammer. She briefly wondered how she was able to manipulate something from the past, but she had to act quickly. She brought it up and smashed the *kouros's* wrist, and its hand fell apart, freeing hers. She stepped back and dropped the hammer. When it hit the stone floor of the temple with an echoing clang, her vision of the past disappeared, leaving her in the library with a stunned marquis and maid.

"My statue!" The Marquis de Monceau pushed past her and ran his finger over the marble splinters. "How did you do that? Why did you have to break it?"

"Perhaps it was already weakened," Iris suggested. Had he not seen the hammer? "As for why I had to do something, it was going to crush my wrist. I suggest you let these things go to the Louvre, Marquis."

The rest of the statues returned to their typical postures, and Iris glanced at the painting of Eros and Psyche. Had the latter's butterfly wings, which were painted in brilliant shades of purple, moved?

"What sort of spirit do you harbor in your house, Marquis?"

"I don't know what you're talking about." He knelt on the floor and tried to pick up the pieces of the statue's hand. "You're speaking gibberish, and I would thank you to leave me be. Haven't you done enough without bringing talk of spirits into it?"

"Your statue attacked us," Marie said. "We were defending ourselves."

A rustling sound brought Iris's attention back to the painting.

"Can you hear it?" Iris asked.

"Only through my connection to you," Marie replied. "But whatever it is, it's big."

They backed away together until their bustles met the library doors, which remained locked fast. The marquis now stood by the statue and tried to piece its hand back together in his handkerchief.

Iris knocked on the door. "Hello," she called. "Can someone out there hear us? We're trapped."

But no reply came, only the jaunty sound of Bach played by Johann and the ensemble.

"Everyone is probably in the ballroom or kitchen," Marie murmured.

"Let's think this through." Iris tried to clear her head of the impressions of the past to focus on the present. "If this creature wanted to harm us, it would have done so by now."

"Or it was waiting to see what the statues would do."

"Good point."

The marquis looked at them, his eyes hard. "You have ruined him," he said. "My poor little *kouros*. This one was my favorite."

"I'm truly sorry," Iris said. "But he wouldn't let go of me."

"No, Mademoiselle, that was your imagination running away with you. It happens to young women here in the library with all these ancient things whispering their secrets. But it is impossible for a marble statue to grab something."

"He's mad," Marie murmured. "Or maybe we are."

Iris bit back a sarcastic reply and tried to allow the facts of the situation to click into place—like the parts of a clockwork, which would be meaningless separately but made complete sense as a whole. The marquis responded to whatever the spirit of the place was driving him to do, and somehow the music made it worse. The dominant piece of artwork was a painting of Psyche and Eros, favorites of the Pythagoreans, and the statues came from one of their temples, as yet undiscovered in Rome. Meanwhile, the marquis advanced on them with a crazed gleam in his eye, and they stood with their backs to a locked door.

Or was it? A click beneath Iris's bustle warned her to straighten before the door opened behind her, but a strong hand on her back steadied her anyway.

"You're needed back at the hotel," Patrick O'Connell said.

"Yes, go." The marquis clutched the statue's ruined hand in his own. "You are no longer welcome in Paris. If I hear you are in the city tomorrow morning, I cannot guarantee your safety."

29

Hôtel Auberge, 13 June 1870

Doctor Radcliffe dropped a solution of foul-smelling chemicals on the handkerchief that had held the poison case, and he and Edward watched to see what colors it would turn. Both men jumped when the door to the room flew open.

"Where is she?" Johann looked around, wild-eyed. He carried his violin case in one hand and ran his other through his hair.

"Where is who? Iris?" Edward rose. "What happened?"

"I don't know. I was playing with the other musicians in the ballroom when she and Marie ran through the room, up the stairs, and into the front hall. By the time the piece finished, I couldn't find them."

"Did you check their room?" Radcliffe asked.

"If they're in there, they're not answering."

"Where's O'Connell?" Edward asked. "He was supposed to be there to protect her. What if Scott got hold of her?"

"I don't know," Johann said, "but we need to pack to leave. She managed to break the hand off one of the marquis's statues, and he's in a snit over it. He's powerful enough to make staying in Paris very unpleasant."

"Does that mean we'll never be able to come back?" Edward had looked forward to exploring the city with Iris when he was well.

"No, he's leaving for his summer home on the coast tomorrow afternoon, and he'll be over the incident by the time he returns, especially if we can manage to find a good archaeological gift for him."

"I will not entrust anything of historical significance to that man." Iris strode in followed by Marie and Patrick. Edward walked to her and took her hands in his. Her fingers trembled, as did her lip. He resisted the urge to kiss her and lend her his strength, such as it was.

"Are you all right?" he asked. "I was worried."

"I'm fine, although shaken up. It's been a strange evening."

"Where were you?" Johann asked Marie.

"Talking to my mother," she said. "She is sending someone within the hour to get us out of Paris quickly. I think the marquis meant to have us attacked—he's angry about his statue —but Mister O'Connell's clever driving got us away."

"What?" asked Johann. "Do you know where we're going next? And what happened?"

"Rome," Iris said. "We're going to Rome. As for what happened, I'm not sure." She glanced to the side, and Edward felt the weight of her secrets.

"I thought our next stop was Florence?"

"No, it will need to be Rome. There's a site where the Pythagoreans had a temple. I don't know exactly where, but I know it was underground." She lifted her gaze to Edward. "I wish there was some way we could explore without digging."

"Ah." With reluctance, he let go of her hands and walked to the table where he and Radcliffe had been doing their experiments.

"There's nothing on the handkerchief or the case," Radcliffe said. "Whatever killed Anctil, he must have ingested it at breakfast or sometime after."

"Very well." Edward reached past the table to his valise, from which he drew the clockwork worm. He turned and presented it to Iris. "Here's the present I promised. It can crawl into small crevices, but it will emit its capture alarm sound and record the presence of echoes. That way you can see if there's a large chamber."

The delighted look on Iris's face made his troubles and the few times the thing had tried to split his eardrums with its whistle worth it. "Oh, thank you!" She threw her arms around him, and he embraced her back.

"This is all lovely," Johann said, "but we should get going."

"Yes, Mama will be sending her coach for us in half an hour." Marie glanced at the clock. "Pack quickly."

With reluctance, Edward pushed Iris away. "We need to keep you safe. Go, and we'll talk on the way to Rome. I want to know what happened."

IRIS WOULD HAVE to lie to him again. The thought beat in her head as she and Marie threw whatever they could into trunks. She didn't have the chance to change, and she knew she'd feel ridiculous, not to mention uncomfortable, wearing her formal clothing to travel.

"Mademoiselle?" Marie asked.

"Yes?"

"Have you always been able to do that, to see things when you touch different objects?"

Iris couldn't lie anymore. Besides, Marie obviously had been able to sense some of what Iris could do and try to keep her from falling into the past.

"Since I left childhood," Iris said.

"So when you touched my brooch…"

"I could tell something happened to you with Parnaby Cobb. But remember, I'm not very knowledgeable about certain things."

"Probably more than you allow yourself credit for." Marie closed the trunk Lucille had sent them back with. "This should do it for the new clothing. Do you have your valise?"

"Yes." Iris wanted to ask Marie about her special ability, which Iris suspected had something to do with making people believe things about her. "What about you?"

"I have my valise."

"No, I mean, what can you do that no one else can? I know it's something because of whatever your mother did to us."

"I am very good at disguising myself," Marie told her. "My mother swears it's more, but I'm a good actress, that's all. I believe you have something special you can do, but I'm a plain person like anyone else."

Iris doubted that, but there was no time to argue. Soon they were in the Théâtre Bohème carriage headed toward the train station south of the city to catch the morning train to Rome. Iris hoped their plan to bypass the main city stations would avoid the marquis's men and Jeremy Scott as well as anyone else who might follow them. But in the confusion and rush to leave, had anyone been on guard and searching for the clockwork butterflies? She certainly hadn't.

"So what happened?" Bledsoe asked and snapped Iris's attention back to the inside of the carriage. "I want to know what you did to anger our Parisian patron to the point he kicked me out before I finished my concert. A concert, by the way, he's been after me to give for years."

Iris glanced around their conveyance. It was more comfortable than the claptrap coach they'd taken to Paris, but they sat in close quarters, and all eyes were on her. She noticed

Radcliffe gazed at her with the same expectation as the others, and she remembered his particular interest in diseases of the mind. Would he think her insane?

"I can't explain it," she said.

"Then describe it." Bledsoe's tone had an edge of impatience.

"Leave off the lass," Patrick said. "Whatever it was, it bothered her."

"Did he hurt you?" Edward asked. "You've been rubbing your wrist."

Iris hadn't removed her gloves, but she suspected that when she did, she would find bruises where the statue grabbed her. "The marquis didn't, no." She braced herself. As much as Bledsoe annoyed her, she could tell them what happened outside of her mind, at least where Marie could back up her story. She described the statues moving in response to the music and trapping Marie, then her. As for using the hammer from the past, she said she managed to twist free, and the statue's hand came apart when she did.

"And that's what angered the marquis. He didn't believe me that the statue grabbed me and wouldn't let go, so I had to break it to get free. Monsieur Anctil told me the marquis refused to house the statues at the Louvre for fear of them getting broken on the journey from Monceau to downtown."

"And can Marie verify all this?" asked Bledsoe. "And are you all right?"

Marie nodded. "It all happened as she said, and I'm fine. She and the marquis stopped the statue from squeezing me to death."

"So the frequency of the music made the statues move," Edward said. "And the more complicated the music, the more movement. How? Aren't they all of a piece?"

"No," Iris said. "Sometimes if they didn't have the right size block of stone, they would attach pieces to each other with iron joints."

Edward nodded. "But that doesn't explain the one statue acting unlike the others unless it was put together differently."

"Did you consider there might be somethin' else to it?" asked O'Connell. "Somethin' otherworldly, so to speak?"

"Patrick, we've talked about this," Radcliffe said. "There's a rational explanation for everything even if we haven't figured it all out yet."

"Fine," O'Connell huffed. "Have you considered a force that —for now—defies rational explanation?"

"No," Edward told them. "I refuse to consider the possibility. Everything is rational, and we have the tools to investigate it. Perhaps it was something about the place where the statue stood or the orientation relative to the sound. Or something about the room caused the sound waves to eddy there and nowhere else."

"Like the square root of two and Pi?" Iris couldn't resist asking. "Those aren't rational."

"Cheeky girl." But he didn't look offended. "Now you're mixing up your terms."

Iris and Marie exchanged looks. Iris didn't know about Bledsoe, but it seemed that O'Connell may believe in her special abilities. Edward and Radcliffe never would, and the thought of having to keep that part of herself from Edward saddened her.

EACH OF THE miles between Paris and Rome pinched Iris in her dress corset. She knew Edward must feel worse, but he didn't complain. Instead, he questioned her and Marie over and over about the statue's attack in the library and had them draw a rough plan of how everything was laid out in the room on the back page of a booklet he had in his valise.

"There has to be some reason that one acted as it did," he said. "Tell me how the bookshelves were arranged."

"We have no more information to give you," Marie told him. "You will have to make do with what you have."

They didn't have a private car on the train but did have a compartment to themselves. Each of them took turns sleeping while the others watched over their luggage and looked out for spy devices.

"Can you tell me anything else about the poison that killed Anctil?" Iris asked Radcliffe when they were both awake keeping watch. "Other than that he likely ingested it at breakfast."

"From what you described, belladonna seems the most likely culprit. Its berries have been blamed for several accidental deaths, and in a high enough dose, it will kill a man in hours."

Coldness settled into the pit of Iris's stomach. She recalled Anctil's fondness for the jam and how he'd alone eaten it. "I doubt this was accidental."

He didn't argue and left her to her thoughts. One—what if she had put jam on her croissant?—particularly disturbed her.

Nothing odd happened, and they arrived in Rome in the late afternoon.

Although they arrived two days early, the hotel Parnaby Cobb's agent had secured for the group in Rome was willing to accommodate them and had an extra room for O'Connell and Radcliffe. The money hadn't run out yet, but the group still had no word from Cobb, nor did they know how the airship had fared under the attack of the Clockwork Guild.

Iris left Radcliffe and the other men to settle Edward in his room. She and Marie took turns bathing, and once she was out of her dress clothing and into her comfortable-if-slightly-wrin-

kled walking dress, a certain restlessness possessed her. She
needed to stop thinking about how close she'd come to her own
dramatic death in the Louvre, and she was happy to follow the
signal of something else that tickled the back of her brain.

The unassuming hotel had been a stopping point for travelers for centuries, the clerk had proudly told them, and much
of the original stone made up the walls, although some had
been destroyed in an effort to modernize the building with
steam-powered indoor plumbing and electricity.

"What do you feel?" Marie asked.

Checking in and using Cobb's voucher had reminded Iris
that Marie was not necessarily to be trusted, although she'd
saved Iris's life and had been mostly kind to her. She hated to
admit it, but she now depended on the maid, and she appreciated Marie knowing of her ability but not judging her or
treating her any differently because of it.

"It feels like something important is very close, as if the
music from last night sank into my bones, and now it echoes
around me. I need to find what will give me peace." The words
didn't make complete sense to her as she said them, but that
was as close as she could get. The volcano egg had called her
with a similar feeling, but this was on a much grander scale.

"Perhaps we should take a walk."

"Should we bring one of the men with us?" Iris asked. "Oh,
let's see if Edward is up for it. He probably needs to stretch his
legs."

30

Hotel Segreto, Rome, 14 June 1870

Edward had never thought he'd be so far away from his home and family, but on this lovely Italian evening with the Clockwork Guild and other troubles so far behind them, he enjoyed it. The determined woman beside him with her hand on his arm didn't hurt, either. She had the same look on her face that he'd felt on his own when closing in on a discovery, and he thrilled at the thought they were so alike in yet another way.

"Are you ready?" she asked. They stood by the front door of the hotel and watched the chaos outside. There was a square beyond the street, and in the middle, a large stone structure with two arches.

"So explain to me how you know we're close to something?"

She gave him a wistful glance. "The hotel was built during the same time period the Pythagoreans were active here, although secretly, in the first century AD. There are symbols and characteristics that have not been obfuscated by time and renovation, indicating that there is something important close by."

Marie looked at Iris sideways. "You're sure?" she asked.

Iris grinned at Marie. "A good archaeologist always has multiple sources of proof for her speculations."

"That's smart," Edward put in.

Iris squeezed his arm, and he preened.

"Let's get this over with," Johann said. He'd offered to accompany them and escorted Marie, who was not dressed as a maid.

Like Paris, Rome was busy, but with a more frenetic air. Small steam-powered vehicles that carried one to two passengers, like small horses but with wheels, zipped in and out among the carriages and steamcarts, which didn't seem to follow any kind of traffic logic with regard to lane or direction. The people expressed themselves more than the Parisians, and Edward had to admit to some anxiety at these non-reserved individuals who said as much with their hands as with their eyes and mouths, and a lot with all of their parts. And he'd thought the Parisians were open about their feelings.

"What are they saying?" Iris asked Marie after they'd passed their second shouting steamcart driver.

"Mostly to get out of the way. We'll have to be careful crossing the street."

They made it across with the help of a soldier who looked like he was dressed in a French uniform. Marie thanked him with a *"Merci."*

"Why are there French soldiers?" Iris asked.

"There is a garrison stationed here," Marie said. "It's hard to tell, but there is some tension between the new Italian government and the Pope over where his territory ends and the city begins."

Once they stepped onto the square, a certain weight settled over the quartet. The arched structure loomed large ahead of them.

"What is it?" Johann asked.

"It's the Porta Maggiore," Iris said. "It was built in the first century AD as part of the aqueduct system and then incorporated into the city walls in the third century."

Her hand trembled on Edward's arm as they walked through one of the arches, and he squeezed her fingers. She smiled at him.

Beyond the structure, a group of children played jacks or something like it. The rubber ball took a funny bounce to the side, and it rolled between two flagstones. With disappointed cries, the children gathered around the crack, and no digging with their little fingers could extract it. Iris narrowed her eyes.

"What are they saying?"

Marie spoke to the children and translated, "They say that in this part of the square, if something goes underground, it can't be found again, even if they pry the flagstones up, which the soldiers don't like them to do."

"Do you have your device?" Iris asked Edward.

"Of course." He took the clockwork worm from his pocket and wound both cylinders with a small key. He knelt on the ground by the crack. The children gathered around and looked at him with wide brown eyes.

"My niece educated me on worms," he said. "I'll have to tell her she wrote a very good paper. And one that was useful." He glanced at Iris, who smiled at him.

"I'm glad you've moved into the realm of practical science," she said. He let the wriggling device go between the flagstones, and the children cheered when their ball popped out. Edward handed it to the biggest of them, and they ran off.

Soon a crowd of curious onlookers gathered around them, and Edward made sure he stood close to Iris, who sat on a large rock, her palms flat against it and her eyes closed.

"What are you doing?" he asked.

"If I told you, you wouldn't believe me."

The worm re-emerged and wound down on the stone by

the crack before Edward could ask her to clarify her strange response. He picked it up and started to brush the dust off, but Iris stopped him.

"It may be useful to see what it crawled through," she said. "Can you put it in a handkerchief?"

"Certainly." He coiled the worm and put it back in his pocket after wrapping it in his handkerchief. The onlookers dispersed, and the quartet made their way back to the hotel to analyze the etchings on the wax cylinders that would tell them if the worm found a large enough space to cause an echo.

THE YOUNG MAN who sat behind the counter at the Vatican permitting office pushed his pince-nez up his nose and secured it more firmly on the bridge. Iris tried not to have uncharitable thoughts about him, his country, and the extreme inefficiency of everything Italian, but her patience wore thin. She, Marie and Bledsoe had spent the previous day at the Rome permitting office, where once they spoke to someone, they found the land they wanted to excavate belonged to the Vatican, which held much of the city inside the ancient walls. Now she and Marie stood in the church offices, where they had elected to come without the men, who kept an eye on the site.

"I'm sorry, Signorina, but the land you want to dig on has already been permitted to someone else. Another English person."

"Can you tell me who it is?" Iris asked. "Perhaps I can send a telegram to England or contact him if he's in the city."

"No, Signorina, but I can tell him someone is interested. It seems he wants to move quickly—he was here yesterday and also got the permits to hire the workers, disturb the historic site, and block the road if necessary."

"Yesterday." Iris clenched a fist below the counter. Damn these Italians and their disorganization.

"Are you sure you can't tell us who it is?" Marie flashed a smile and a bank note. "We could collaborate."

"No, Signorina. I will pass along your information to the permit holder should he come in. *Pronto!*"

With the indication to let the next person in line know it was their turn shouted in Iris's face, she knew it was futile. She hated to ask, but once they jolted along in a steamcart—they'd soon decided to let the Italian drivers handle the Italian roads and hired one—she turned to Marie.

"We can't have come all this way to be stopped by a permit, of all things." She hated bureaucracy and was surprised to find it to such a degree in a place that seemed so very chaotic. They couldn't even figure out how to unite and become a country, for goodness's sake. But it made sense if the part of Rome they wanted to dig in belonged to the Catholic Church, a bastion of rules and regulations.

"It's frustrating," Marie agreed.

"I hate to ask you this, but can you contact Cobb and see if he can use his influence for us? We haven't seen anything about his dirigible crashing in the papers, so I assume he's alive." They had seen a blurb about an incident in Paris at the home of the Marquis of Monceau. Iris's name hadn't been mentioned specifically, but she cringed at the thought and hoped they could return to England without going through Paris.

"And you're sure this is the place."

"As sure as I can be. I saw it in two visions, and the echo-worm readings show it's the right size."

Marie gazed at the street. "If Cobb wanted to be contacted, he would have been in touch. I suspect he's sitting back and monitoring us to see if we succeed."

"So you're not communicating with him?"

Marie shook her head. "Not in any great detail. But I haven't heard back from him."

They rode the rest of the way in silence. They found the men at the cafe across the square, from where they could monitor the site but stay out of the sun. A stone carafe of wine with condensation beading on the outside sat in the middle of the table, and Iris swallowed against her thirst.

"Pour me some?" she asked once they added chairs for her and Marie.

"It went that well, did it?" asked Bledsoe. "You're not one to drink in the middle of the day. Or at all."

"Someone already pulled the permit," Marie explained. "But they wouldn't tell us who."

"It's too strange," Iris said. "Too coincidental. I thought we got out of Paris without anyone seeing us, but maybe someone did. Maybe they followed us and decided to let us do the work of finding the place."

"But how would they know to go to the Vatican permitting office first?" asked Marie.

A shadow fell across the table. "Some of us are better at hiring people to do our work for us. It does make things more efficient, Miss McTavish."

Iris looked up to see the smug face of Lord Jeremy Scott.

"Surprised?" he asked.

Big hairy ox's bollocks!

EDWARD WANTED TO DO SOMETHING, but he waited to see what course of action Iris would prefer. There was something in the lordling's smile that made Edward want to step in front of Iris to protect her from... Well, he wasn't sure, but Lord Jeremy Scott seemed up to no good.

"How did you find us?" Iris asked.

Edward nodded internally. *Ah, investigation, a logical course.*

Scott studied his nails. "The clerk at the Hôtel Auberge sent me a tube when you checked out, and by the time you had your luggage loaded onto the theatre's coach, my men were in place to follow you."

"But we didn't see anyone," O'Connell said. "We were looking, especially for your men."

"Live and learn, gentlemen. I hired professionals for this job. It didn't come cheap, but it was worth it because now I'm able to join you for a lovely lunch. Let's discuss how to proceed with this archaeological dig that will make my name in the field." He gestured for a waiter to bring him a glass.

"We didn't invite you to join us," Iris said.

"Ah, but you don't have any say, do you, Miss McTavish? Considering I hold the papers on your house, you should try to stay on my good side."

"But how did that happen?" Edward asked.

"There was debt after my parents' illnesses," Iris said.

Something wary about her demeanor reminded Edward of how he felt when the dean approached him. Now Edward knew he could comfort her because he recognized this dance. "I know we don't make much at the University, but your father should be able to pay off most of it with his salary even if we don't succeed with this venture. You won't be in this person's debt for long."

"Ah yes, your father." Lord Jeremy raised his glass. "I have a toast to make to the great man."

"Don't," Iris said through clenched teeth. "Don't you dare."

With a triumphant expression, Lord Jeremy Scott said, "To the late Irvin McTavish, may his soul rest in peace."

"He's dead?" Edward put his hand on Iris's wrist. "My condolences. This must be horrible news for you."

"It's not news, though, is it, Miss McTavish?" The odious

lordling inclined his head at Iris, who looked like she wanted to snap his head off like a brittle statue's, although she would never destroy a precious artifact. But why didn't she look more distraught at such horrible tidings?

"I don't wish to speak of this," Iris said at the same time Scott added, "She's known all along."

"We found out in Paris," Marie put in. "But we didn't tell you, Professor, because you were on pain medication, and we needed to keep it a secret. Miss McTavish would have had to go back to England if word got out, and our goals would be compromised."

Now Iris shot Edward a fearful glance, and he remembered her promise not to hide anything from him.

"You could have told me," he said. "If it's important, no matter how much medication I had, I wouldn't have said anything. Why didn't you trust me?" As much as it hurt, he could admit it was the logical thing to do. He'd blurted out their purpose in going to Paris to Radcliffe, and thank goodness the doctor had remained trustworthy.

"I'm sorry, Edward." Iris drew her wrist from under his hand and looked at him with tears in her eyes. "But I've lied to you all along."

"You've lied to everyone," Scott said. "Now I know why you were so confident your father wouldn't approve of my suit for you. He was already dead."

"But that happened before we left Huntington Village." Edward tried to put all the pieces together to make sense of them, to convince himself she had only lied about her father's death since Paris, but he couldn't. "So you knew he'd died when you accepted this assignment on his behalf."

She nodded and wouldn't meet his eyes. "I had to. I couldn't keep up the household on what we had left, and this seemed the perfect opportunity to get out of dire financial straits." She glared at Scott. "I didn't count on my maid betraying me. Or was that your doing too?"

"I might have arranged for her and my footman to meet, but she caught his eye long before I got involved."

Johann put his cup down on the table hard enough that the noise directed everyone's attention to him. "This is all very well, but we need to figure out what we're going to do. Obviously Miss McTavish needs the money to rescue her house."

The sun seemed to beat down on Edward, and he squinted against the tears the bright light brought forth. The tendril of jealousy that he had fought at seeing how Iris and Johann interacted now curled inward and stabbed him through the middle of his chest, then expanded into a root-web of anger when he thought about her lying the whole time. The two thoughts batted his mind back and forth like sadistic cats. Why hadn't he jumped in to defend her rather than letting Johann do it? Oh, right, because she'd lied. He should have known all women were the same.

Time to celebrate another bloody brilliant Edward Bailey discovery.

He had a small sample size, but it was large enough for definitive conclusion: women were not to be trusted. He poured himself a half cup of wine and downed the sour liquid in one gulp.

It's interesting how something can be cold and hot at the same time.

He poured and drank another one.

"Edward," Iris pleaded. "Edward, please look at me."

He blinked and saw she seemed blurry at the edges but still attractive. That wouldn't do. He reached for the wine carafe again, but she stopped him.

"Let him drown his sorrows," Scott said. "It's about time he found out your true nature. Thankfully I'm willing to rescue him from you."

Iris withdrew her hand. "What do you mean?"

"If you want access to the site, you need to do one simple thing for me."

"And what is that?"

"Agree to marry me. I have the contract with me now."

31

H otel *Segreto, Rome, 16 June 1870*
"You don't need me to marry you if you have the rights to the site," Iris told him. "I am willing to trade my cooperation and help with the excavation and cataloging since I know you don't have the knowledge to make sense of what's in there."

Lord Jeremy smiled at her, but no amount of wrinkling at the corners of his squinty eyes could make him look warm or generous. "Even so, you need access to it. And I want your father's notes, particularly on discoveries he hadn't published yet. His acquired knowledge will become the property of the University since there is no male heir, and we will both lose access to it."

Iris saw the logic in his statement, but her father had not wanted her to marry Lord Jeremy, and she recalled the vision of him from Irvin's things. She knew humiliating him in front of the others wouldn't help her case, so she stood and gestured for Jeremy Scott to follow her. They walked into the hotel lobby, where she found a quiet corner.

"This is more than about his notes, isn't it?" she asked. "You want revenge on him for something."

Now all pretense of joviality dropped from Scott's features. "Your father thought I cheated in his class and kicked me out."

"Did you cheat?" Iris crossed her arms and scowled at him.

"Don't give me that school marm look, Miss McTavish. I didn't cheat, I delegated."

"You had someone write a paper for you." She knew from his expression she hit home. "Why would I want to marry a cheater?"

"Why would anyone but me want to marry a liar? You said yourself you're not the type for marriage, but you don't have a home to go to since I hold the deed to your house. Do you really think you'll be able to survive on your own, especially if you turn back from your quest now? I can't imagine your patron will take kindly to your willfulness."

"Willful child, you'll never find a man to put up with you." Iris's mother's voice came into her mind, and her father's chimed in with, *"You have to look at all the evidence and see what makes the most sense. Even if it's a conclusion you don't want to be true, you have to accept it and move forward without bias."*

She had to try one more thing. "What if I give you access to his notes before the university gets to them? Then will you allow me to assist with the excavations without having to marry you?"

"There's no guarantee you'll be able to do that." He put his hand on her waist and drew her to him. His breath smelled of garlic, and she turned her head away. "Marry me, Iris. It's the only way you'll get what you want."

She drew away from him and walked into the sunlight, which now seemed mocking in its cheery brightness. She gazed across the square at the arched remnants of a civilization long dead and felt the eighteen hundred years that separated her from its builders and the designers of the space below. What was one lifetime of misery in the context of history? How could she deny the good this discovery could bring, a power source that would lift the poor from slavery to coal? She'd lectured Edward on the need to remain practical in his science. Perhaps her mother was right—as a woman, it was her lot to sacrifice herself, and at least she could to pursue her intellectual hobbies. At least as much as Lord Jeremy—Jeremy now— would allow it.

Don't be foolish, of course he'll allow it. He can't do it without help.

That felt like a hollow victory compared to what she was giving up, most of all Edward. But she knew that was futile from the beginning. He valued honesty above all else, and she'd lied to him. The Maestro was right—she should have left well enough alone.

Iris walked back to the table at the cafe. She felt the other men's eyes on her, but she gazed at Edward. He stared into the bottom of his wine cup. She so badly wanted to take him aside, to make him believe she'd done what she had to do to survive, but a little voice said she should have trusted him all along. Maybe it was for the best. A deeper attachment would have hurt him more. As for Marie, the expression on her face was unreadable aside from a hint of sympathetic pity. Now Iris's stomach flipped with shame at having judged Marie for what- ever had happened with Cobb. Perhaps he'd put her in a similar situation, given her an impossible choice. Iris wanted to hate all men, but that wasn't reasonable, either.

"I have an announcement," she said. "I have consented to marry Lord Jeremy Scott. Excavations at the site will begin as soon as we can gather and organize the crew."

She turned and fled into the hotel before she had to face their halfhearted congratulations or Jeremy's smug smirk.

THE FOLLOWING MONDAY, Iris stood at the edge of a ramp that led down into the gloom. Lord Jeremy Scott stood beside her, and on the other side, Marie, who had proved adept at getting the Italian workers to move in a less chaotic and more efficient way. Consequently, they broke ground the Friday after Iris agreed to marry Scott, and rather than having to dig, they had to remove rubble that had been put into the space, which ended up being some sort of underground chapel with a skylight on one end, and settled enough to create the chamber the echo-worm detected. Patrick O'Connell had rigged a pulley system to clear the rubble quickly. Now Iris and Lord Jeremy— she couldn't think of him as simply Jeremy—were to lead the others into the space for the first time to discover what had been left behind and see what condition any decoration might be in.

Iris couldn't help but check behind her to see where Edward stood. As usual, he didn't meet her gaze, just stared straight ahead. While she, Marie and Lord Jeremy oversaw the work, the others had hired an academic translator and gone around to the libraries in Rome to see if they could find any mentions in old manuscripts as to what the space might have been. So far vague clues hinted that this might have been some sort of neo-Pythagorean gathering space, but as they were persecuted at the time it was built in the first century AD, secrecy surrounded it. If it indeed had been used by the cult, this discovery would make Iris's—no, Lord Jeremy Scott's— name in the field.

It's worth it for the discovery, Iris reminded herself, but she resented the situation.

"Are you ready?" her fiancé asked.

"Yes."

One of the workers handed him a torch, and he reached for her hand, but she folded her arms. "After you," she said. "It's too narrow for both of us." *But Edward and I could have fit.*

She followed him into the space, which smelled of stone dust and now the sulfur of the torch. It brought back memories of the visions she'd had, and something told her this was the right place.

The flickering torch and the light from the skylight opening revealed a room that would be considered small by Roman basilica standards, but the structure reminded Iris of the large chapels with a central aisle and another on either side. The sun illuminated an altar, on which a box lay on its side. Lord Jeremy started toward it, but Iris held him back.

"Remember, we have to look first, catalog second, and then we can pick them up and take them apart." She kept her voice low in respect for the sacred space. People had died there.

"Right." He squeezed her hand. "I lost my head with the excitement."

Or you never bothered to learn how you're supposed to do this. But she gave him enough of a smile to placate him.

As they walked through, the torchlight illuminated scenes in stucco. Iris itched to stop and sketch them, but she reminded herself to get the overall impression of the place, and she could study the details later. She glanced back to the others and saw her own sense of wonder reflected on their faces. Even Edward dropped his stone-faced sneer, which she had to admit was a slight improvement over the pout he often sported at the beginning of the trip, and gazed at the stuccoes and columns with awe and respect for the long-dead architects and artists. She paused so he moved closer to her before he realized where he stood and moved back a step. Iris sighed, but when she looked up, she found the angle of the light to be familiar and maneuvered so the vision of the past and perception of the present merged.

When Iris stepped on the spot where the slave girl had stood, probably as the finishing touches were put on the chapel, a shiver ran from the soles of her feet to the crown of her head, and she couldn't stifle her gasp.

"What is it?" Edward asked. "Are you all right?"

Another layer of the past, this one from the previous week, superimposed itself, and Iris blinked to bring herself back into the moment. "This looks familiar."

"How?" He frowned. "You've never been here."

I promised myself I would be honest with him, and I have nothing to lose by telling him at this point. "Objects tell me things. It's like they give me their memories. One of the statues in the Louvre was of a person who had been here. A *kore*, or female *kouros*, which were sometimes made to commemorate someone. She must have been a beloved slave girl."

"You don't expect me to believe that, do you?" Edward asked, but his frown deepened. "But my brother said your father had an uncanny ability to make conclusions about finds that were borne out by evidence later."

"I suspect he had a similar gift," Iris said. "He hinted, but we never talked about it directly."

Lord Jeremy approached them, and Iris moved to a spot that didn't call to her as much. Before she did, she noted which of the stuccoes were best seen from that location. Perhaps they were the key to what they sought?

"Have you noticed anything interesting, my love?" Scott asked.

Iris kept her expression neutral. "Not yet. You?"

"I want to see what that box on the altar is. It's in a unique enough place that surely we can move it and open it."

"Wait a moment." Iris sent one of the workmen for the sketch pad and tools she'd acquired and measured exactly how the box sat on the altar and where with details down to the exact angle it lay at. Then she nodded to Lord Jeremy. "Now you can open it."

The box proved to be a small trunk, and it contained a device with, of all things, gears.

"What is it?" Bledsoe asked.

"It looks like some sort of calculating device," Edward said. "But I'll need more light to look at it. Miss McTavish, if you would care to assist me?"

"Very well." Was he interested in her archaeological knowledge, or was this a peace overture? Not that it would help her situation, but perhaps he would move more quickly toward healing if he wasn't furious with her.

"I'll come as well," Lord Jeremy said.

Of course Iris didn't want him along, particularly as they had only shared the broadest details of what their patron had hired them to do, so she suggested, "Why don't you see if you can find any other interesting objects? You can catalog them like I did the device and bring them up. The credit for those finds would go to you."

"A brilliant idea, my dear. But do bring Marie to chaperone you with the professor."

As they ascended the ramp into the sunlight, Edward reminded himself he didn't want to have anything to do with Iris. She had lied to him, and he felt more heartbroken than he had with Lily, whom he never respected as an intellectual. But throwing himself into the work of investigating the underground chapel as well as indulging in replacing his aether isolating rig through the excellent Italian craftsmen put him in a more reasonable frame of mind. He hadn't forgiven Iris for lying to him, but he could somewhat see why she had. Now if only he could sleep again, as emotional pain had replaced physical discomfort.

They covered the short distance from the ramp to the small building they'd rented as a place to store and organize the finds, but not before some of the Italian children who had been on the square the day of their initial discovery saw them. They ran over, and Marie had to tell them to back away.

"This won't stay secret for long," Iris murmured once they entered the building and placed the box with the device in it on an empty table.

"Nothing ever does," Edward replied. "We better figure out what this does quickly in case the church decides to take it."

"Right." Iris wrote the necessary details on a card and tied it to a splinter protruding from the box. "Go ahead, Professor."

Edward removed the device, which looked like a clock but with dials on the outside instead of a face, from the box and set it on the table. Greek writing, which hadn't been evident in the dim light of the chapel, was inlaid in some sort of metal around the dials.

"I don't suppose you know how to read Greek," Iris said to Marie.

"No, don't you? I would think it's required for archaeologists."

"If I were to go to school, I'd learn."

"Perhaps I could help." Doctor Radcliffe entered the room. "I had to study both Greek and Latin in medical school."

"Please." Edward gestured to the device. "I've seen plenty of clockworks, but none like this."

The doctor squinted at the writing. "May I have a piece of paper? I need to transcribe the words as I read them so I can translate them all together."

Iris provided a pen and paper to the doctor, who mouthed the Greek words and phrases, as he wrote them down. "It may take me some time to figure this out."

"Please hurry. Once word of this gets to the church, there's no way to know whether they'll want to requisition it."

"Give me an hour. Oh, and Professor? You may want to get your aether rig set up. This might be the clue we're looking for."

32

Rome, *21 June 1870*

Iris watched Edward set up his new aether-isolating rig. He had also acquired a new set of tuning forks and laid them in a precise row. She recalled that the first time she'd seen him work with them, she'd been annoyed with him. Now the tension around his jaw and eyes said he was still angry at her.

Radcliffe emerged from the office where he'd been working. "It appears to be some sort of astrological device," he said. "Maybe to predict dates of certain events, but there also seems to be some sort of code underneath the instructions."

"How can you tell?" Iris asked.

"The way the words and phrases are laid out doesn't make sense. It could be that it's very old Greek—that's what took me so long, I had to remember back to reading some of the original old texts from Hippocrates in my History of Medicine course—but there's something strange about it. But do you know when the next full moon is?"

"No." Iris looked at Edward, who shrugged. "Why would I need to?"

"If you were practicing a mystery religion, it would be important." The doctor reached for the device, then stopped. "Can I touch it?"

"Try to do so as little as possible."

"Right." He turned two of the large dials on the top, and three of the smaller ones on the face turned on their own. Iris followed his actions but couldn't figure out what, exactly, he did.

"What are you doing?"

"The first two dials are indicators of season and month. The calendar changed from Greek to Roman times, so I adjusted for that. The others show what day of the month and time the full moon will occur."

Edward leaned over and squinted at the dials. "That's brilliant, but I can't tell what they say."

"Again, making adjustments for calendar changes, it says the full moon will occur July 12, and the new moon will be in one week, June 28."

"That's amazing!" Iris clapped her hands. "What else can it tell you?"

"It will require more study, but it's a fascinating device."

"Can you teach us how to read it?"

"I could, but I think it's more important I work on breaking the code. I suspect it has something to do with the harmonies of the spheres, but that's a physics problem. Professor, perhaps you could help me with this."

The two men bent over the device and Radcliffe's translation, and Iris stepped back. She knew she had done her part by finding the chapel, but she resented the feeling of being pushed aside.

"Doctor, was Lord Jeremy in the chapel?"

"No, Miss, I believe he's broken for lunch."

"Good." Iris gestured for Marie to follow her. "Let's explore now that there are no distractions."

"Is it as you expected?" Marie asked once they were back underground.

"Mostly. A lot of things are missing, unfortunately. Perhaps vandals got in before it was filled in." This time Iris held her own torch, and the sunlight came more directly through the shaft in the ceiling, so she got a better view of the stuccoes. She also filled in the statuary from memory from her two visions, which seemed all too accessible.

Iris glanced at Marie. Part of her couldn't believe the other woman accepted her abilities and didn't think she was some sort of freak. But now they had more in common than Iris would have thought at the start of this strange adventure.

Marie seemed to read her thoughts because she asked, "So you're going to do it, then? Marry Lord Jeremy?"

Iris gazed at a stucco relief of a butterfly-winged woman being lifted in the arms of an angel-winged man: Psyche and Eros. "You see that one?"

"Yes," Marie said. "Lots of wings, like the painting at Monceau's house. Must've made for some interesting coupling."

Iris's cheeks heated, but she laughed. "Are you going to take it upon yourself to educate me in such things before my wedding?"

"Well, you said your mother was dead. Someone needs to, although since you're into these old statues, you've at least seen what a man looks like under his pants."

Marie's statement reminded Iris of the point she was going to make. "So you see those two. That's Psyche and Eros. He was a god, the son of Aphrodite, the goddess of love. She was a princess who was said to be as beautiful as Aphrodite, which made the goddess jealous."

"Yes," Marie said. "It's not a good idea to mess with powerful beings."

"So she sent Eros to make Psyche fall in love with someone ugly or otherwise inappropriate, but he fell for her. He brought Psyche to his palace, and they married and coupled in the dark. She thought she was married to a monster, so she lit a lamp one night while he was sleeping and was so shocked at his beautiful appearance she spilled oil on him, woke him, and drove him away."

"She couldn't feel he was good-looking and well-built?" Marie shook her head. "Some women are so dumb."

"Or innocent." Iris lifted the torch. The lovers' apparent expressions of bliss made heaviness settle in her chest. "Of course, this being a temple, they're portraying the ideal, the happy ending. I saw from my parents that's not likely to happen no matter how much either might want it to. So I'm hoping that if—when—I marry Lord Scott, I will discover something redeeming about him."

Iris refused to look at Marie, to face the pity on the other woman's face, but she did find the weight of Marie's hand on her shoulder comforting.

"Keep that optimistic spirit, Miss. You're going to need it. But what does Eros have to do with aether and what we're looking for? And what does it have to do with the device upstairs?"

"There is no greater power than love, some would say passion. What better name for an extremely strong source of energy? As for the device, perhaps it will show Edward, I mean Professor Bailey, what he needs to add or do to isolate it. Meanwhile, I'll study the stuccoes and try to remember the statues that were here to see if I can offer some guidance."

Heavy footsteps down the ramp heralded the arrival of Johann Bledsoe. "I'm sure Professor Bailey will appreciate your help," he said. "But he and Radcliffe are shut up in the office, and I'm left to entertain myself, so I thought I'd come down and see what you ladies were doing."

"Where's Mister O'Connell?" Iris asked.

"Keeping an eye on your fiancé."

"What? Why?"

"We know he's not the most upstanding individual, and we'll try to come up with some way to keep you from having to follow through with wedding him. In the meantime, we'll make sure he doesn't try to force you to do something you're not ready for and trapping you in a situation where you have to marry him sooner rather than later."

Suspicion rose to cloud Iris's mind. "Why are you helping me? I thought you would rather have me out of the way so I won't hurt your friend any further."

"He's handling this better than I thought he would. He's grown a lot through all this, and he seems to realize you did what you did out of a need for survival, and you wouldn't deliberately hurt him. Whereas with Lily, she used him and didn't care at all about him."

"Like Lord Jeremy is doing with you," Marie added.

Iris had to look away from the torch because tears came to her eyes. "Why are you being so kind to me?"

"Because you're a kind person, more than I gave you credit for," Bledsoe told her.

"We all feel that way," Marie said.

"Thank you." That was all Iris could get out before she fled up the ramp and into the daylight. Now that she had friends, she would have to give them up, for she knew Lord Jeremy wouldn't want her associating with a musician or a maid, and he certainly wouldn't allow her to socialize with Edward. Although their work would make a huge difference for many people, it seemed an unfair sacrifice.

WITH RADCLIFFE'S help in translating and interpreting the

markings on the ancient device, Edward thought he calculated the correct frequency to isolate the aether. The tone was much higher than he'd tried previously, and he had to have special equipment made that would transfer it to the vacuum quickly enough before dissipating through the materials. Finally he was ready to try it, and the others gathered around to watch. They did the procedure in the underground temple, which seemed appropriate. Also, the angle of the light coming through the ceiling aperture at noon was perfect for the aether isolation.

The situation reminded Edward of his teaching days, which now seemed so long ago. "I wish all my students were as invested in the results of my experiments," he said and started the burners. "Goggles on, please."

He tried not to look at Iris, whom he acknowledged as the originator of this exciting opportunity. At least that was the direction he moved his thoughts whenever he saw her. Thinking of her like that seemed to make the most sense rather than attaching the labels of "liar" or "desperate," or "willing to sacrifice herself for all of them". At least Lord Jeremy had stayed upstairs. He'd tried to argue to be included, but since he wasn't authorized by Cobb, they had reason to leave him out. Radcliffe and O'Connell technically weren't supposed to be there, but as Edward wouldn't have been able to do anything with the device without Radcliffe's help, the doctor stood with the group in front of the altar, and O'Connell stayed at the bottom of the ramp and served as a guard.

Edward went through the procedure to isolate the aether by creating a vacuum in the small glass sphere and striking the tone to make the substance appear. "And now I shall attempt to stabilize it with this higher tone." He struck the tuning fork and held it to the copper globe. It grated his ears, and Marie actually put her hands to the sides of her head, but no one said anything. He glanced at his watch to note the time, and once the higher sound faded, counted the seconds before the aether disappeared.

"Fifteen seconds beyond the end of the tone," he said. "That's progress, but not what I hoped for."

"It did seem to last longer," Iris said. "Try a different tone?"

"That's the one according to the device." He set the tuning fork down too hard and enjoyed its plink of protest. "What are we missing?"

He mentally went through the calculations again, and Radcliffe stayed behind as the others filed up the ramp.

"There has to be something else," Edward said once he and the doctor stood alone in the temple. "Something simple we're missing."

Radcliffe sighed and shook his head. "You're right. There's something obvious. You work better when you and Miss McTavish are getting along. Talk to her."

"What's the point?" Edward picked up the little tuning fork. "She lied to me, and now she's engaged to someone I have no desire to maintain an acquaintance with."

"But she's your friend. Those are hard to come by."

"Thanks for your advice, but I'd rather ponder the mathematics than the emotional aspects of this."

"Even though it's the Eros Element we're trying to derive?"

"A clever name, that's all. Cupid is not to be trusted."

33

Underground Temple, Rome, 27 June 1870
U
    Several days passed with no progress. One afternoon Iris stood in the chapel and sketched the set of stuccoes over the altar when Marie came puffing down the ramp. The air stood heavy with humidity and dust over the city, so they all got short of breath moving through it except Patrick O'Connell, who grew up around a forge and so could breathe through thick air.

"Iris," Marie said, "I've word from Cobb." She held a letter. "I telegraphed him the result of the professor's experiments, and this came through the tubes."

"He must have wanted us to get it quickly to pay to tube it so far. Have you read it yet?" Iris turned from the altar, and anxiety shot through her middle when she saw Marie's face. "We need to get the others."

They all gathered at the cafe, again without Lord Jeremy, and Marie read the letter.

. . .

My dear explorers,

I am aware of the progress, or lack thereof, of the experiments to stabilize aether and therefor isolate the Eros Element. Due to a change in my own financial circumstances including costly repairs to my airship from the Clockwork Guild's attack, I am no longer able to finance this expedition as I have been. Your stipends from the trip, including my donation to Professor Bailey's department, will also be halved. Before you become angry at me, look to your companion Johann Bledsoe, whose gambling debts prompted the attack. Lest you think I am a monster, I will pay for another three days in Italy and your return passages to your respective countries including that to America for Doctor Radcliffe and Mister O'Connell, whose assistance Marie said you have found invaluable. Thank you, and I wish you godspeed.

Yours truly,
Parnaby Cobb

ALL EYES TURNED TO JOHANN, who gazed imploringly at Iris. She shrugged—what could she do? She'd kept his secret without threat or malice. All she could do now was not harangue him like the others would and turn her mind more intently toward figuring out the problem with their now very short deadline.

"You're the reason we got attacked?" Edward asked. "I lost my best copper globe up there."

"And my best set of clothes," Marie said.

Johann held up his hands. "I'm sorry, especially about your injuries, Edward. But Cobb knew, or he must have known. He approached me about this expedition a week before he appeared at the University and said he knew I would be interested in a potentially lucrative opportunity."

"But he didn't mention your gambling debts specifically."

Marie toyed with a knife, and Iris wondered if the maid was pondering sticking it in the musician.

"No, but he implied them."

Radcliffe and O'Connell exchanged looks.

"What is it?" Iris asked, happy to divert the attention from the maestro, whose face was as red as the tomato sauce they'd come to like.

"I've met Cobb," Radcliffe said. "At Harvard. Patrick and I were having lunch one day at a restaurant off campus when he approached us. Of course I knew who he was—everyone in Boston does. He asked if I was the talented colored physician he'd heard of who had a knack for Greek."

"Don't let Chadwick fool you with his false modesty," O'Connell put in. "He took highest in the class."

"And would have gotten the tar beaten out of me for it if Patrick hadn't stepped in. But I told Cobb yes, I was. He paid for the trip to Vienna, and when we got waylaid in the north of France, he sent us a message to stay put because his airship would be landing. He had a chance for me to use my skills in Greek and medicine, and O'Connell's tinkering might help as well. He told us not to say anything about it, but to make ourselves useful so you'd want us along."

"So why did you tell us?" Marie asked. "You were lying all along too, but it would have been easy enough for you to keep your secret."

Radcliffe inclined his head toward Iris. "She's probably figured it all out."

The parts of the conversation dropped into place like puzzle pieces in Iris's brain. "Cobb didn't want us to know he's the puppet master. If you look at history, savvy emperors had networks of spies unaware of each other. Remember, we're supposed to be posing as Grand Tourists. Perhaps if we seemed too cohesive a group, we would have alerted Cobb's competitors." But she sensed Radcliffe wasn't telling them something important. She caught Marie's eye, and Marie nodded. The link between them continued to strengthen, and Iris knew Marie shared her suspicion.

"Meanwhile, what do we do?" Edward asked. "We're close—I can feel it—and perhaps if I make this discovery, I can save my department, if not my job."

"We keep working," Iris told him. "The stuccoes in the chapel have to have something to do with the device we found. I need to take another look at it."

And I need to get my hands on it to see what it can tell me.

Edward's face showed his distress at his friend's betrayal, but he set his mouth in a line, and Iris admired how he refused to let it deter him from their mission.

He has definitely changed. We all have. The memory of the first crack in his emotional armor showing at the airfield swirled around in her head along with grief—yes, more grief—at their group being broken up and the thought that her marriage to Scott would come sooner rather than later. She would try to wait until the heavy mourning period for her father was over, but she suspected Scott would find some way to force the issue. Even if she could put him off, he would be a large and annoying part of her life from this point on.

The group split up with Iris and Marie going to the rented offices, Johann disappearing, and the other men heading back to the site to see if they could see anything in the chapel that had eluded them to this point but that could help.

"What will you do?" Iris asked once they walked out of the sun and into the dim but stuffy office building. "Do you have to go back to him?"

"What concern is it of yours?" Marie asked. She turned her back on Iris and looked at the objects on the shelves in front of her.

"I'm worried about you. You know what I can do—your brooch told me some of what happened."

Marie turned toward her. "Don't be. He's doing with me what he does with everyone else in his life. He's used me, and now he's sending me back to the theatre. He sent a separate note, that he'll pay my passage back to Paris, and he no longer needs my services."

"Isn't that good? You'll be away from him."

"And back with my mother, who will take every opportunity to remind me how she told me taking up with him was a bad idea. I'll have to become an actress again—it's the only profession that will suffer my ruined reputation now that I'm no longer in Cobb's employ. Well, the one I'm willing to do. At least with my training, I can fight off any man who thinks actresses are for more than acting."

"Is that why you don't want to go back to it?"

"That and when I'm on stage, I feel like I lose part of myself, my true self, with every role. I wish I could go back to being a ladies' maid, but as much as I've traveled with Cobb, I'm too known in the big cities, as is my reputation."

Iris knew Marie spoke truly. "I'm sorry. I wish there was some way to help."

"Figure this thing out." Marie gestured to the device, which sat on the table between them. "At least make it so this journey will have a good outcome for someone."

"If we do, we'll have to hide it from Lord Jeremy and test it and patent it before Cobb finds out."

"Go ahead and see what it has to tell you," Marie, apparently done with talking about Cobb, said. "I'm surprised you haven't already tried to read it."

"I wanted to figure this out with my archaeological training and knowledge. Plus, Doctor Radcliffe and Ed—Professor Bailey—have been doing well with this part of the puzzle. I feel they're close."

"But not close enough for the time we have."

Iris pulled off her gloves. "Right. Not nearly close enough."

She flexed her fingers. "If I'm in the trance for too long or if you sense that something is very wrong, do what you need to get me out of it."

"You can trust me."

And oddly, Iris knew she could. She pressed her fingertips to the wooden sides of the device, caressed the gears with her thumbs, and closed her eyes.

IMAGES AND FEELINGS tumbled through Iris's mind. First there were Edward's and Doctor Radcliffe's excitement at working with the device, a shared joy in a good challenge that was both academic and practical. Edward's feelings at Iris's betrayal floated in, as did his sadness that she would be marrying someone else but then relief that he'd escaped the clutches of another deceitful woman. Iris pushed through those emotions —she didn't want to intrude on his privacy—and Radcliffe's strange sense of wild hope at what they would accomplish. The man remained a mystery, but she couldn't focus on that now. There was a long period of muffled noise as the city changed around the little temple and finally a glimmer of light and flurry of activity.

"Tell me why we have to haul all this gravel down here?" It was the slave girl Iris had read the statue of at the Louvre. Apparently she hadn't been sacrificed in the temple as Iris had thought, and she staggered down the ramp under the weight of a large bag.

A burly man with a similar bag slung over his shoulders replied, "Because he said what they've found is too dangerous. It's two that's required, and he needs this place hidden by the next new moon. The emperor can't get hold of this."

Two what? Iris asked. She didn't know how much her present self could affect the past.

"Two what?" The girl echoed Iris's thoughts.

"Two tones, high and low. They figured it out with the Astrological Calculator. When the moon is dark, there's one source of sunlight, and there's little enough interference to make it stay."

"How do you know this?" the girl asked.

"I assisted at the last ceremony, and my Greek isn't as rusty as yours. Trust me, it's good we're covering all this up, burying it. They don't know what it's capable of, but the emperor don't care about taking it slow."

The warning of the statue came back to Iris, how some sort of primal being would be unleashed, but the slave girl again seemed to share her thoughts, this time her skepticism.

"That's what they say, but they also believe people come back as beans. How much of this is myth and how much is true?"

"It doesn't matter. Do you think they'll let us live after we do this? The secret will die with us."

The girl nodded, a resigned expression on her face. "I always thought it would come to this. I hope I won't come back as a bean."

Iris recalled her first vision, which must have been the girl's death in the coliseum, and whispered, "I'm sorry for what will happen to you." The slave looked to where Iris stood, and Iris recognized she wasn't in anyone's perspective this time, but rather watching from the altar like a ghost from the future. Or maybe there was something in the device. But objects couldn't have spirits, could they?

Either way, a tug brought her back to the present and Marie.

"Are you all right?" Marie asked. "You look like you've seen a ghost."

"I think I might have been one. I wasn't in anyone's head this time."

"How? You're not dead."

Iris shivered. "I hope not." But then she remembered she would be marrying Lord Jeremy Scott soon, and part of her felt like she might be. "Come on, we have to tell Edward and the others."

"Wait," Marie said. "Did you see anything else? Before you went into the past?"

It all seemed shrouded in fog now, but Iris dug through it. "Radcliffe is really invested in us figuring this out, but I can't determine why."

Marie held up the echo-worm, which they'd found would also record voices. "I saw him and Mister O'Connell go into the hotel, and he's been watching the papers from Austria. Perhaps I should have one delivered to them and send this device in to see what they say."

EDWARD STOOD ALONE in the temple and counted the number of stars at the top of the main stucco at the altar. Clues, clues, they had to find clues as to how to work the device and discover the tone that would stabilize the aether into a new element. The Eros Element. It seemed aptly named, for without the partnership of minds, they wouldn't have gotten as close as they did.

"I know what you're missing," Iris said from the top of the ramp. She carried the device gingerly in her gloved hands and descended into the gloom to join him.

Edward stepped back. "Should you be here alone? You're affianced to another man."

"The others are out and about, and Marie had an errand to run. I'll only be here a few moments." Iris set the device on the altar, and it caught a ray of sunlight. It blazed gold, and Edward thought it looked like it must have when new. Like his and Iris's relationship—time had tarnished it.

"What do you mean, you know what I'm missing?" Edward walked to the device. The dials were where he and Radcliffe had left them.

"Look at all the stuccoes." Iris gestured around them. "There are Psyche and Eros. And there's Orpheus and Euridice and Medea and Jason... They're all relationships, meetings of minds and hearts on common ground to form something greater or make a journey of transformation. Perhaps this was an initiation chamber of some sort."

She didn't have to say it. Edward's brain took the leap. "There needs to be more than one tone. A person can't initiate himself."

"Yes. But it has to be the perfect pair."

"Right. Because early experiments with more than one tone proved disastrous. That's one reason we all wear goggles. It's thought that there is no such thing as a perfect combination of tones. There will always be some dissonance, and dissonance can be deadly."

"There's always conflict in the myths. In most fairy tales, if you think about it." She looked at him, and her dark blue eyes held sorrow. "They always have to fight for their love and overcome obstacles to make it work."

"Forgive my skepticism, but I've recently recovered from my airship crash injuries. Are you suggesting I put myself in further danger?"

"Let me do it. You figure out the tones using the device, and I'll run the experiment. I've seen you go through the procedure enough times."

Edward waved her away from the clockwork device. Although she'd betrayed him, he wouldn't allow her to put herself in danger of permanent disfigurement. "I'll do it. I just need to know what settings to start with."

"Whichever ones help you calculate the time of the dark moon. By the way, that's when the experiment needs to be run."

"Are you sure? How do you know?"

She smiled at him. "I know you can't trust me in much, but do me this favor and believe me when I tell you that you need pure sunlight without any chance of reflection from the moon for this to work."

"Very well. The moon turns new tonight, so I will run it at dawn tomorrow."

WHEN IRIS EMERGED from the temple, a rough hand grasping her elbow made her struggle against the bruising hold before she recognized her fiancé.

"Let me go," she said and pulled her arm away.

"Were you alone down there?" he asked. The muscles of his face clenched so hard that lines appeared under his round cheeks and jowls.

"No," she said, "I'm not going to lie to you. I was discussing the experiment's next step with Professor Bailey."

"Are you an idiot?" Scott snapped. "You're an engaged woman, but that doesn't preserve your reputation."

They walked across the square toward the hotel, and Iris counted the steps until she could feign a headache and escape from his company. No, she couldn't do that. She would honor Edward by sticking to a strict code of honesty.

"I'm not stupid," she said. At least that was the truth. "And we don't have much time. I can't accomplish what I need to if I have to go running for a chaperone every time I need to talk to one of my male colleagues."

"Enjoy it now," he snapped. "Because once we get back to England, you're not seeing any of them again."

Iris managed to slip away from him on the crowded sidewalk and stalked into the hotel. The first person she saw was Marie, who stood between Radcliffe and O'Connell with a guilty look on her face.

"You seem to have lost something," Radcliffe said and handed her the limp clockwork worm.

34

T rattoria Domani, Rome, 27 June 1870

"We have to stop meeting like this," Iris told Radcliffe once the four of them were seated at a corner table at the trattoria they frequented regularly. It was off the square and therefore quieter. "People will start to talk."

He didn't crack a smile. "You didn't need to spy on us. If you had questions for me, you could have asked me. I'm not interested in playing your and Mister Bledsoe's game."

O'Connell's size had struck Iris as potentially dangerous, but Radcliffe's intensity and the way his gray eyes hardened with anger made her want to scoot away.

Big hairy ox's bollocks, I've already been manhandled by Jeremy Scott today, and I'm not backing down from this. Iris tried to assume a stern expression. "You say you're not deliberately keeping secrets, but there's something you haven't told us. Don't ask me how I know, I just do. Why are you really along on this crazy mission? It has to be more than showing off your Greek."

Radcliffe and O'Connell exchanged glances.

"She's a smart one like Claire," O'Connell said. "Even if her maid isn't as sneaky as she thinks. Maybe they can help, give you a woman's perspective."

The doctor held his hand up to the waiter, and once the stone carafe of wine appeared, and four cups had been poured, he looked at Iris, and the way his eyes filled with pain, which must have taken a lot of energy to suppress, nearly broke her heart. Nearly.

"There's a girl from Boston," he told her in the sort of tone men used when they spoke of their true loves. "She's white. I'm..." He held out his hands. "Well, as you know, I'm not. She didn't care, and her father was a tinkerer and her mother a tutor, so they had more liberal views on such things. But she had an aunt who didn't."

"A narrow-minded, stubborn woman if I've ever seen one," O'Connell added. "I studied with the girl's father, and her aunt manipulated the family through money, and they were always short."

"But Claire saw through it." Radcliffe spoke with a kind of professional detachment, but sorrow came through. "I managed to enlist in the army as a field hospital doctor to save some money so I could marry her. I proposed to her at her eighteenth birthday party—I was on leave for the holidays—and she accepted though all I could give her was a small ruby."

"It was a lovely ring," O'Connell said. "Everyone thought so too, until the aunt saw it."

"She wasn't supposed to be there, but I went ahead and proposed. The look on her face, as sour as Claire's was happy. Her parents felt badly and allowed me to drive her home in my new steamcart. I should have known better."

"What happened?" Marie asked.

"A horseman, one of the draftee hunters, came out of nowhere. It reared, and its hooves landed on the boiler, which exploded and sent the cart flying. Claire caught the worst of it on her hands and arms and tumbled out of the cart and down an embankment."

"How awful!" Iris said.

"Yes, for when she awoke, she had no memory of what happened and very few of the year leading up to the accident. The doctors cautioned me and her parents that seeing us could trigger further injury to her mind. So, with the aunt's help, Claire went to college in Vienna. She's almost done, and my time of mandatory service is over, so I hoped..." He looked into his now-empty wine cup. "I thought I could go and see if she would react negatively to seeing Patrick, whom she also knew during the time she'd forgotten but who wasn't on the list of people she shouldn't see."

"Did she?" Iris asked.

"Looked right through me like I was invisible," O'Connell said. "Didn't respond when I spoke to her or called me by name."

"Her mind is still injured," Iris said. "That must be horrible for you."

Radcliffe continued, "So when I got a message from Parnaby Cobb that he would allow me to join this expedition, I had a faint hope that whatever we discovered may help her, heal her. Asylum doctors have been working on electricity and the brain, and while their results have been promising for melancholia, they haven't done anything for psychic shock. It's a small chance, but I'll take anything."

Iris fiddled with the buttons on her gloves. "I wish I could give you some hope, but I don't know what we're dealing with."

The bell over the trattoria door opened, and Jeremy Scott walked in. Iris shrank into the shadows and hoped he wouldn't spot her. He didn't seem to.

"If nothing else, listen to me," Radcliffe said. "You don't get many chances at true love. Some say you get one. Don't throw that away out of fear."

"I can't go back on my word, and he holds the mortgage on my house."

"You're clever. You and the professor will figure it out," O'Connell said.

Formerly, Iris would have thrilled at someone acknowledging her intelligence, but now it didn't seem like enough. "I don't even know if Edward has feelings for me after my betrayal."

"Love isn't so easily killed," Radcliffe said. "I believe Claire loves me, that her regard for me is somewhere in her fractured mind. Edward has been moving toward healing in both mind and body, and his feelings for you are part of that."

If only it was that easy.

"Well," Iris said, "shall we order an early dinner since we'll be stuck here for a while?"

SOMETHING different about the atmosphere woke Iris before dawn the next morning. Marie snored through the wine she'd drunk as she slept on the cot in the room. Iris's head felt stuffed with gravel, but she wouldn't have traded the previous evening with Radcliffe and O'Connell for anything except maybe a similar one with Edward where they could bare all their secrets and interact as themselves. She grabbed the courtesan's poison case from its hiding place and put it in her pocket to serve as a reminder that no matter what happened, history would erase all but the most solid of details.

That line of thought produced more stomach upset, so Iris rose, dressed, and tiptoed from the room in search of tea. Or one of the coffee and milk concoctions the Italians drank in the morning would do. The morning kitchen staff gave her a cappuccino and two sweet rolls, and she carried them outside.

Light barely streaked the sky, and something tugged Iris

toward the temple. Had Edward solved the puzzle? Would he be there doing his experiments in the pure dawn? Before she knew it, she was across the piazza and descending the ramp. The fog hung heavy around the entrance as if it guarded the place from prying eyes.

Iris plunged into the gloom and emerged into a candlelit world. *Is this romantic or some other sort of atmosphere?* Edward stood behind the altar, and the circles under his eyes told Iris he hadn't slept. He set up his apparatus and kept consulting his watch. His movements were slow like one of the statues.

"Do you need something to eat?" Iris asked. The ordinary question hung in the air between them, but it pulled Edward out of whatever trance he'd been in.

"Iris? What are you doing here?"

"I brought you something." She held out one of the rolls and handed him the rest of the coffee drink. "You can't work on an empty stomach."

She thought she remembered her mother saying something similar to her father back when the two of them got along, and she couldn't imagine herself taking care of Lord Jeremy like that. Not that he would need it—he would always put himself before his work.

"Thank you." He quickly ate and returned to calibrating his equipment. "I'm going to try this at sunrise. You're welcome to remain, but please stay back since I don't know what will happen. It could be dangerous."

He's concerned for my well-being. That's a start. "You've calculated the proper frequencies, then?"

"There are a couple of possibilities based on Pythagorean mathematical principles such as the Golden Mean. I'm going to start with the most likely one. Will you assist me by watching and taking notes? Here's a spare watch."

Iris took a set of goggles out of the box by the altar and moved to the aisle on the side so she could duck behind a pillar if she needed to. A ray of sunlight passed through the high windows and hit the altar above where Edward's glass globe stood.

"How soon?" she asked.

"Two minutes."

Iris counted heartbeats, but hers was faster than the second hand of Edward's watch. *It's amazing how emotion and frequency can be linked.*

"Starting the vacuum process," Edward said.

Iris noted the time and smiled at the excitement in his voice. No matter how far apart they ended up, they would always have the joy in scientific discovery in common. The sunbeam now pierced the top of the glass.

"Vacuum chamber closed."

Iris hardly dared to breathe so as to not create any interfering noise.

"Striking tuning forks. Silence, please."

If Iris listened hard enough, she could hear the two frequencies, but they were complementary enough they augmented the tone that vibrated through the air as a single sound.

That has to be it. Iris peered around the pillar and watched as Edward touched the two tuning forks to the copper globe. The aether formed in the glass one, but it looked the same as before, and it dissipated as soon as the sound did.

"What happened?" Iris asked.

"Nothing." Edward rested the tuning forks on the altar. "Now we try the other one. Stand back because it will be less harmonious and therefore more dangerous."

Iris moved one pillar back and again kept notes and watched as Edward went through the procedure. Although the two new tones made Iris's ears buzz at first, they intertwined and formed a new sensation. Edward touched those forks to the copper globe, and while the aether remained stable for longer and glowed brighter, it disappeared after about thirty seconds.

Edward looked at the two tuning forks in his hands and frowned. "That second one should have worked."

In spite of the space being small, it had some reverberation, as Iris found when she walked to the altar. The air hummed with the second new tone.

"Perhaps we should try it all together."

Edward's frown deepened. "That could be dangerous, unpredictable. Are you sure you want to risk being injured and disfigured?"

"What do I have to lose? A marriage to a man I don't love. And I have a major scientific discovery to gain if it does work."

"Very well. You strike the first two tones and hold them to the copper globe, and I'll do it with the next two. But if the glass looks like it's going to shatter or the aether threatens to expand beyond it, duck under the altar. The stone may protect you."

Iris nodded. Now her stomach fluttered with a new frequency, but she didn't show her anxiety.

They made sure their goggles were firmly in place, and she struck the two original tuning forks on the altar. The vibrations traveled up her arms and felt like they went to her heart, but she ignored the strange sensation and placed their ends on the copper globe. The aether appeared much as it had in Edward's lab, as a glowing, writhing, opalescent snake eating its tail. Then he struck his forks.

A note of dissonance came into the sound, and he hesitated, but Iris mouthed, "Do it." He placed the ends of those tuning forks on the copper globe, and the aether brightened considerably. It also increased the frequency of its undulations until its motions were too fast for them to see. Iris had to look away from the searing glow, and when she tried to blink the after-image from her eyes, she noticed the sound waves had quieted.

"I think it worked," Edward whispered. He gazed at the

glowing mass at the center of the glass globe. "It's not dimming or disappearing."

"You've made a new element." Iris placed the tuning forks on the altar. Edward swept her into his arms like the hero of the novels she'd stolen from her mother long ago, and their lips met. Now the opalescent colors bloomed behind her eyelids, and her heart beat in harmony with his. She wanted to merge with him to become a new, different, better person.

"Professor Bailey, I would thank you to unhand my fiancée."

35

Hotel Segreto, Rome, 28 June 1870

Marie woke when a stray sunbeam speared her left eye. She listened for Iris's regular breathing and bolted upright when she didn't hear it. Relief that Iris's breathing hadn't stopped was replaced by panic—where had she gone? Marie didn't know exactly what had transpired between Iris and Edward or between Iris and Lord Jeremy, but she hadn't missed how Iris rubbed her left elbow off and on all evening or the mumblings in Iris's sleep, mostly to let go of her and she didn't love him. Marie had seen all kinds of men at her mother's theatre and knew better than most how some were not to be trusted with a woman's well-being, either physical or mental. Lord Jeremy's expression, which contained a new level of hardness since they unearthed the temple, had made it quite clear that things would not go well for Iris, and Iris's stab of fear when she saw him enter the trattoria confirmed Marie's suspicions. He'd hurt her and promised more if she didn't obey him. Knowing Iris, she wouldn't.

So if Iris had gone to the site, and if Edward was there and Jeremy walked in on them... He might do something to eliminate the competition permanently. Or eliminate Iris before she further injured his pride and caused him more trouble.

Marie dressed as quickly as she could and rushed from the room. She ran into Johann Bledsoe on the stairs. His bloodshot eyes, disheveled clothing, and alcohol odor told her all she needed to know of how he'd spent his night. She gave him her best Lucille glare. *I know what kind of man you are.* But he blocked her way.

"Where are you off to in such a rush?" he asked.

"Iris and Edward might be in danger."

He blinked, and the foggy expression on his face cleared. "Where?"

"The temple."

He followed her down the stairs. "Why do you think they're in danger?"

"I don't have time to explain. Call it a sixth sense."

"Nothing's ever normal with you is it?"

Now they crossed the hotel foyer. "No. Nor is it boring," Marie shot over her shoulder.

"I have no doubt of that."

Was he flirting with her? No time to think about that now. The edge of the sun peeked over the horizon, and a new sense of urgency bloomed in Marie's gut. "Hurry!"

THE ODIOUS LORDLING stood at the top of the ramp and held something in his right hand. The early morning sun streaming into the chapel glinted off of the object. Iris didn't need to look closely to see it was one of the long, thin stiletto knives the Italians favored.

Edward tried to shove Iris behind him, but she wouldn't let him rescue her. Lord Jeremy was her problem, not his.

"I can't marry you, Jeremy." She moved around the altar to

block the globe with the aether from his view. "You and I both know it wouldn't be good for either of us."

"I don't care what would be good for you. I warned you to stay away from him, and you said your relationship was professional. Apparently it isn't."

She tried again to appeal to his self-interest. "I watched my parents have a loveless relationship. I'm not going to inflict that upon myself or anyone else."

He moved toward her more quickly than she thought he could, and she turned to flee, but her skirt caught on a rough corner of the altar, and the pocket that held the courtesan's poison case caught and tore. The gold container clattered to the floor, and when Iris reached for it, Lord Jeremy grabbed her arm with one hand and the golden object with the one that held the knife.

"What's this? Have you been hiding temple treasure from me along with your dishonorable behavior?"

"Give it back," Iris twisted and tried to grab it, but he held her firm against him.

"What is it?"

"It's an Italian courtesan's container. Completely wrong period for this place, which you should know. My father gave it to me."

"Fine. It along with everything else will become my property when we marry." He dropped it into her hand.

Images flooded through Iris. Hands opening the container in a ballroom in London and pouring something into her father's drink. Lord Jeremy watching the whole proceeding. The lordling receiving payment from a shady-looking character in an alley and passing it along to another one. Iris couldn't see the first criminal's face but did see the tattoo on his wrist, of the same symbol that had been etched on the study window and that was on the piece of paper the doomed Monsieur Anctil gave her.

"You killed my father!" Iris kicked him in the shin, but he held her tighter. "You took bribe money from the Pythagoreans and paid the Clockwork Guild to finish him off."

"How do you—? Never mind. Stop struggling, or I'll cut your throat."

"No!" Edward moved toward them, but Jeremy held the knife to Iris's neck.

"One step closer and neither of us will have her," Jeremy said. "Yes, I arranged for your father's illness, Iris. He humiliated me in class and was going to have me kicked out of the program. Luckily his unfortunate and sudden need for a sabbatical made sure that wouldn't happen. But I didn't mean for him to die."

"I don't believe you," she said. "Lie all you want to me, but I'll never marry you."

"You gave your word. Or were you lying about that as about so much else? Either way, what you discovered in here including this glowing thing in the glass globe belongs to me, as do you."

Edward picked up two of the tuning forks. "Then allow me to demonstrate." He gave Iris a significant look.

"Don't," she said. "It's not worth it. I'm not worth it."

"What's another copper globe in the grand scheme of things?" He struck the two forks on the altar, and a discordant combination of tones slithered through the air. He held the tuning forks over the copper globe but didn't touch them to it. The air vibrated with the discord, an almost solid manifestation of what was happening among them.

"What are you doing?" Jeremy asked.

"Augmenting its power. Look at it."

The mass grew, and its edges became ragged.

"How much will that be worth?" Jeremy leaned in to see better, but to do so, he had to move the knife away from Iris's neck. She let her muscles relax but couldn't pull away without focusing Scott's attention back on her.

At least I can breathe. She watched Edward's face. His expression was that of a patient teacher, but behind his goggles, his eyes held a ruthlessness she'd never seen in them. Was he willing to do it, to destroy the temple and everything in it, including them, to keep the Eros Element away from Scott?

"It requires testing and development to make it practical," Edward said. "But once we do figure out how to harness it, it will be a new source of power, particularly important because it's self-sustaining." He glanced at Iris and then down. She understood his message: *duck under the altar.* She shook her head—*not worth it*—but he ignored her.

"Self-sustaining power. I can be like those coal moguls, but without having to bleed resources on personnel and property," Jeremy mused. He leaned in closer so his nose almost touched the glass, and Edward put the two now barely vibrating tuning forks to the copper globe. The mass inside expanded, and Scott put his hands to his eyes, releasing Iris. She dropped to the floor and darted under the altar. Shattering glass filled the air, and two bodies hit the floor.

Iris curled into a ball under the altar. The air buzzed with the dissipating energy, and the next two noises—a loud bang and footsteps—made her cringe further.

"Oh my god!" It was Marie. "Dammit, Johann, I told you to break the door down."

"I tried. Who knew Italian construction could be so strong?"

"They build churches that last for centuries, you ninny. Iris? Iris, are you here?"

Iris crawled toward where Edward lay with an arm over his face. The fabric over his elbow hung in ashy shreds, and his skin blistered. Iris moved his arm out of the way and was relieved to see it had blocked his nose and mouth, but his face also showed burns, and worse, he didn't breathe.

"Edward?" she tried to ask, but all she could manage was a moan. "Edward, please don't be dead. I can't lose someone else I care about."

Marie knelt beside her and put two fingers to Edward's neck. "I'm not feeling a pulse."

Iris put her head to his chest and remembered how good it had felt in the train when they'd all ended up tumbled on the floor and he supported her. Nothing. Marie removed his goggles, and he lay there as if asleep.

"No!" Iris pressed her hands to his chest and moved so her face was a whisper away from his. "No, Edward, please don't leave me." She took a deep breath and parted his lips with hers. She exhaled into his mouth, then breathed again and again for him.

EDWARD STOOD to the side and watched Iris breathe into his mouth. It didn't make sense, but his mind kept going back to the discovery. The experiments had disappointed him so, but Iris's genius suggestion that they combine the two new tones—well, it was called the Eros Element, after all, so it made sense that simple things would beget a new, different whole.

But then Lord Jeremy Scott had threatened her with that long knife. A simple mistake, an unintentional slip, and she'd be maimed or worse. Not that he wouldn't still love her—and his mind tripped over that word too—if she had a scar on her face, but he didn't want her to be killed. Lord Jeremy's motives were easy enough to read, so Edward had lured him in with the promise of wealth and power, and—

And that was where Edward's mind didn't want to venture. He'd killed a man. With science, which he'd come to believe was to be used not only to gain knowledge, but also for the common good. And after he took that man's fiancée and kissed her like he was some sort of savage laying claim on another man's property. What must Iris think of him? What should Edward think of himself? He'd gone so far beyond the bounds of what he considered reasonable, but he'd done what he had to protect her. And himself. That part was jumbled too. Had he died? Well, empirical evidence suggested otherwise. Or did it? He did stand outside himself looking down and feeling happy he couldn't feel the burns on his face and arm. Iris breathed into him, and he wished he could feel what it was like to have her mouth on his again.

Edward looked around at the others assembled there. Iris's hands glowed gold. She'd said something about her sense of touch, how it told her more than it did other people, and Edward suspected her father could do something similar. The existence of such a talent didn't make sense in the normal world, but here, in this space outside reality, more seemed possible. Did others have abilities like that? A golden film stretched and waved over Marie's face like a mask. Then Radcliffe came down the ramp and broke into a run when he saw Iris kneeling by Edward. O'Connell followed him. Radcliffe shooed her aside and pulled his stethoscope out.

"There's something," he said. "Keep breathing for him, Iris. Whatever you're doing, it's helping."

Is it? I don't feel any different. Edward looked at his own hands. He could see the chapel floor through them.

"You need to get his heart going stronger," Radcliffe said. "His pulse is fluttering."

"Wait." She looked back at the altar. "I need the two he tried first. I felt the frequency in my own chest. Which ones were they?"

She stood and ran to where the tuning forks had fallen after Edward destabilized the aether and destroyed the globe. "Big hairy ox's bollocks, I can't tell which ones they were!"

Edward stood beside her in his transparent form and

picked them out, but he couldn't grab them. Standing so near Iris, he heard her thoughts.

"Eros, if you're there, if you're listening, you can't let it end like this. Whether you're a force or a god, Edward kept your element from being poached by an evil man. Doesn't he deserve some sort of reward?"

A deep voice resonated through Edward. *"And what price will you pay? No one can come back from Hades without a fee."*

Edward found himself in his body, and the pain kept him trapped there.

THE VOICE SOUNDED like it echoed around the temple, but a quick glance told Iris none of the others heard it. She'd read enough mythology to know that gods were tricky and would twist words, so she had to choose carefully.

"I will give up my house in Huntington Village."

"That is not yours to give."

"I will give Father's papers and artifacts to the University rather than keep them for myself, which I had planned to do in secret. I will make my career on my own rather than rely on building upon his." The grief-crack in her heart throbbed at the thought of losing that tangible connection to her father.

"Giving up one link of the heart for another will suffice. Have faith, little sister. You will need it for what's to come. The rose is opening."

The next breath brought a gasp from Edward, and Iris moved back so he could sit with the support of Radcliffe and Johann.

Iris collapsed with relief against Marie, and a lava mix of emotion welled from her center. Relief mingled with grief, happiness with loss, and soon Edward held her as she released the sobs she'd held back since her father's funeral, the ones she said she couldn't allow herself because she had to put her energy into figuring everything out. The tears subsided, and the crack down her middle felt smaller.

She looked up at Edward and blinked the last of the salt out of her eyes. "I'm sorry," she said.

"For what? You're supposed to cry when you're sad. It's a perfectly logical thing to do."

"No, for lying. For not trusting you."

"I forgive you." And he kissed her. It was a gentle kiss at first, a butterfly landing on a flower, but it deepened, and Iris kissed back with a wanton fierceness she didn't know she possessed. They broke apart when someone cleared their throat.

"Ahem, I don't know if I'm still supposed to chaperone you," Patrick O'Connell said. "But it seems like you need one. Hands where I can see them, you two."

Edward stood and helped Iris to her feet. The burns on his face and arm had mostly healed, leaving streaks of pink as if he'd been sunburned, not aether burned. Iris had heard of aether accidents and knew how bad they could be. While she was grateful for the miracle, she also wondered what price might be exacted from him. The gods were a capricious bunch, after all.

Iris glanced to the corner, where Radcliffe and Johann had laid Jeremy Scott's body.

"Don't look at him," Johann said. His face had lost its usual high color, and his paleness made him look younger. "It's not pretty. I'll spare you the details."

Iris thought about telling him she wasn't a weak woman, she could handle it, but she also knew she wouldn't be able to un-see the mess that had become of Lord Jeremy. "I won't look."

"We'll notify the authorities," Radcliffe said. "Go on back to the hotel. Both of you need to rest."

36

P *orta Maggiore Plaza, Rome, 28 June 1870*
With Iris's and Marie's help, Edward crossed the square at what he hoped looked like an ambling gait. His mind reeled through the events of the morning.

"Are you all right?" Iris asked once they cleared some of the crowd.

"I'm not sure." He answered her with honesty because he didn't want there to be any deceit between them ever again.

She looked up at him with a small curve to her lips, a secret smile just for him. "I feel the same way. Physically I'm fine, but I'm shaky through my spirit, and I fear it will take a long time to sort everything out."

They crossed the street and entered the hotel, so Edward didn't say anything, but he squeezed her hand. She squeezed back, and he knew she understood.

~

WHEN THEY ARRIVED BACK at the hotel, the clerk behind the desk raised an eyebrow at Iris's and Edward's dusty, wrinkled clothing. Iris guessed she and Edward looked like they had been engaged in naughty activities in the temple. Granted, they had, but nothing near what the young man behind the desk seemed to think, judging from the smirk on his face.

"Signorina McTavish?" he asked. "A letter arrived for you this morning." He handed her an envelope bearing a return address from Paris and a seal with the image of a Roman coin on it.

"What is it?" Edward asked.

Iris's fingers trembled, which echoed the shakiness in her core. Could the Marquis have decided to charge her for the damage to his statue? Or was this another surprise from Jeremy Scott—would he continue to torment her now from beyond the grave? Her thoughts shied away acknowledging Lord Jeremy was dead and Edward was capable of—

"I don't know." She peeled the wax seal and extracted the letter.

"'Dear Miss McTavish,'" she read aloud because her mind slipped over the words. "'Congratulations on your discovery of the temple at the Porta Maggiore! The archaeological community here in Paris has been abuzz with it, and we would like to invite you to be a student in our inaugural class at the new *Académie de l'Archéologie*. Classes will start in September, so please give us your answer as soon as possible. Sincerely, the admissions committee, Monsieur Roget Firmin, Chairman.'" For the second time that morning, tears made it difficult for Iris to see three feet in front of her, much less three months.

"Aren't you happy?" Marie asked. "This is your dream."

"Well, yes, but school requires tuition, and tuition requires money."

"You'll have the stipend from Cobb," Edward said.

Iris did some mental calculations. "But it will not be enough. Plus there's room and board to consider. Paris isn't a cheap place to live, and I have to worry about the Marquis de

Monceau." She rubbed her eyes. "I need to lie down." She broke away from them and rushed up the stairs to her hotel room, where a clockwork butterfly lay on the bed. The rest of the room was pristine, and nothing seemed to be missing, so Iris took it as a message: they were still being watched.

EDWARD DIDN'T KNOW how he was going to face his friends. He'd left a mess in the temple, and they'd stayed behind to clean up after him. But when Johann came to their room, he greeted Edward with a tired wave and collapsed on his bed.

"Italian women, Edward," he said, "are a tireless bunch. And thankless. I'm lucky to have escaped yesterday evening with my balls intact."

Edward looked at him, open-mouthed. "What does that have to do with anything?"

Johann sat. "What do you mean? Oh, good job eliminating Scott, by the way. He was a nuisance. He'd've hurt Iris if they'd married, I have no doubt."

Edward sat across the room from his friend. "But I killed someone. That makes me a murderer, a horrible person."

Johann stood and crossed the room to stand next to him. He put a hand on Edward's shoulder, and Edward braced against being hauled to his feet, but Johann patted his shirt.

"You did what you had to do. It was a tough decision, but you risked yourself to save her. That counts for a lot. Come on, the others are going for lunch and a big carafe of wine. I suggest you join us."

He didn't haul Edward to his feet, but he did manage to get Edward up and out the door.

When Edward walked onto the sidewalk, he expected to see people sneering at him or pointing at him in judgment, and it struck him as strange that the world hadn't changed because of his deed. The same old men sat at the edge of the piazza and played chess. The same women sold flowers on the corner, and the trattoria had the same tattered curtains in the front window. The main difference he noticed was how Iris's eyes lit up when she saw him. Now there were no traces of caution, only happiness he was there, and he felt an answering smile on his face in spite of his dark musings.

"How are you holding up?" she asked.

He thought about the clockworks. "I feel like I've been disassembled and put back together into something else."

"Me too." She squeezed his hand, and the tension around his heart eased. She'd hated to lie to him—he knew that now—but she'd done so to survive. It wasn't exactly murder, but it was something he could now understand about her, and he hoped she would not judge him for his grave misdeed.

They ordered, and when the waiter stepped away, Iris dug something from her reticule. She put a clockwork butterfly on the table. It didn't have a wax recording cylinder in it.

"This was on my bed when I went up to my hotel room," she explained.

"A warning," Radcliffe said, his tone flat. "They're still watching us, and they know we've found something."

Now Edward's anxiety returned. "And they might know what happened this morning."

No one contradicted him. In the excitement, it was unlikely anyone noticed whether a butterfly was flitting around the temple, particularly if it stayed in the shadows.

"So that makes three people or organizations we have to beware of," Marie said. "The Clockwork Guild, the neo-Pythagoreans, and Cobb."

Iris looked at Edward, her face stricken. "Mister O'Connell and Doctor Radcliffe can escape to the American front, but the rest of us have to go into hiding. But where?"

"You're not giving up this opportunity in Paris," Marie told her. "We will make it work. And there's nowhere better to hide than a big city, especially if you're under the protection of the owner of the Théâtre Bohème, who knows everything that's going on at any moment."

"And the theatre will be the perfect place to test out the EE," Edward said. "As I recall, the gas system had problems, so Madame St. Jean want to replace it. Think of how beautiful the theatre lighting will be with power from an aether-derived element."

Iris looked up at him. "And you'll be there?"

He thought about the University, how his office had been painted over, his beloved ivy stripped away. Now he only wanted to be with her, a true source of strength and steadiness. "I think it's time for me to bring my research from the theoretical into the practical. And it's difficult to court long-distance."

She blushed and looked away, but she licked her bottom lip, and Edward knew she thought about their kisses. Now there would be more.

"So it's settled," Marie said. "I'll send a telegram to *Maman* and let her know to expect three guests for an undetermined amount of time."

"Are you sure you're okay going back?" Iris asked.

"I will be as long as it's not just me."

"Make that four guests," Johann said. "I can't go back to England, at least not yet, and I should try to smooth things over with the Marquis when he returns from holiday. I can at least do that for you, Iris."

"Six, if there's room," Radcliffe said. "I continue to hope this will help Claire."

"And you'll need an engineer to come up with a way to actually use the element," O'Connell added.

"So it's settled," Edward said. It felt strange to take charge of the group, but Iris smiled at him, and he knew she would be there by his side. Hades, she'd probably take charge when necessary.

Hades? Where did that come from?

"To the Eros Element," Edward said and raised his glass. "And to friends."

THANK you for reading Eros Element! I hope you enjoyed it. If you'd like to keep up with me and my writing, and to get a free short story, please join my author newsletter at: http://www.ceciliadominic.com/newsletter (tap link to follow).

ALSO, if you have the chance, please leave me a review at the site where you bought the book and at Goodreads. Reviews are so important for us authors so we know what to do differently, but most importantly, what readers want more of. Even a single sentence like, "I liked it" is greatly appreciated.

ABOUT CLOCKWORK PHANTOM

Everyone wears a mask. But the deadliest secrets hide in plain sight.

Marie St. Jean's supreme acting talent comes with a price: Every spellbinding performance extracts a piece of her soul. When she reluctantly steps into a role abandoned by another leading lady, she encounters the ghostly spirit that caused the other woman to flee in terror. And who promises to fix Marie's affliction – for a price.

Marie's other problem – her attraction to alluring violinist, Johann Bledsoe, a temptation she dares not explore. However, with the Prussians surrounding Paris, she is well and truly trapped.

Johann left disgrace and his gambling debt behind in England, but a murder outside the Théâtre Bohème makes him fear he's been exposed. He'd love nothing more than to claim Marie as his own, but after the siege is over, his past will catch up to him again.

Under the baleful eye of steam-powered ravens, more murders drive Marie and Johann closer to the truth of what really lurks below the stage, and what dangers hang over their heads. Their only hope could lie in exposing their darkest secrets—and surrendering to the Eros Element in a way that could push them irretrievably close to the edge of madness.

"This deftly woven adventure is cast with well-developed characters that round out an entertaining mystery...a complex tale of murder, mayhem, and romance." - Romantic Times

Clockwork Phantom is available from most major book retailers in ebook and paperback formats. You can order it directly online or ask your favorite bookseller to order it from Ingram. You can even make it easy for them by giving them the ISBN: 978-1-945074-47-9

CLOCKWORK PHANTOM EXCERPT

Please enjoy this preview of Clockwork Phantom, the next book in the Aether Psychics series.

Théâtre Bohème, Paris, 1 December 1870

Screams were not uncommon at the Théâtre Bohème, mostly because on stage, one was expected to express emotions in an exaggerated way for the benefit of the audience. But the scream that sliced through the usual midday din of the theatre held a note of pure terror, and Marie nearly dropped the costume she held up for the examination of modiste Madame Beaufort.

"*Sacre bleu,*" Madame said. "What could that have been?"

"I don't know, but I'll check it out," Marie answered. "I'll let you know if the Prussians are upon us." She handed the dress to Madame and lifted her own skirts to make her way through narrow hallways from the costume room to the theatre itself.

Now shouting echoed through the wooden and brick hallways.

"I will not go forward with this!"

Marie recognized the slightly nasal but resonant female

voice as Corinne, her mother's go-to lead after Marie had left. She had become quite the *premiere femme* while Marie was away, but rather than sounding snobbish, her tone held an edge of panic.

"You must. The first performance is next week, and I don't have time for this nonsense."

And that was Marie's mother, Madame Lucille St. Jean. Marie took a shortcut through a secret passage, which allowed the sound to carry. She emerged in the theatre to see the two women almost nose-to-nose.

"What's wrong?" Marie asked before she could stop the words from tumbling out of her mouth. "You two do realize others are trying to work here."

"Oh, Mademoiselle." Corinne's face melted into a mask of tragedy. "I saw a ghost backstage. It raised its finger at me to tell me I am doomed. I must get away from here!"

Lucille looked at Marie. "What are you doing here? I have told you that if you refuse to take the stage, you do not belong in the theatre. Go back to helping Madame Beaufort with her pins and pinches."

Marie ignored Lucille. *This is the most interesting thing that's happened since I returned.* "What did the ghost look like?"

"He was tall and thin, and his hand looked like a skeleton's. He wore a long robe, and I could not see his face. He was Death come for me!" She placed the back of her hand on her forehead and swooned.

"Actresses." Marie sighed. Two stage hands came and picked Corinne up from the floor—she'd pulled the fainting trick before, but this time she didn't jump up with protestations at the "filthy peasants'" hands being on her.

"Well?" Lucille asked, apparently forgetting she'd banished Marie. "What are we to do now? I have a play with no lead actress and apparently a ghost has taken up residence in the theatre."

"Not my problem." Marie turned to go, but her mother grabbed her arm with surprising strength.

Lucille switched to English and lowered her voice, both signs she didn't want the workers and other actors to hear and understand what she was going to say to her daughter. Since the American "Civil" War had become a proxy war between England and France, not knowing English had become a point of pride among the common folk, particularly as the hard consonants and flat vowels sounded a lot like Prussian, spoken by the invaders who massed outside the city.

"And 'ave you forgotten that I am housing you and your friends for free?" she snarled in Marie's ear.

"And have you forgotten we're trying to help replace the faulty gas lighting system?" Marie snapped back. "You can't have a performance without light."

"The professor isn't proceeding as I'd hoped." Lucille's eyes glittered as the gas lights subsided and then flamed back to light. "I doubt he will have anything installed in time for dress rehearsals, and I am not sure I want to try the holiday play with an untested system."

Marie couldn't argue. "Science takes time," she said, echoing Professor Edward Bailey's oft-repeated sentiments. But she'd watched him in the laboratory they set up in a room at the top of the apartment building. The space itself received a lot of illumination, but the scientist within didn't seem to. Seemingly mesmerized by the isolated drop of aether within the glass globe, he would only sit and stare at his equipment. Inventor Patrick O'Connell proceeded better with developing the actual aether lighting equipment, but without the substance itself in usable form, the system would be useless.

"I cannot support you if we do not have a performance. We cannot have a performance without a leading actress. You are her understudy. Therefore, you must take the stage again."

Lucille punctuated that last statement with a finger held up in triumph.

"The only reason I accepted the understudy role was because I knew there was no way Corinne would back out. She may still do it." Marie looked to where the actress had been set, but—uncharacteristic for her—Corinne had left quietly and without any kind of announcement. "*Merde*, she really was frightened."

"Congratulations, Henriette," Lucille said. "You have tonight to memorize your lines. Rehearsals start for you tomorrow. Now Gerard, let's get back to the scene in the graveyard. I'll stand in for Marie as Henriette today."

Violinist, artist, and now disgraced gentleman Johann Bledsoe snuck in the back door of the theatre. Or at least he tried to, but he ended up holding the door open for the blonde actress he'd bedded two nights previously. Or had that been three? Either way, he tipped his hat and smiled, bracing himself for an onslaught of emotion and reproach.

"*Merci*, Monsieur," she said with uncharacteristic meekness, at least from what he could remember. She'd been a tiger in bed, or at least an alley cat. This change in character intrigued him.

"Where are you going?" he asked.

"Away. Death has come for me, and although I know it is futile, I shall run to the ends of the earth to escape her."

"All right, then. It figures death would be female." He watched Corinne hurry away, but before she reached the end of the alley, she turned.

"Beware, Monsieur! *La Mort* has come to the theatre, and she will not leave until she has claimed enough souls to satisfy her insatiable hunger."

"If it's insatiable, then she won't be sated," Johann pointed out, but she only shook her head and picked up her pace, her satin slippers splashing in the puddles from last night's rain.

Johann tried to enter again, but this time Marie St. Jean dashed out and nearly bowled him over.

"Where is she?" she asked. Her chest heaved, and Johann dragged his eyes away from her generous décolletage, which didn't need that much help from a corset. Not that he would know. She'd kept a careful distance from him since the incident in Rome when it was revealed how much of an ass he was. Had been. All right, was.

"Who?" His befuddled mind wondered if Marie ran after death.

"Corinne, the lead actress in *Light Fantastique*," she said and gave him a look that would have shrunk the balls of a lesser man back into his torso. Johann's balls barely took notice except to shoot an impulse to his brain to kiss her. They said such things frequently about Marie, so he told them to shut up.

"She ran that way," he said and gestured to the end of the alley.

"*Merde,*" she muttered and picked up her skirts to run after the escaped actress, but a gust of wind made her gasp.

Johann followed her through the alley. Now he really had to try not to look at the front of her dress to see if the wind had done him a favor and peaked her nipples. "You really shouldn't be running about without a coat. You'll catch your death of cold."

Another cool gust ruffled both their hair, and he shivered both internally and externally at his unintentional mention of whatever had scared the actress.

"I should be so lucky," Marie said through gritted teeth. They reached the street and looked in both directions, but the only thing to be seen was the disappearing back of a cab.

"Damn, now we'll never catch her." She dropped her skirts and rubbed her hands over her bare forearms.

"What was that all about?" Johann took off his overcoat and draped it around her shoulders.

"I don't need your help," Marie told him, but she tugged the wool closer around her.

Lucky coat. "I wasn't offering it, merely curious, that's all."

They turned back and walked toward the theatre's back door. The alley concentrated small gusts of wind into blasts, and Johann tried not to flinch whenever one hit them.

"But perhaps your way with women could be useful," Marie told him with a sideways glance that brought surprising warmth to his middle.

"How so?"

"Something spooked her. She said it was a ghost that looked like Death."

"And it wasn't the costume they're using in the play?"

"Of course! Someone was playing a trick on her. She's certainly been nasty to enough people to warrant it. Thank you!" Marie stood on her toes and kissed his cheek. "I'm going to her lodgings to explain. Then she'll come back."

Once inside, Marie handed his coat back to him and with a grin dashed off, presumably to get her own cloak and go to Corinne's apartment.

"Shall I accompany you?" he asked.

"Normally I would say no, but..." She sighed, and she hunched her shoulders when Lucille's voice floated down to them from the backstage area.

"Marie, come quick. The new phantom costume has arrived. You must see this."

"Your mother isn't good for your posture," Johann observed.

Marie straightened. "Or my sanity."

Reluctant to let this moment of detente pass, he followed her up the narrow wooden stairs.

Lucille held the mask for Marie to admire. "It is made from a material that will appear to glow, or at least I hope it will, in the Professor's new aether light."

"What happened to the old costume?" Marie asked, afraid of the answer. "And when did this one arrive?"

Lucille waved a hand. "I sold the previous one to one of our noble patrons for his parlor games. He has a mistress who likes strange bedroom role-plays. Death should be tattered, but that old costume had so many holes you could see the person underneath. Another reason it was perfect for the Count."

Marie had long since grown out of the tendency to blush at the mention of sex, but the image of her and Maestro Bledsoe playing out a scandalous scene with the costume flashed through her brain. He stood beside her, and she couldn't help but be aware of his broad shoulders and chest that tapered toward a narrow but still manly waist.

"Well, this leaves us with a problem," he said.

"Several," Marie murmured and widened the distance between them as she reminded herself that he was a selfish sort, as the English would say. "But yes, we're back to needing to know what frightened Corinne."

Lucille put a hand on Marie's cheek. "*Mon Dieu*, your skin is cold. What did you do, go chasing after her, you silly *fille*? You need to preserve your voice, not risk it by running into the cold without a cloak."

"I had a coat," Marie said with a sideways glance up at the musician. He grinned but didn't say anything, for which she was grateful.

"As for what frightened Corinne, bah!" Lucille banged her cane on the floor. "She was always a silly, superstitious girl, particularly once she became the *premiere femme*. As for you, go to the *Chambre d'Etoile*. You need to practice your lines, and I will send Madame Beaufort to start fitting the costumes to you. They will all need to be let out." She pinched Marie on the waist.

Marie moved away from her mother's critical, prying words and fingers. "Yes, that would be wise, so I don't burst through the seams on opening night." The look on Johann's face made heat bloom in her chest. "I mean, it's not going to be that kind of show." *Still not helping. I need to get rid of him.* She curtsied and said, "Maestro, thank you for your assistance. I'm sure you preserved my ability to perform in this detestable play."

"Any time," he replied with a cough. His cupid's bow lips were pulled back into a grin that said he tried not to laugh at Lucille's ridiculous antics. "And I think the costumes will look better on you, anyway. You have a more classical figure."

"Thank you. If you'll excuse me."

Marie fled from the genuine admiration in his eyes and the answering expansion of gratification in her middle. *Silly girl, you can't get stupid over a man who does something nice for you.* But her mind turned to the feel of the soft wool coat being placed on her shoulders by his large, strong hands.

Maybe having to take the lead in this play is a good thing. If I'm going to lose part of myself, I'd prefer it go to a role than to a man.

Now anxiety replaced any warm feeling she'd gotten from the maestro's complimentary look, and she had to catch herself and lean against the nearest wall while waiting for her heart to stop its pounding in her throat. She would have to take the stage again and face the loss of part of her soul.

Order Clockwork Phantom today!

ABOUT THE AUTHOR

Cecilia Dominic wrote her first story when she was two years old and has always had a much more interesting life inside her head than outside of it. She became a clinical psychologist because she's fascinated by people and their stories, but she couldn't stop writing fiction. The first draft of her dissertation, while not fiction, was still criticized by her major professor for being written in too entertaining a style. She made it through graduate school and got her PhD, started her own practice, and by day, she helps people cure their insomnia without using medication. By night, she writes fiction she hopes will keep her readers turning the pages all night. Yes, she recognizes the conflict of interest between her two careers, so she writes under a pen name. She lives in Atlanta, Georgia, with one husband and two cats, which, she's been told, is a good number of each.

You can find her online in the following places:
    Web page - ceciliadominic.com
    Facebook - facebook.com/CeciliaDominicAuthor
    Twitter - twitter.com/ceciliadominic
    Instagram - instagram.com/randomoenophile/

Newsletter (receive a free story)
    ceciliadominic.com/newsletter

ABOUT NOBLE SECRETS

Don't miss the other titles in Cecilia Dominic's Aether Psychics Series!

Noble Secrets

If you'd like to see where the Aether Psychics series began, check out Noble Secrets, a prequel novella.

A dangerous man from her past.
A handsome duke in her present.
Secrets that threaten their future.

After tragedy hits and danger moves in, Pauline Danahue flees London, searching for sanctuary and a way to start over. A job at a small university provides the escape she needs. Keeping recalcitrant professor Edward Bailey on task after a shattered heart renders him broken and destroyed becomes her daily routine. But when the same vicious man from her past sets his malicious sights on Pauline, her safe haven comes crashing down.

Duke of Waltham, Christopher Bailey, never counted on the gentle commoner, Miss Danahue, to save his brother–and himself–from broken pasts and a lifetime of mistakes. But she does just that. As their love blossoms, danger closes in, threatening Pauline and Christopher's lives. Together, they are forced to face their biggest fears, revealing secrets that could ruin them both.

Noble Secrets is available in ebook and paperback. Order your copy today to see where it all started!

CPSIA information can be obtained
at www.ICGtesting.com
Printed in the USA
LVHW031432310122
709622LV00001B/45

9 781945 074554